SKUNK
CREEK

"With his melding of magic realism in the front-porch-sittin' tall-tale tradition of the Ozarks, Todd Parnell weaves a story about the bigger-than-life citizens of Edenesque Hardleyville that is a Scheherazade tapestry involving a coven of cultists, corporate hog farmers, and, of course, murder."

– FRED PFISTER, former editor of *The Ozarks Mountaineer*, Branson, MO

"A wonderful chockablock story, a memorable group of richly drawn characters and community, and a whopping good tale with a passel of good stories running throughout. Just when I thought I was headed to a finale, there was another twist! Absolutely, positively, just terrific. I didn't want to put it down!"

– JANE BRITE, New York, NY

"Skunk Creek is a brilliant read, full of vivid imagery, zany situations and memorable characters who come to life through Todd Parnell's delightfully pungent prose. It takes you on a breathtaking ride through the hills and hollers of the Ozarks. That's a trip well worth taking."

– DR. CHARLES TAYLOR, Professor of Communication, Drury University

"Amazing! What an imagination and natural storytelling ability. I also liked the 'Arcadian' references to the Ozarks glorious natural beauty. So few know of that!"

– KAREN FOSS, retired anchor, NBC affiliate KSDK St. Louis

"Skunk Creek takes the reader on a rollicking, wild fantasy/adventure through the dark side of paradise – from murder to worse, from occult mysticism to pig farm politics. It is not without charm but never seeks to be charming – squarely in the tradition of Ozark folk tales . . . Take a deep breath before you start. This book will not be well reviewed (but might be widely read) by the church ladies."

– TOM PARKER, artist

SKUNK CREEK

THE OZARKIAN FOLK TALES TRILOGY
—— BOOK ONE ——

BY TODD PARNELL

P
Pen-L Publishing
Fayetteville, Arkansas
Pen-L.com

CONTENTS

DEDICATION

The Ozarkian Folk Tales Trilogy is dedicated to my wife, Betty, who challenged me in retirement to write fiction. When I complained that I had been raised to tell the truth and wouldn't know where to begin, she advised, "Start with something you know—the Ozarks, small towns, creeks, and rivers—then make it a mystery. Add a little violence, sex, humor, politics, exaggeration, even a hint of the supernatural. And have fun!"

I am grateful for her recipe. The first words I wrote were Skunk Creek, and the rest has just followed. I can only hope that this celebration of life amidst chaos and confusion entertains, as well as frames an often misunderstood culture as brave, resilient, and deeply rooted, with ultimately Village as hero. It has been fun to try.

Thank you, Betty, for pushing me and my personal envelope!

AUTHOR'S NOTE

A creek is a peek at Earth's fate.

This is a novel about the Ozarks—that vague notion of geography and culture tucked into Southwest Missouri and Northwest Arkansas. I was privileged to grow up here, and I treasure the history, the beauty, the humor, the toughness, the kindness, the independence, the gentleness, the lore and legend, the bonds that bind us.

Skunk Creek is an Ozarkian folk tale* with the village of Hardlyville as hero and a large support cast of colorful Hardlyvillains facing grave natural, unnatural, and environmental threats to their way of life. It is a mystery grounded in Ozark waters, culture, and history, and set in the tragedy, love, lust, and resilience of a fictional Ozark village. Crafted in the long tradition of Ozark storytelling, *Skunk Creek* is bawdy, irascible, and irreverent. It is the first in a trilogy of Ozark folk tales, which seems a natural way to tie characters and history together, as well as provide timeless context.

The Hillbilly caricature of bibs, corncobs, white lightning, ignorance, and bliss is often a self-inflicted and profitable iteration of the hardscrabble life many of our forefathers experienced in forging an existence in a beautiful but unforgiving landscape.

Dark tales of violence, drugs, and abuse are but one side of the Ozarks. Herein I have sought to meld the tragic with the exaggerated to honor the mythical Arcadia of ancient lore and the dogged resilience of a people and place beset with myriad contemporary challenges. Humor underlies all, as it has served as an antidote for tough times and rough lives throughout Ozarkian history. And yes, the threats to tradition and precious natural and water resources are real and ongoing.

I was raised in a giving and extended family and community—short of perfection, but long on love. Characters and locales featured herein are fictional but grounded in the imagination and tall tales of my youth. At the same time, jabs at prevailing political and moral hypocrisies play out every bit as well alongside a beautiful Ozark stream as in a teeming metropolis. Earthy and ribald language and situations are meant to soften body blows and bring an occasional chuckle, not to offend. Beyond all, I smile at my homeland, its rugged elegance, its many special characters, real and imagined, fond memories, and huge hopes.

Todd Parnell

DECEMBER, 2014

* *Folk tale: A tale or legend originating and traditional among a people or folk having to do with everyday life, and frequently featuring wily peasants getting the better of their superiors.*

List of Locations

Hardlyville – Fictional Town
Hardlyvillains – Residents of Hardlyville
Skunk Creek – Fictional Creek

List of Characters

Sheriff Sephus Adonis – The Law
Pierce Arrow – Editor, *Hardlyville Daily Hellbender*
Lucas Jones – Genuine Hero
Lettie Jones – Wife of Genuine Hero
Jimmy Jones – Cousin of Genuine Hero
Pastor Pat – Minister
Ms. Octavia Rosebeam – Latin Teacher
Dylan "Ol' Dill" Thomas – Deaf Owner of Family Still
Donald "Dinky" Doodle – Village Jester
Doc Karst – Town Physician
Bud Boswell – Bank President, Civic Leader, Crook
Lois Boswell – Banker's Wife
Sally Boswell – Banker's Daughter
James Bond (PB) – Postmaster, Civic Leader
Bob Klunkerkokatus – Undertaker, Civic Leader
Matilda Peaches Klunkerkokatus – Undertaker's Wife
Josephus Dudley – Mayor, Civic Leader
New Chairman – Chair, State Oversight Board (SOB)
Larry Larrsnist – Congressman
Demon Lady, Devil Woman, SHE – Lady with Graying Ponytail
Holly Howell – Sheriff's Occasional Girlfriend
Flotilla Hendricks – Bakery Owner
Sabrina Hendricks – Pregnant Daughter

Henry Hoary – Noodler
Dr. Felix Feelgoode – Pierce Arrow's Classmate
Florence (Flo) Hormel—Feelgoode's girlfriend
Rifleman – Small Businessman
Steele – Rifleman's Wife
Norm Seaton – Manager, Skunk Creek Ranch
Bilious Bloom – Librarian
Tiny Taylor – Owner, Greasy Spoons Grill and Bar

CHARACTERS: (HISTORICAL)

Thomas Hardly – Founder, Hardlyville
Petunia Perfidy Hardly – Thomas Hardly's Second Wife
Hardlita Hardly Rosebeam – Thomas and Petunia's Daughter,
                              Ms. Octavia Rosebeam's Mother
Herman Rosebeam – Hardlita's Husband
Pornopoly Rosebeam – Octavia's New York City Aunt
Sardo – Octavia Rosebeam's Italian Lover
James Qingdao – Early Hardlyville Settler, Friend of Thomas
Anny Qingdao – James's wife
Mr. Garth – Federal Marshal, sort of

LIST OF INSTITUTIONS

Hardlyville Daily Hellbender (Newspaper)
Bank of Hardlyville
Skunk Creek Church of Christ
State Oversight Board (State Water Quality Board)
Skunk Creek Ranch (Hog Farm)
Big Pork (Pork Lobby)
Coven of Evil (Religious Cult)
Hardlyville Cemetery

GRISLY

His canoe drifted silently along the current's edge. Top water bite for smallmouth at dawn was as good as it got. Water erupted behind a rock-sheltered still spot adjacent to the current as brownie leapt skyward, then dove for its life. *I could spend every morning of my life on Skunk Creek,* he mused. Five minutes later, he freed the twenty-inch, red-eyed warrior and immediately recast downstream.

Skunk Creek. The ancient name was formalized by Thomas Hardly, founder and original resident of namesake Hardlyville, which sits midway between the creek's origin and its merger with a mighty river along the Missouri and Arkansas' border. Heart of the Ozarks. Home to so many clear, karst, limestone bottomed tributaries to larger waters. The Ozarks. Land of beauty and headstrong, independent cusses. Settled by those fleeing structure and order, set on freedom and independence, in a harsh but plentiful landscape. Some God-fearing, others godforsaken, most there by default. The Ozarks. Yet to escape its history, choosing instead to cling to it for sustenance and deep rooting among those who find comfort in such. Skunk Creek, aptly named in that context. As for Thomas Hardly?

Dead. Soon after founding, brutally murdered. Some say worse. No suspects. No motive. No nothing, beyond grieving wife, young daughter, and new village left behind, more than a century past.

Lucas Jones had put in at his secret access spot less than an hour earlier. He could care less about the history but knew firsthand that there was nothing more spectacular than a crisp, clear sunrise in the Ozarks, skimming slowly along a glass-smooth surface of crystal, with mottled rock bottom beneath. Sun creeping over the horizon slanted soft light through trees, bringing a pink glow to most beneath it. A kingfisher screeched, and a plaintiff owl hooted. He even heard a buck deer snort in the foreground. This was indeed a heavenly palate of color, sound, and texture, and it was all his to share with only him or them or that who made it. No, Lucas had not been many places in the world, well, none really, but he would stack up what he was part of this morning with any picture in any magazine he had ever seen. If the fish weren't biting, he would simply sit and drift through it all, hoping that some of it might rub off on him to take home to his wife, Lettie, and their two young'uns. But there was clearly brownie action on this stretch this morning, and he cast his Zara Spook ahead at a slight angle, again along the current's edge between rocks. Nothing this time, but bound to be next.

Lucas Jones lived a simple life. He loved, he fished, he hunted, and he fixed things. There was not a broken object he could not repair. It was the way his mind worked. He could absorb, in a glance, what something looked or worked like, what it had used to look or work like, and how to return it to its original state. This was an innate visioning capacity, as Lucas had barely passed high school. And beyond fixing things, Lucas wasn't much good at anything that could earn him a living or support a family.

Lucas charged by the hour and worked only when he wanted to, allowing him to pursue his other passions when and however he wished. He generally liked to fish in the morning, hunt during season, and love Lettie whenever she was in the mood. He occasionally got his priorities mixed up a bit, but Lettie always had a way of helping him reorder. This assured him of plenty of time to fix things.

He was a tall, strapping, handsome chunk of manhood, with a disarming smile that served him well when he got in trouble, an occurrence of some frequency. He considered himself the most fortunate human being in the world. He was also a little naive and self-absorbed, rarely innocent, mostly guilty, and occasionally beyond comprehension, his or another's.

This magnificent morning, Lucas rounded a bend left to the facing bluff before noticing the still, graveled campsite across. He would seek to drift by and honor the "do not disturb" sign implied thereon. It was then that a quick glance changed his life forever.

A form extended from the open tent door. It was a body, that of a man—nude, spread eagle, face up, splotched with red. Blood. And closer to the creek's edge, a young woman, similarly adorned.

"Oh, my God," he gasped to no one in particular.

He reluctantly moved closer to inspect the carnage. He pulled ashore and sat in stunned silence. Blood caked along gashes on both throats. Both had been murdered in cold blood and apparently sexually assaulted. Both were shot execution style, single bullet hole in the forehead to certify death. Brutally ravaged bookends to unspeakable acts of violence. Evil doings by evil men. Had to be men, from what he could see.

He sat in the canoe in stunned silence, unsure of what to do next. He threw open the cooler and grabbed a Bud Light. After three long gulps drained it dry, he grabbed another. It was early, but he had to find a clear thought somewhere.

It was then that he wondered for his own safety. He or they could still be about. He himself was subject to offing for no other reason than wrong place and time. He would even make a fair suspect, if framed properly. He vomited violently, spreading his DNA around the crime scene. He quickly grabbed a third beer to wash away the sour remains in his mouth.

There were, in fact, several pairs of eyes on him as he ruminated over what next.

He quietly pulled his cell phone from a waterproof bag, pushed the "camera" icon, and snuck several photos of the whole bloody mess, including close-ups of the mangled victims. He tried to cover each body as best he could with a single bed roll and several brightly colored beach towels, still scented with soap.

He reboarded his canoe, tucked the rod beneath the bow seat, and shoved into the current, paddling rapidly downstream. He had thought about carrying the bodies with him but didn't have the stomach for it.

Thirty minutes earlier, he had been one with Skunk Creek and her surrounds. Now, only shock and fear.

Once he rounded the downstream bend, eyes in the woods took shape as several forms slipped into view. They built a large fire creekside and burned everything that would ignite, including the deceased young lovers. The stench of burning flesh mingled with the acrid undertones of smoldering camping equipment, fouling a beautiful, early morning spring bouquet. Partially baked remnants were doused with water and air cooled before loading into trash bags. A canoe was pulled up into the woods, attached to a waiting plow horse, trash bags were dumped into an empty cavity along with that which couldn't burn, and trekked a mile or so to a dirt road and a pickup truck bed for hauling to a private landfill. Smoldering human remains were shoveled into the moving current for random distribution downstream.

Drill complete, she ordered the assailants to move on, and they were joined by an upstream sentry for a walk out beyond the pristine gravel bar. No hint of campsite or former tenants remained. It was a shame the weak-stomached bystander had floated by before cleanup was initiated, but better then than later in the process when they would have had to kill him as well.

Skunk Creek, Dead Creek, whatever, they laughed among themselves. They had taught the young sinners a lesson, saved their putrid souls, gotten a little pleasure in the process, and done so in gory glory.

BYWAYS, BLUEWAYS, AND BLACK HELICOPTERS

Pierce Arrow, semi-acclaimed editor of the *Hardlyville Daily Hellbender*, sat in his office contemplating the Ozarks. "Daily" was a misnomer in itself as the *Hellbender* only appeared when Pierce had something provocative to write about, which was generally a monthly occurrence. All agreed he was good with the big words and a very likable, if strangely dressed and spoken, character. Pierce was educated somewhere back East and had been named after the luxury auto of his father's youth. He had sought the solace of a small town after a debilitating stint as a crime reporter in Philadelphia, Pennsylvania, wherein he barely avoided a mob hit and a disenfranchised voter's pipe bomb, among his many brushes with destiny.

Seems one of Pierce's ancestors to the fourth power had once owned land outside Hardlyville and had, in fact, been a trusted confidante of Thomas Hardly at one time, according to family lore. As Pierce scanned the nation for proverbial Arcadias, Hardlyville quickly caught his attention and became his peaceful haven of escape. He had started the *Hellbender* not long after relocating and fit into the Hardlyville social landscape comfortably, apart from being widely regarded as a likely closet liberal.

Pierce Arrow embraced his name as appropriate for an honest print man: straight, true, on the mark. He went to great extremes to live down the "liberal" rumor with his editorial policy and would do so again with this whole "National Blueway" thing.

Seems that the United States of America's federal government in Washington, DC, had decided to bestow a coveted honor on the Ozarks. The mighty river that spanned both sides of the Missouri—Arkansas' border would hereafter and forever be designated a "National Blueway" in honor of clean and bountiful waters, rich history, and unique culture. It would be only the second time in all of the nearly two hundred fifty years of the republic that such formal acclaim had been bestowed.

Obviously, the first should have something to do with the original thirteen colonies and the Connecticut River, which had survived gristmills, sawmills, animal and human waste, chemicals, dams, and most recently the daily dumpings of 2,400,000 citizens through its four hundred ten mile course touching Vermont, New Hampshire, Massachusetts, and Connecticut to the ocean.

The mother river of the Ozarks was the next rare national treasure so designated. Almost twice as long but half as populated, she had survived the same gauntlet of user affection along her course to the Mississippi River. This broad-reaching designation superseded previous watershed honors for National and Scenic Rivers and America's first national river, the Buffalo, and added regional balance to federal outreach. While no direct aid was promised, it was implied, as was enhanced coordination and communication amongst stakeholder groups.

Only problem was that Washington forgot to ask, mused Pierce. He looked at the AP byline, proudly announcing the designation in a liberal big-city newspaper, and began writing his lead editorial on the matter immediately.

Pierce knew his town's temperature. It was typically Ozarkian, insular, bent to looking in rather than out, taking care of their own when their own were in bad enough shape to need help, but subtly rather than overtly. A plucked chicken at the back door, a can of gas next to the family truck, a half-used bottle of castor oil in a sniffling kid's knapsack, all without notice or ownership. Pride in this neighborhood ran as deep and strong as the powerful pulse of neighboring Skunk Creek, and what little crime that occurred was generally rooted in wounded pride, with a dose of alcohol seasoning. National designations of Blueways, Highways, Byways, and Heritage Areas raised fears of infringement on personal property and individual rights, a cause to die for.

We don't own much, he smiled, but what we do belongs to us and no one else, particularly a bunch of thieving government officials. We pay our taxes only because we have to or go to jail. That was the local mantra and easy to editorialize to. For the *Hellbender* to survive, daily or otherwise, it needed to reflect the local conscience, if indeed such individualized context could be collectivized. Pierce tried his damnedest and had made a living out of it for ten years now.

Hardlyville history was rich but undocumented, beyond word of mouth. Founded in 1882 by Thomas Hardly, an itinerant farmer and merchant, on the banks of beautiful Skunk Creek, it was nothing but a small settlement for many years. Hardly moved there with his second wife, the former Miss Petunia Perfidy, from a farm farther south. Thomas Hardly did all things founders were supposed to do. He named the place after himself and promptly had a child, a daughter in this case, named in a similar vein, Hardlita Hardly. Then he upped and got brutally murdered. Some said for stealing a map. Some said for messing around with a neighbor's wife. Some said both. Times were rough in the Ozarks then with bullies, warmongers, and even vigilante groups raising hell each morning of their lives. Could have been anyone or anything back then. Probably outsiders, guessed Pierce. Outsiders still stirred suspicion and stares. Had to earn their way in, even today.

Pierce, in fact, carried a great deal of affection in his heart for the good citizens of Hardlyville and the cultural milieu that had left them as they are. Some would say "behind." Pierce would claim that as an advantage. While course and rough in some aspects—particularly talk, whiskey, and sex—they were deep-hearted and soft-souled, for the most part. Their lives weren't easy, but they made a lot of them. Beneath their rugged construct was a humorous take on life that was infectious, once grasped. Did Ol' Dill Thomas really eat worms? Probably not, but all said he did, rendering it a God-fearing truth. Some kids even tried, on occasion, to the disgust of that same all.

He wouldn't trade a single one, no matter how backward, for some of the urban beasts he had dealt with in his previous lives. He loved Hardlyville and her hearty residents, warts and all, but feared that not just they but that their way of life would not stand the test of time, would not pass beyond this or the next generation.

While Pierce hadn't experienced it personally, he had heard talk of blue-helmeted United Nation's soldiers in black helicopters and their secret plans to take over the Ozarks. Something that got locals particularly riled back in the '70s related to secret "Man and the Biosphere" incursions into sparsely-settled, high-value acreages around the world—all courtesy of this United Nation's coven, which was governed by Russians, liberal Europeans, blacks from all corners of Africa, Orientals, Arabs, Mexicans, and the like, who had no interest in or knowledge of Hardlyville or individual rights.

One of Pierce's neighbors swore that his grandfather once saw a squadron of at least twenty black helicopters, some of them gunships, some double bladed, sweeping at treetop level over the woods next to his farm. Said he ran them off with his shotgun but had a tremor for the remainder of his life.

Stories abounded about similar clandestine encounters over the years since. Marse Tucker even claimed to have seen a green-looking black helicopter pilot peering into his window one midnight, shining a tiny moonbeam flashlight into his eyes to temporarily blind him. Marse had no idea what the probable Martian stole from his farm, but was certain his liquid corn stock had been diminished, and he swore it had not been at his own hand.

Pierce dutifully reported each encounter to the community, in line with his promise to be eternally vigilant and aware of threats from the outside.

This National Blueway hoopla had a similar feel. It reeked of the same kind of governmental incursion stench as Biospheres and Ozarks National Heritage labels. As Pierce wrote in his lead editorial, "Scream loudly to your representatives, state and national, then scream again, and surely we will defang this scourge." He was proud of his choice of words.

He would happily report, barely two weeks later, that the National Blueway designation for their mighty river had been withdrawn, and that bureaucrats, tree huggers, and land-grabbing opportunists had been sent packing by their indignation. He praised the local populace for its passion for the land, the water, and its neighbors. Didn't sound much like a back-East liberal to himself.

He even got to report, at a later date, that the whole Blueways takeover had been shelved in Washington, DC, a rare example of democracy in action. America was stuck with one Blueway, this in the radical Northeast, and that was a long way from the Ozarks, thank the Good Lord!

Just now, Pierce Arrow heard the makings of a commotion outside.

HARDLYVILLE

Hardlyville was abuzz. Just minutes earlier, a partially soused Lucas Jones had stumbled into town from Skunk Creek bridge several hundred feet away with a tale of terror that stunned even the most cynical of hometowners. A brutal double murder with apparent sexual assault of two young floaters camped several miles below the AA put-in and cell phone photos to prove it provoked immediate community outrage. Lucas had shown his grisly images to any who would look along his staggered walk down Main Street to the sheriff's office.

Sheriff Sephus Adonis presented as an overweight, under IQed, duly elected public servant, whose favorite phrase—"shit, brothers"—endeared him to all, despite his lack of formal credentialing. He chose that phrase as his signature brand because of its unique versatility. "Shit, brothers" as a command was clear and crisp, as an adjective, properly pejorative, and as an expletive, firm enough to garner attention without crossing the line into impropriety. It struck a public pose for him that balanced earthiness and approachability with strength and authority, a positioning with which he was both proud and comfortable. He had never lost an election.

The sheriff was giving his new girlfriend, Holly Howell, the pleasuring of her life in a conference room behind his cramped office when Lucas burst in screaming about rape and murder. Amidst the sheriff's protestations and Holly's panted affirmations that theirs was very much a consensual act and both were clearly alive, Lucas shoved a graphic photograph in Sheriff Sephus's face to demand his attention.

No one knew from whence Sheriff Sephus or his strange last name were sourced, but as a local lover, he was legend. From rumors about an otherworldly tenderness of touch and technique to size and endurance, Sheriff Sephus Adonis stretched imaginations.

Sheriff Sephus cursed Lucas, cell phones, and goddamned murderers between bookend "shit, brothers" before regaining his composure. He pressed Lucas for details, which were slurred out in broken sentences.

It was then that Lucas's pretty wife, Lettie, barged in without knocking, berating Lucas for being drunk before noon again and demanding that the sheriff lock his sorry ass up until he could pass that Breathalyzer thing. She was sick and tired of his early morning fishing trips becoming all day soirees, alone or with his buddies, but never without Mr. Bud Light. Maybe this would teach him a lesson.

Pierce Arrow, editor of the *Hardlyville Daily Hellbender*, joined the melee, demanding an interview with Lucas and wanting to know what Sheriff Sephus was going to do about the situation. Lucas thrust the ghastly photos at Pierce Arrow, who immediately vomited on the cell phone images and was charged on the spot by Sheriff Sephus with tampering with evidence.

While order was beyond restoration, chaos gave way to an eerie silence far beyond the norm of daily life in tiny Hardlyville.

NOTHING BUT THE FACTS

Sheriff Sephus urged several townsmen to posse up. Dill Thomas, short for Dylan, eighty-plus-year-old, third generation native of Hardlyville, and deaf as a dead cottonmouth, thought Sheriff said "pussy up." He limped to the front of a long line of volunteers, pronouncing himself ready for action. Too old, he was told. He indignantly announced he could get it up with the best of them. Sheriff told Dill that if he couldn't hear it, he couldn't do it. Ol' Dill wondered aloud what that had to do with the challenge at hand before Sheriff gently nudged him aside with the admonition that there was a genuine crisis going on, adding that unfortunately he, Ol' Dill, was not to be part of the solution. Though Dill was still confused, he complied with Sheriff Sephus's mandate and cranked up his $13.99 hearing aide as high as it would go.

Sheriff hollered an aside to Lettie that Lucas would spend that night in jail for public drunkenness, but that he needed the lad just now to locate the scene of a purported crime. She nodded her approval.

Sheriff and his men loaded into an aging pickup truck that doubled as squad car and fire wagon. Several canoes filled with paddles were strapped atop the wooden truck bed rack. Sheriff slapped Lucas soundly on the cheek to hasten his sobriety. He then shoved him into the front seat as Lucas tried a wild swing back. "That will cost you another night in jail" was about the only response he earned.

The truck sped toward the AA put-in upstream as Sheriff asked Lucas to recount how he came upon his grisly discovery. A slowly sobering Lucas was fixated on the story of his monster smallmouth until another sharp slap redirected his memory. He recalled the ghastly scene as something out of a movie, with blood and the smell of death spread all around. He threw up again, right on the sheriff's dashboard, which earned him another swift slap and a hardy "shit, brothers." Sheriff slammed to a stop and threw Lucas in the truck bed with the others.

Upon arrival at the AA put-in, Sheriff Sephus deputized all, including Lucas, and ordered him to steer the lead canoe with the sheriff in the bow. This was not an easy task for a half-drunk cowboy unused to a three hundred pound bow anchor. Lucas over-steered through the second rapid, throwing Sheriff Sephus into a stand of willows and inducing a monumental weight shift that dipped the upstream gunnel beneath the fast current. The ensuing dump was quick and total.

Sheriff Sephus was apoplectic as he blubbered to the surface, sentencing Lucas, on the spot, to an additional thirty days for endangering a Hardlyville official, and demanding another stern man. He pulled his dripping pistol from its holster, pointed it at Lucas's head, and fired just over it with a hardy "shit, brothers," which is precisely what Lucas did. With weapon drawn and aimed at Lucas's now soiled backside, the sheriff and his chastened entourage resumed their downstream paddling with some urgency. Lucas begged the sheriff for a cleansing dip but was advised such would have to wait until they arrived at the crime scene. Lucas's canoe mate was none too pleased with the sheriff's edict.

Lucas finally advised the sheriff that it was around this bend on the left, facing the bluff they could now make out in the distance. It had taken most of the day to get there. All steeled themselves for what lay ahead as Sheriff's canoe moved to the head of the pack.

Sheriff Sephus tried to rise in the bow for a better look but re-sat quickly as the canoe wobbled like the crippled minnow bait that Lucas so loved. His stern man shoved the canoe into a gravel bar as the sheriff stepped out with a whispered "shit, brothers" belying his confusion. Lucas pulled in next, more anxious about cleaning his drawers than revisiting the gruesome scene. Head down, he waded past waist deep and pulled off his soiled britches. Thankfully, he hadn't bothered with underwear this morning and had only one garment to clean. The running water felt cool and cleansing until the deafening silence caught his attention.

A quick glance at the gravel bar was all he could stomach until he realized it was clean as a whistle. *What the hell,* he wondered, *was going on,* reorienting his gaze both up and downstream. Wrong place, he challenged himself before dismissing such a foolish conclusion. This was definitely it—a sordid spot he could pick out with precision from any gravel bar lineup.

Sheriff Sephus ordered Lucas ashore, a demand with which Lucas complied. Between curses, the sheriff issued a follow-up edict demanding that Lucas put on his "goddamned trousers" before he shot his tiny pecker to pieces. Again, Lucas was quick to comply, quietly objecting to the descriptive. Lucas stood in stunned silence exactly where he had eight hours and ten Bud Lights earlier.

When Sheriff Sephus asked Lucas what he had to say for himself, Lucas could think of nothing. That is until Sheriff Sephus aimed his revolver at Lucas for the fourth time that morning.

"They was right there," whined Lucas, pointing at two separate spots before hypothecating aloud that someone had cleaned up one hell of a mess. He had the pictures to prove it if someone would just clean Pierce Arrow's puke off his cell phone.

Sheriff Sephus waddled slowly up to Lucas and whacked him upside the head before calling him a no-good, besotted, worthless drunk. Lucas wondered aloud where sheriff had learned "besotted," earning a second blow to the head and a trip into the heart of darkness. Which is what the party paddled in by. Thankfully, there was a full moon.

CASE CLOSED

Lucas awoke with his head on fire and water dripping down his chin. Sheriff Sephus loomed overhead, waving the large glass he had just emptied in Lucas's face and demanding to know where he had gotten those "danged" pictures.

Sheriff had asked Holly if she would clean up Lucas's cell phone so he could examine the evidence more closely. She reluctantly agreed, wondering if this fit into a girlfriend's job description without response. Her efforts were rewarded with a peck on the cheek and the grossest images she had ever seen. All of this occurred while Lucas lay unconscious in Hardlyville's only jail cell, courtesy of the good sheriff himself.

As Sheriff Sephus scrolled through Lucas's Photo Stream, it became apparent to him that Lucas had not lied about location. Sheriff was an astute observer, and several background scenes carried landmarks that were instantly recognizable to the sheriff himself. He just couldn't figure out where the graphic photos came from.

He called the sheriff in an urban district, and without revealing details of why, inquired about this Photoshop process he had once heard about. Sheriff didn't read much and paid scant attention to technology, beyond that required to rustle up a little online porn from time to time. He wondered if Lucas could have created the disturbing images and somehow transposed them to a previously photographed background. That neither he nor others recognized either person set him thinking in that direction. Talk about a contradiction in terms. How could anyone recognize an attractively-endowed, naked female body covered in blood with a gaping slice through her neck? Urban sheriff's answers were vague and left open the possibility that most images can be digitally altered.

Sheriff figured the only way to get to the bottom of Lucas's horseplay was to beat it out of him, so that he did. He started with the cold water in face moment before placing the "Sheriff Out" placard in a front door slot and locking up. He then waded into the task at hand, starting with Lucas's gut, moving quickly to ribs, and finally whacking the groin a time or two for good measure. With Lucas reduced to a slobbering shadow in the jail cell corner, the sheriff obtained the confession he sought. Yes, Lucas had made the whole thing up, had pulled images from computer film clips, and had superimposed them on a background photo he had taken of his favorite gravel bar on the entire upper Skunk. Why? Sheriff supposed he simply wanted to get Lettie off his back for drinking so much and perhaps her on her own a little more often, sleeping with a hero and such. She was a purty one.

In any event, no evidence, motive established, confession obtained, and case closed, with the rascal incarcerated for thirty additional days owing to him endangering an elected official by flipping his canoe in the waters of Skunk Creek.

Where in gospel's name had Mr. Hardly come up with such a grotesque name for a beautiful creek, anyway? He had heard the explanations. Everything from getting squirted by a skunk while bathing in the creek on a spring day, to finding a putrid dead skunk floating through his favored fishing hole, to even a misspelled Skink Creek, named for the tiny lizards that were found in abundance along its banks.

Whatever the reason, Skunk had stuck through the ages. Maybe Mr. Hardly didn't even name it. Skunk Creek it was, is, and will be evermore.

And, more importantly, a potentially ugly blemish on the community and a prolonged investigation were thwarted at the pass. That's what good sheriffs are for, Sheriff Sephus mused.

A CONVERSATION

"Lucas Jones, what do you believe in?"

Lucas was clearly confounded by the sheriff's question. His flip response was that he truly believed in sheriffs who kick innocent ass to get false confessions.

No, sheriff explained, just doing his job, restoring law and order and some semblance of sanity in the interest of peace in the neighborhood. No, he really wanted to know what big things Lucas believed in. Things like God, heaven and hell, love and marriage, sex, and the like.

Lucas didn't know where this was headed, but he sure as hell didn't want another broken rib, so he started spewing right and left. Yes, he believed in God because it was the right thing to do. Plus, it was safer than choosing not to.

"If God was here, he would obviously be pissed if I said 'no way' and probably strike me dead by lightning. If he wasn't and actually no more than a crutch to help me cope, I can find comfort in that as well."

God is definitely win-win, concluded Lucas. He was a simple thinker, but could not find fault in his own logic. Sheriff did.

"Come on, Lucas, dig deeper," was his challenge. "You're using tired old logic that doesn't require much effort."

He really wanted to know whether Lucas believed in God or not. Lucas confessed to not having a clue what God might be or may look like, let alone what interest God might have in him, Lucas.

"No, sheriff," was his response, "think I'll just stick with good old cause, effect, and probability." He reasoned that if he believed in God it was more likely that good things would happen than if he didn't. Sheriff shrugged but didn't whack him.

About hell, Lucas didn't know but was quite certain that whoever did those ghastly acts on two young people would find out long before he would. Sheriff Sephus cautioned Lucas against clinging to the fantasies of his overwrought imagination, but Lucas refused to back down on this one.

"I seen what I seen," was his last observation on the matter, and the sheriff let it slide this time.

"Don't ever say that in public," Sheriff admonished, "or I'll lock you up in here for months, with nothing more than a weekly bath and beating to boot."

"Any thoughts on education?" the sheriff inquired of Lucas.

"No," was Lucas's quick response.

"Not one?" pushed Sheriff Sephus.

"Okay, just one," responded Lucas. "I met Lettie in eleventh grade. It was sex at first sight. If it wasn't for education, she'd be sleeping with someone else. Come to think of it, education is just fine."

Of love, marriage, and sex, Lucas liked sex the most. It was so clean and natural, well, maybe a little messy, but for all the right reasons. Sex felt good, looked good, and lasted a lifetime, if you simply paced yourself.

"What's not to like about that?" mused Lucas.

He had had his share with and before Lettie, his own little spitfire. He even confided in Sheriff Sephus that he had stepped out on Lettie a time or two, maybe even three or four. Nothing serious, and generally only when she was pregnant or otherwise indisposed. No love wasted there. When you get the itch, gotta scratch it. Right, Sheriff? Surely God could forgive a small indiscretion or two, or three or four. What God wouldn't forgive is what was done to them two innocent kids. Lucas was sure of that. Sheriff Sephus gave him another pass but repeated his earlier warning.

Sheriff Sephus Adonis smiled slightly. He liked to pass his time in this manner. Lucas was not the first to bare his mortal soul to Hardlyville's dispenser of justice. He liked to play out life with his prisoners when life got a little boring. Sheriff then raised the question in reverse.

"What if she gets the itch and you're the one indisposed?" he pondered.

Lucas supposed that would be an okay itch to get scratched, as long as it wasn't Lettie's. Sheriff smiled again.

Lucas asked Sheriff if he could have a beer. Sheriff politely declined but promised to buy Lucas one when he was out of there.

"Why would anyone live in Hardlyville?" was another question Sheriff enjoyed throwing on the table.

"I like the creek," was the best Lucas could muster. "It's pretty, it's clear, it's clean, it's fast and furious in spring and after heavy rain, low and slow late summer and fall, generally full of fish, and empty of people. It's just not that complicated, particularly compared with other stuff. Now if someone messes with my creek, they will pay," Lucas declared with passion.

He recalled what had happened when large-scale livestock farms had dotted the edges of a Texas creek a friend told him about. All in the sole interest of money. All that chicken, pig, horse, and cow shit that greened water and smothered fish. He couldn't imagine which would stink worst. He would never allow that to happen on Skunk Creek. He would die first. Sheriff Sephus nodded in agreement.

"So what else, beyond animal shit, do you hate, Lucas, really hate?" the sheriff pushed.

Lucas proceeded to unload on his favorite subject, except perhaps sex: how much he hated government. Said he got the hate from his pappy, and his before him.

"So this is a genetic predisposition?" the sheriff asked.

Lucas wasn't sure about Sheriff Sephus and his big words, but he had already shared with him his cheating on Lettie, so he let it rip. When he was finished, there was no doubt that his hatred of all things government was real and deep. Real deep. Didn't much matter if it was national, state, or local. Lucas was convinced that them that set the rules, them that interpreted the rules, and them that put them in play was out to get him. That included sheriffs, Lucas confirmed.

Lucas could feel another beating coming on, so he set out to get his money's worth.

What's more, Lucas concluded, if there weren't no rules set by them seeking to protect their power, no one would need to be arrested, and presidents, governors, mayors, and the like would be out of a job lording over folks like Lucas and have more time to go fishing and hunting. Yes, that included Sheriffs too, and everyone would be in a much better mood. He probably wouldn't have to drink so much beer to get happy either, which would further please the misses. Lucas self-congratulated himself out loud for his impeccable logic.

Sheriff Sephus started to open the cell door and whack Lucas, but concluded it wasn't worth the calorie burn. He could only mutter "shit, brothers," which brought back horrible memories of self-soiling to Lucas and served as an adequate reprimand, unbeknownst to the sheriff.

Sheriff asked how Lucas felt about one more big thing: forgiveness.

Lucas went on and on about what a big heart it took to forgive. He could forgive about anyone or anything, except maybe those butchers on the river.

"There you go again," Sheriff quickly cautioned. "Hard to forgive what hasn't happened," was his bent. Lucas rolled his eyes but wisely decided to stop there.

Sheriff asked Lucas whether he thought Lettie would forgive his occasional wanderlust, if she found out. He sure hoped so. Sheriff then asked Lucas whether he could forgive Lettie, if he found out she was occasionally cattin' about. Lucas chewed on that one a minute, then answered hesitantly in the affirmative. He wondered aloud why she would even consider doing that, not expecting an answer. Sheriff spared him one.

Sheriff closed by asking Lucas if he preferred that ladies maintain their private parts as God intended, all wild an' wooly, trimmed like a manicured lawn, or bald as a baby's butt? Lucas pondered this because he had seen variations on all three. His response was measured but sincere. He would stick with style Lettie, just like a black bear's back.

Boy, was Lucas in for a surprise when he got home, thought Sheriff Sephus Adonis.

It had been a long and emotional interview, observed the sheriff. He had appreciated Lucas's straightforward style and naiveté. He offered that he would call Lettie to pick her man up before noon that very day. Time off for good behavior, and one less lunch to pay for out of the community coffers.

Next day, Sheriff Sephus found himself mulling over his conversation with Lucas. He concluded that, while Lucas was not the brightest penny in the pocket, he seemed like a decent kid. He was refreshingly honest with answers to challenging questions. Simple, big, rawboned, honest. Sheriff even had a passing thought that perhaps Lucas had been telling the truth about the purported gravel bar massacre. But he flushed that idea down the toilet stool with his daily constitutional. Reopening closed cases, particularly the nastiest ones, served no constructive purpose. Sheriff had learned that long ago. Let dead cases and, in this case, the thought of dead bodies, lie.

Weeds Among Bulrushes

Jimmy Jones lay giggling with Sally Boswell. They stretched naked together on a wool army surplus blanket where they had just completed the dirty deed. Jimmy couldn't help but wonder why it was called that. It felt really good, and you only got dirty if you got a little wild and slid off the blanket. And a little Ozark clay on your butt never hurt anyone he knew of.

They both stared into the brilliant-blue sky, the sun slowly headed to rest behind them. The corner of this field, nestled next to thick oak, hickory, and beech, sprinkled with dogwood blossoms and a few remaining redbud clusters beneath a high, greening canopy, had become their own special nesting place—spring, summer, and fall the past year, and back to late spring again. It enveloped them in the love of being alive and pleasured by and with each other.

Jimmy was Lucas Jones's first cousin, and he idolized him. Sally was also purported to be a cousin to some degree or another. Most folks around Hardlyville were. But that shouldn't keep them from some good, honest fun every now and again, they reasoned. A little weed, a little laughing, a little loving, sweetened with a beer or two, and what's not to like about that?

They didn't do the hard stuff, and Jimmy always wore a rubber, which is the way he was raised by his Uncle Norvel.

Jimmy had inherited this large parcel of land from Uncle Norvel, who died without heirs. Norvel had helped raise Jimmy, whose own father had served time for crystal meth trafficking most of Jimmy's youth. Jimmy couldn't even recall Dad's face, and Mom had passed on of pneumonia while Jimmy was in high school. Jimmy was an only child, given his dad's incarceration and his mother's admirable, if misplaced, loyalty.

Norvel and Jimmy had fished, hunted, and drunk corn whiskey together as Jimmy grew to manhood and became a nice, if somewhat lazy, young adult. Jimmy had no use for meth, due to what it cost his dad. But Jimmy had a fondness for weed and, in fact, farmed it in another corner of this field, shielded from view by a rogue hedge line. He didn't make much working at the gas station and needed to supplement his meager income, as well as cut the cost of his favorite pastime, getting stoned.

Jimmy was not alone in his passion for pot. Most of his buddies took the edge off life from time to time. It just slowed things down to a comprehendible pace. Lucas particularly enjoyed fishing with Cousin Jimmy after a fresh harvest. You could smell them coming downriver two bends away, but then again, no one was ever on their stretch of Skunk Creek. Throw in a case of Bud Light and a couple of lunker smallmouth, and life became one big rainbow for a while.

Sally was small and pretty and the proverbial banker's daughter. She loved doing it outdoors, which was just fine with Jimmy. He was an outside kind of guy. That they had to pick a few ticks off each other after a roll on the blanket only presented an excuse for more foreplay and perhaps another roll. There was the time they were going at it and a large copperhead snake had sidled up next to their blanket, striking both with a bad case of coitus interruptus.

Jimmy had learned that word in Ms. Rosebeam's Latin 1. Hardlyville had to be the only high school in the county, perhaps the state, that required a dead language to graduate. But Ms. Rosebeam was an old maiden of eighty-some years, a direct descendent of Thomas Hardly through his daughter Hardlita and her betrothed Herman Rosebeam, and Latin was the only thing she remembered from her youth. So who was going to say no to history and culture, dead or not?

She even had her seniors dress up in sheets for an annual toga party. It was a ritual worthy of its Bacchanalian roots that demanded a dollop of Dylan Thomas's white lightning in the grape juice, which even Ms. Rosebeam enjoyed without acknowledging its presence. It was on one occasion, after two cups of joy, that she slyly shared that famous Latin descriptive cited above. She had found Johnny and Susie going at it in the ladies' restroom, togas thrown asunder, and had scared the hell out of them before realizing what a unique teaching moment had been presented. She ushered them back to the party, togas properly back in place, and announced that she had caught them fornicating. The giggles all round were deafening. Beyond saving them from consumption and sure repository in hell, she had taught them a new "Beam-phrase," which others would do well to commit to memory, as it would be on the final. Neither they nor the other toga revelers ever forgot that Latin lesson on coitus interruptus.

As for the copperhead intervention, neither Jimmy nor Sally felt like picking up where they left off after bludgeoning the deadly viper with a large stick. They would never forget that one nor the Latin phrase that described it.

Another fond dirty deed memory involved getting it on in Jimmy's truck beneath Skunk Creek Bridge. At peak of passion, Sheriff Sephus came roaring up with siren blasting and spotlight flashing, asking them for their drivers' licenses. We weren't driving, observed Jimmy, which got him a knot from Sheriff's nightstick up top his head. They immediately reached into pockets for ID's, then sat covering their privates while Sheriff read their birth dates out loud, followed by the riot act for doing the dirty deed under age. There was that misleading term again, thought Jimmy. Sheriff said they could be put away for statue rape or something like that. Sally was offended and offered that she was much more lively than some cold statue. Sheriff could only shake his head. He ordered them to get their clothes on and go finish what they were doing at home before he booked them. Hard to do, Jimmy observed, with everyone still awake. Sheriff cracked his nightstick on the hood of Jimmy's truck and told him to get his dumb ass out of there. Sheriff had clearly lost patience with the two.

Jimmy didn't know if they would marry someday. Probably not. Cousins, even to the third degree, weren't supposed to. He had learned that in Mr. Pelvic's biology class at Hardlyville High. But they were sure having fun, living in the moment.

Next to Sally and Lucas, Jimmy's best friend was a big, black dog named Bob. Jimmy called him Bobbers and had no idea of Bobbers' ancestry. Bobbers went everywhere with Jimmy. Jimmy had even begun to include Bobbers on their trips to the blanket in the woods after the copperhead scare. Bobbers would share their peaks of glory, occasionally running in a circle around the blanket at full throttle and barking loudly when they got particularly wound up. It only added to their sense of excitement and fulfillment. Another plus for Sally. Several of Jimmy's prior blanket mates didn't display such patience with Bobbers, hurting his feelings and Jimmy's as well. Sally was the real deal.

Back to Jimmy's weed patch.

Why did Jimmy and others like him risk it? Getting caught could catch you a long stay in jail, and we're not talking Sheriff Sephus's hometown pokey here. Why? Money. And because it was easy. Conditions for growing marijuana in the Ozarks are perfect. First of all, you couldn't grow much else amongst the rocks and brambles, except tomatoes and berries, so no competition for growing space. Second, you could hide your plants all around the Mark Twain National Forest, and no cop could ever find them. Occasionally, another local would rip you off, but not enough to dent income stream, if you kept moving your plantings around.

There were more than a few major growers operating around the county, who provided Jimmy seeds on a regular basis. Jimmy sold strictly to repeat customers within his small market segment, never crossing paths with the big guys, who supplied all through the Midwest. Jimmy dealt only in cash and never had a problem keeping same in his pocket, which impressed young Sally to no end.

Jimmy knew there were some major meth cookers in his neighborhood as well, but he steered way clear, as did most of his friends. Meth was really bad shit, and he had seen more than just his pathetic father trampled in its wake. Sheriff Sephus seemed more intent with taking on meth than pot, providing Jimmy and his buds a lot of space to play. Weed was just plain fun—no more, no less.

Closest Jimmy came to getting busted was on one particularly dry summer day when his entire crop caught fire and burned up. Seems Sally had not been careful with her match, all caught up in the rush of a post-romp joint, and had flipped it beyond the blanket edge into dry grass. Try as he might, Jimmy could not control the spread of flames. He even tried peeing a small fire line in the beginning, as he had drunk a good bit of beer, but his pant cuff caught fire, and he had to rip them off. So he hustled Sally, Bobbers, and the small herd of grazing cattle downwind to ride it out.

As fire and bouquet filtered across his field, Sheriff Sephus and several volunteers, who had caught wind of the marijuana conflagration, drove up to offer help. One sniff told the whole story, and Sheriff asked Jimmy what he was burning, after he ordered him to put his singed pants back on. Just weeds was all, Jimmy allowed. Sheriff smiled wryly and commented on what a pungent patch of weeds it must have been. Funny thing, even after Sheriff left, a couple of volunteers insisted on walking the fire line, breathing heavily of smoke and bursting forth in giggling fits from time to time. Even the cattle acted giddy.

Cousin Jimmy's life was a happy, if not overly productive, one. He treasured each moment with Cousin Lucas, Sally, and Big Bobbers, appeared at work on time, pumping gas and washing windshields, as his boss insisted, and spent most of his time high and dry.

Like everybody else, Jimmy went to Skunk Creek Church of Christ on Sunday to pray for forgiveness. Whether it was weed, statue rape, envy of your neighbor's wife, an occasional bout of lust in your neighbor's back shed, or borrowing a tool and forgetting to return it for a while, Pastor Pat was generous in his forgiveness. Not that he condoned the excesses or excuses of his flock, he simply abided them.

He actually sported a few vices of his own, including a fondness for sweet wine and one of his choir members, often simultaneously, for which he forgave himself periodically. She was married to a traveling kitchen utensil salesmen and had her needs, like every healthy human might. Pastor Pat knew that her husband took care of his own through his frequent confessions, and as an unwed man of God, viewed his pastoral stewardship through an expanded lens.

There was a small contingent of practicing Catholics in the community, but they seemed to prefer living with their guilt over driving two counties north to flush it out in priestly confession.

Pastor Pat was occasionally asked to forgive one of them as well, and in keeping with his ecumenical outlook on life, he was proud to comply with any and all requests.

Strangely enough, no one knew Pastor Pat's last name. Everyone assumed he had one, but Pastor Pat had introduced himself as such to the church board of trustees, who hired him, and had proudly embraced this aura of mystery and anonymity as a holy attribute. He had been referred by a cousin of one trustee, who lived in Phoenix, Arizona, and had attended Pastor Pat's church there. Cousin didn't share that the good pastor had been busted for three DWI's in four years, all attributed to sweet wine consumption, only that he was a kind and gentle man.

Pastor Pat, on the other hand, didn't want anyone looking up his arrest records and figured a last name could only cause him grief. He had toned down current consumption in the interest of keeping his new job but occasionally shared that fond weakness with his favorite choir member, who became quite amorous after just one glass of heavenly elixir. Their private communion commemorations were rumored but never confirmed beyond an occasional wild scream of joy from Pastor Pat's church office. He always acknowledged and confirmed the salvation of another tortured soul. Just doing his job.

So how could a legitimate church hire a Pastor without a last name? "Didn't notice," "quaint," and "down homey" were among trustee responses when occasionally asked. Nor was the applicant pool for a leadership post at Skunk Church brimming with qualified candidates. Three of the six formal petitioners had served jail time for offenses of varying degrees of severity. One had a Hispanic surname. Another was a woman. No, Pastor Pat had risen to the top of the milk can, like a fine layer of cream, last name or not. All said, all happy.

Several of Pastor Pat's congregants' pleas for mercy and forgiveness had confronted Pastor Pat with ethical dilemmas.

TODO PARNELL

In one recent case, a loyal parishioner was curious to experience a unique and one time only sexual experience and had sought out well-known local lover Sheriff Sephus Adonis to provide it. She swore it was over, and despite being worth it once, it would never happen again. She asked Pastor Pat to forgive her for her selfishness. Pastor Pat knew all parties in passing, including the unsuspecting husband, whom he knew had strayed occasionally as well from other tearful confessions of her friends. He felt justice had been served and, rather than give her the "eye for an eye" speech, simply excused her indiscretion, warning that another would likely be less tolerated in the eyes of the Lord. She had nodded "yes" through her tears of shame.

Another involved a lonely single soul, who got so drunk one night he mistook his short-haired coon dog for an ugly damsel and woke up next to her the following morning. This was far more difficult for Pastor Pat, a clear violation of the most basic Biblical laws, and was probably illegal, in addition to immoral. He asked the litigant for time to pray on it before dispensing God's will. Several days later, he found peace in offering conditional forgiveness to the poor mess of a man, who promised it would never happen again, no matter how drunk he got. The lot of a rural preacher was a strange and rewarding one.

One ritual Pastor was most proud of was the Bulrush Festival. He, of course, administered traditional Skunk Creek Church celebrations, Christmas, Easter, Halloween, and the others, but had added one of his own creation. His very favorite story in the Bible was about how baby Moses was placed by his mother in an ark of bulrush to save the newborn boy from the pharaoh and in the hope of a kindly adoption. In one of the most ironic Biblical twists, Moses was saved and adopted by the pharaoh's daughter, only to later save the Israelites from a pharaoh's wrath. Talk about the ultimate end game. Pastor Pat believed this miracle should be commemorated annually and launched his festival in mid-summer years ago, providing a church-wide celebration to fill pews and spill out into Skunk Creek between Easter and Christmas, and when water flows were generally low. There was no celebration quite like it in all of Christendom, and folks drove in from miles around to observe.

He would begin the service, fourth Sunday of every July, by reciting Biblical evidence of the episode: *Exodus*, Chapter 2, Verses 1-10. He then called forth several of the more talented basket weavers in the community to seal the bulrush ark they had previously constructed with pitch and slime while he preached the Moses story, the burning bush, the plagues, the pillars of cloud and fire, the parting of the Red Sea, and on and on to his exhaustion. He would then ask the costumed mother of Hardlyville's Moses to place her baby boy in the ark for hand delivery to shallow waters just beneath Skunk Creek Bridge. If there were no baby boys, a baby girl would do in a pinch. He had even had to use a doll on one occasion, when no one birthed a young one the entire winter past. Ark and baby were placed in Skunk Creek and allowed to drift downstream a few yards to waiting parents and gravel bar.

On one occasion, the ark drifted away with Cletus and Glory Hampton's baby aboard and bounced down Skunk Creek a good quarter mile before Sheriff Sephus and several of his deputized buddies could catch up to it in a still pool along a rock bank. They also stumbled onto Henry Hoary, buck naked and noodlin' catfish in the small caves along same bank. For those who don't know, noodlin' is the ancient hillfolk art of grabbing big catfish by the mouth bare handed and dragging them out of their water dens to skin and eat. Many still ask why, even after explanation.

Sheriff asked Henry what he was doing, and Henry claimed to be taking a bath. Sheriff asked where his soap was, and Henry said he didn't own any. All knew what Henry was up to, that noodlin' is illegal, that his alibi was leaky, and that Henry had simply been caught red-handed and cheeked. They also knew that Henry rarely had much to eat. So, as he often did, Sheriff Sephus looked the other way, pretending to be absorbed with what was going on upstream, while Henry reclothed and fled on foot, one noodled ten pounder tied to his belt. Baby Moses survived nicely.

Pastor Pat always ended his service with verses twenty-two and twenty-three of *Galatians* 5:

"But the fruit of the Spirit is love, joy, peace, longsuffering, gentleness, goodness, faith, meekness, temperance: against such there is no law."

Such were God's demands of the citizenry of Hardlyville. Such were the core values of this special community. And such was the basis of Pastor Pat's mission: to offer forgiveness when each fell short, as all did from time to time, some more than others.

With all of his wisdom and forbearance, Pastor Pat hadn't a clue that Hardlyville would soon have an entirely new context in which to consider religion.

A RIGHT HONORABLE COMMUNITY OF CHARACTERS

C ivic leadership in Hardlyville was entrusted to four white males: the banker, the postmaster, the undertaker, and the mayor. To understand the interactions of these fine men is to understand the machinations of one small Ozarkian town. Civic leaders indeed, subject to several obvious anomalies.

First and foremost was the notable absence of women. Not that most women were deemed inferior to their male counterparts, just that they were comfortable with duties they were bred and raised to perform, like cooking, washing, child bearing, and cleaning. Of course, both genders enjoyed sexing as a shared responsibility. To bear the burden of keeping a village running, meeting its financial obligations, and planning its future would have put too much pressure on the already heavily laden and brave wives, widows, and young maidens awaiting marriage. At least, that's how this civic leadership saw it.

These four were never elected, appointed, or otherwise imbued with authority. They just assumed it. They had the wisdom and stamina to lead, and Hardlyville could not care less. That no one had the slightest interest in doing what they did, which wasn't much, never hit their radar gun.

There were, of course, other able men in town, most of whom delivered specialized yet indispensable doses of expertise. Sheriff Sephus Adonis faithfully kept law and order, more or less. He had earned the trust and respect of voters, as well as the civic leaders, and was legend in certain other circles, as previously noted.

Pastor Pat kept the faith and forgave the missteps of many. His sunny outlook was contagious and uplifting.

Doc Karst cared after the health of the community with a curious combination of the traditional melded with magic. Most of his diagnoses and remedies were close, and those which weren't did more good than harm. Doc Karst endeared himself to all with a heavy dependence on moonshine whisky as a base prescription. For pain or as a sleep aide or anesthetic, Doc Karst prescribed liberally.

He excelled at deliveries at all hours of night and day and had never blown a live birth. He had even delivered a calf or two. There was the time he called the Bledsoe boy a girl at birth because the peepee had not yet popped, but two days and one name change later, the record was set straight. Hardlyville was indeed blessed with those who knew their role and their place.

The majority subset of male citizens contributed less societally but generally had a good time and harmed not. Lucas Jones and his Cousin Jimmy come to mind.

And then there were the old timers, those whose institutional memory of Hardlyville lore and legend, and occasionally history, provided crucial, if generally inaccurate, grounding. They were a colorful lot, who made up what they could not remember and were held in some degree of reverence by most.

Dylan Thomas, Ol' Dill, was their spiritual leader. Long of tooth and short of ear, Dill was famous for his misinterpretations of the spoken word and clear corn mash. He had inherited an old still, hidden in a cave close by, from his grandfather and had handcrafted high-quality product for a generation. He lived off welfare, which met his every need and allowed him to be generous in distribution. When someone was down in the dumps for any reason, he or she could expect to find a mason jar of Dill's finest on the back porch to lift spirits. One new to town would likely receive a pawpaw cake from Flotilla Hendricks and a jar from Dill in welcome. The former was frankly inedible without a nudge from the latter, which Pastor Pat assured recipients knew before jumping into either. He greeted each newbie with a personal prayer and promise of forgiveness for whatever it was they were bound to do beyond the boundaries of righteousness before sharing their welcoming repast.

Dill claimed to be in his early eighties, which immediately raised the question of whether he had ever gotten it on with the similarly aged Ms. Rosebeam, the official community old maid and Latin teacher. He couldn't rightly recollect but suspected he had as there weren't many options back then. She acknowledged having had a crush on Ol' Dill when he was really young, but poo-pooed the notion of intercourse with anyone that undependable. No, Ms. Rosebeam was saving it for someone responsible. "Veni, Vidi, Vici," so to speak.

Flotilla Hendricks had once married, but to a genuine scoundrel, who had left her with two children, a wooden shack, and two acres for a young girl in the city. He had tried to earn his way back into her good graces after tiring of the girl and the city, but Flotilla had spurned his renewed interest. She was making it on her own with a small bakery and was through with men. She raised her children clean and proper, and both had left Hardlyville after high school to return only on holidays. Flotilla's unusual name derived from her two aunts, Florence and Matilda, neither of whom could spell but were most fond of her from birth.

And every Ozarkian town was in need of a village jester, so to speak, one who devoted every waking hour to making townsfolk laugh. Hardlyville was blessed with one Donald "Dinky" Doodle. He had the upper hand immediately because no one, even his best friends, could say his name without laughing. Donald Doodle was bad enough, but throw in Dinky, which was slang in some parts for a small male organ, and straight faces gave way to guffaws all around. Dinky dressed the part as well, utilizing surprise as a genuine art. Sometimes his clothes were too big, sometimes too small, sometimes a mix of gender specific garb. One would not be surprised to find Dinky sporting a bra with jeans and work boots on occasion. Sometimes Dinky simply went start raving naked, hiding behind corners and leaping forth to startle even the most veteran Dinky watchers.

Sheriff Sephus made a point of ignoring Dinky, for the most part, though he could have jailed him on many counts. Sheriff counted laughter as a key component of protecting the peace, and if Dinky's bizarre behavior caused people to laugh, who was Sheriff to pass judgment otherwise. Sheriff Sephus simply looked the other way when Dinky made an appearance.

Once a big-city newspaper got wind of Dinky's weird antics and sent a young cub photographer to town for a couple of days to follow him around. Dinky made a great game of it, which only made people laugh more. Dinky went into hiding and instead trailed the young man, appearing only when his back was turned. This frustrated the young photographer to no end, and he returned home without a single image of Dinky doing his thing.

"Screw the paparazzi!" Dinky screamed at him from a prominent tree branch as he headed home in defeat.

The young guy slammed on the brakes, as he thought he had Dinky treed in a state of nakedness. But by the time he got his camera aimed, Dinky had vanished into the tree top. He sat at the ready for a couple of hours, as townsfolk chuckled, before retreating to urban civilization and sanity. Dill Thomas was waiting for Dinky as he finally climbed down, wanting to know what it meant to "pop a rotsey." Dinky told him it was equivalent to passing gas, which seemed to satisfy Dill's curiosity. More laughter in Hardlyville. Dinky was truly a master at his craft.

Pierce Arrow chose not to publicize Dinky's aberrant behavior for reasons similar to the sheriff, though he did print a few photos of the cub photographer expressing frustration with Dinky by kicking at shadows and even throwing his expensive camera at a rustling bush or phantom movement on occasion. More community laughter, and peace in Skunk Creek valley.

And there was another, neither male nor old timer. Tiny Taylor owned the local grill and bar. Eat first, then drink on a full stomach. She called it Greasy Spoons. Yes, Tiny was a she, and she was indeed tiny, four foot ten inches and ninety pounds wringing wet, which she was most of the time, cooking up a storm. Who could ever dream she could plate up the greasiest, messiest, best tasting, worst for you food in the history of humankind?

Sheriff Sephus Adonis blamed his bulging waistline squarely on Tiny. He once arrested Tiny on charges of contributing to the delinquency of an elected official, him. Said he was only seeking a thirty day injunction to allow commencement of a diet. He ultimately dropped said charges, fearing a voter recall if he took Tiny to jail and away from her constituents.

Lettie Jones wouldn't walk within a block of Greasy Spoons for fear of adding ten percent body fat from simply breathing.

Pastor Pat absolved all overweight Hardlyvillians of their indiscretions while pardoning Miss Tiny for contributing to the community sin of gluttony. He adored her fresh baked cherry pie.

Doc Karst advised all of his patients to beware Miss Tiny's charms, then bad-exampled them to death.

Even Pierce Arrow's pouch paid homage to Tiny Taylor.

Tiny had moved to town several years back after leaving a rocky marriage behind in the big city. She sought escape and comfort in providing comfort food to others and was quickly embraced by most Hardlyvillians as good for their psyches, if not their waist bands.

Ms. Rosebeam even asked Tiny to cater her toga party every year, hoping to distract her students from sex, if only for the moment. While fried chittlins, fried okra, and fried canned pineapple were hardly Mediterranean, she billed them as exotic imports from the East. It generally took her days to remove grease stains from the sheets she let out for togas.

Tiny never talked much about her past—or the future, for that matter. She lived in the pleasure of the moment, putting smiles on the faces of her customers.

It was rumored that Dylan Thomas had asked her to wed, professing in his proposal the sincere desire to wake up next to a string bean and a fried donut every morning for the rest of his life. He purportedly promised that love would follow. Both he and she denied the rumor, though Tiny did seem partial to Ol' Dill, despite their age difference.

Tiny Taylor was an outsider, who moved in and brightened community life, beyond the health hazard she presented.

Back to civic leadership.

Banker Bud Boswell was one of the four. Middle-aged and well cared for by his hardworking wife, Lois, and beautiful daughter, Sally, Bud was a banker of the old school. Though lacking in formal education, he had a certain dexterity with numbers, and as the third generation to own the bank was never questioned as to his qualifications to protect townspeople's hard-earned savings.

His guiding banking principle, as handed down the lineage, was to only lend money to those who didn't need it. If a young'un needed a truck loan, Banker Bud would lend directly to young'un's parents, who could secure the loan with their bank savings account. Thus, if young'un got drunk and wrecked the vehicle or otherwise mussed it up, Banker Bud would advance the money for repairs directly from parent's savings, pocketing the spread between loan and savings rates to make a reasonable return for the bank. Cash in, cash out, with a small dollop for the facilitator. No disintermediation here.

Banker Bud always wore a black tie and short-sleeved, button-down, white dress shirt to work to reassure Hardlyville's citizens that their money was in good hands. He believed in banker's hours, as practiced by his father and grandfather before him. Bank of Hardlyville opened at nine a.m. sharp, closed for lunch and nap from noon to one thirty p.m., and reopened until three p.m. He had one full-time employee, the good widow Greisidick, who handled teller transactions, opened new accounts, and occasionally provided Banker Bud sexual favors in return for a small bonus.

He spent most of his day at the bank, counting and recounting money—he just loved the feel of it—and looking at old photographs of nude ladies he had inherited from his forbearers. It fascinated him that, while the lure of nude ladies was never changing, the generational differences in presentation were striking, from weight to age to body structure to hairiness, and so on. These preoccupations generally afforded him sufficient time for civic meetings and a respite from the constant stresses associated with leadership.

If he had a weakness, beyond old nude photos, it was for seven card, roll your own, high low poker. Banker Bud had always enjoyed a good game of cards, generally with a bourbon chaser for luck. This is where he differed from his forefathers. Old school to them meant no overt drinking and definitely no gambling. Would people entrust the safekeeping of their money to one who was prone to bet on anything? "No" was their collective answer. And while Banker Bud could hear their admonitions and warnings rattling around in the back of his number processing brain, he left them there, at least Friday night through Sunday morning in time for church, when community leaders hosted a marathon, clandestine, thirty-six-hour poker game, with carefully selected entrants coming and going, as fit their respective busy family schedules.

Banker Bud loved to win and loved to cheat. Being quick of mind with numbers, Banker Bud was an intuitive card counter of the highest order, which translated into consistently winning ways. He also sneaked peeks at others' cards when they reached for nuts and beer or he took one of his frequent leaks.

For instance, when he rolled three aces in the middle of his hand and had an option to go low with a 7-5-4-2 kicker, he would count how many sixes and threes showed before excusing himself to step outside for quick relief and a glance in the mirror behind Dill Thomas's chair to check out his hold cards. It didn't always work, but often enough to fund both his card playing and nude lady photo habits, including additions to inventory. That he was able to keep both his cheating and his collection sacred secrets was further credit to his closed mouth ways and formal manner.

He dealt with his lineage's concerns about bankerly credibility in the context of drinking and dealing cards by simply wearing a large paper sack, cut with eye and nose holes, to every card game. Anonymity was a state of mind, he reasoned, and though all knew who lurked beneath the brown paper, none would acknowledge him as their banker for fear of him lowering CD rates even further. He sometimes even wore the sack to bed with wifey to add a little spice and mystery to their otherwise mundane coupling. This allowed them each to imagine they were doing it with an unknown partner and worked well to relieve the boredom associated with every Tuesday night about

9:30 p.m., just past Sally's bedtime. Tuesdays worked well for both as they fell between poker games and Lois's increasingly frequent midday dalliances with Doc Karst in his exam room. Though Banker Bud found it unusual that Lois had so many health problems, he never suspected the source of her cures.

Banker Bud's life was predictable, safe, and occasionally exciting, in a perverted sense.

The same could not be said for Postmaster James Bond, so named well before Ian Fleming's famous copycat movie role, to which Postmaster Bond could readily relate. Postmaster Bond was a daredevil of the highest order, still hand delivering, by foot or bicycle, Hardlyville's mail, regardless of rain, snow, heat, or critters. PB, as he was affectionately referred to throughout his postal zone, had spent every adult day of his life, beyond Sunday, delivering mail.

PB had been gored by a pissed off billy goat, struck by a copperhead, shot in the arm by Dill Thomas, who mistook him for a revenuer, seduced on several occasions by comely Hardlyville matrons, who waited by their mailboxes in little or nothing while their mates were out hunting or trolling, bitten by countless dogs, hailed on by stones two inches wide, stalked by a twister that swerved a mere fifty yards from sucking him high into a vortex of death, attacked by a black bear rooting around in Doc Karst's trash, and even busted by Sheriff Sephus Adonis for delivering illegal drugs. But the mail had always and would always go through.

Hardlyville's Post Office remained stuck in the year it was constructed, one hundred plus years past, including the horse tie out front and the outhouse behind. There had never been postal boxes therein, not enough room, and never would be as long as PB was postmaster. Mail was meant to be delivered up close and personal so that its arrival could be guaranteed. Mail was vital to the good health of a community.

There were only four absolutes in PB's mailbag, and each was a never.

PB would never marry, he would never get sick, he would never fail to deliver, and he would never miss Saturday night seven card, roll your own, high low poker, where he generally lost half of his bank account. That was his abbreviated version of the *Bible's* Ten Commandments. Everything else in his life was in play and up for grabs, and he intended to keep it that way.

In the context of a civic leadership team, PB was an ideal complement to Banker Bud's conservative philosophy and assured representation of a high community risk tolerance.

In many ways, Undertaker Bob was the perfect bridge between competing leadership ideologies. He believed in nothing. Except Death, always with a capital D. And he made a damn fine living at it.

Unlike Pastor Pat, Undertaker Bob had a last name that was known to all. It was simply too long and difficult to pronounce to use. Klunkerkokatus was purportedly what his line's patriarch muttered upon seeing how ugly his first born son was, and it stuck with the immigrant branch as they left the old country behind. Undertaker Bob saw no immediate harm in leaving it behind as well. When he married his high school sweetheart, Matilda Peaches, she was relieved with his conclusion and was proud to go by her first name as well. The thought of Matilda Peaches Klunkerkokatus was the stuff of nightmares.

Their marriage was a strong one. No fooling around in that house. Matilda had been unable to bear children, so they simply adopted when special needs arose. If A loved B but had cheated on him only to find herself pregnant with C's seed, and infant had red hair to A and B's black, Undertaker Bob and Matilda were there to pick up the slack. Forgiveness was sometimes easier when the evidence didn't wake up underfoot every morning, and several marriages around the county were rescued by the

Undertaker family. They were loving and generous parents, the best of neighbors, and Undertaker Bob's leadership skills were much admired by his civic leader compatriots. He knew his peers' strengths and weaknesses and played to their former, holding latter in hip pocket for leverage in reaching consensus on difficult decisions.

Things like carrying guns into Pastor Pat's house of worship, and his passionate objections thereto, divided the community. Everyone in Hardlyville knew their Second Amendment Rights and didn't fancy anyone intruding on them. Pastor Pat preached a message of peace and love and didn't see a role for firearms in that discussion, at least on premises. If someone was going to shoot another over a horse or a woman or an insult, let them do it on their own time, not the church's. Undertaker Bob proposed a bridge to his fellow civic leaders. Anyone who felt the need to pack at church could simply slip the pistol or sawed-off shotgun into a personal cubbie hole in the narthex, where it could be easily accessed to defend the congregation in the unlikely event of an attack. Both safety and individual rights secure.

Undertaker Bob had actually borrowed the concept from daycare. When he dropped off his children, he loved the convenience of depositing diapers and wipes in bins with their names on them. Personal and sanitary.

Undertaker Bob argued convincingly that such was consistent with early Christian and Byzantine church design, wherein the narthex was not considered part of church proper. Pastor Pat could live with that, and all were satisfied that they had won this one.

Undertaker Bob greased the wheels of civic leadership and kept them purring through collaboration and common sense.

The fourth member of the Hardlyville Junta also went by one name, but only because it was his title, and he was proud to wear it. Mayor Josephus Dudley, no kin to Sheriff Sephus, was serving in his fourth term as mayor and was much beloved throughout the community. He was the token politician in the civic leader group, principally because no one trusted politicians. Mayor was different. He had earned his constituents' and fellow civic leaders' trust by being a politician who did nothing except smile and utter an occasional platitude. An exception was Pierce Arrow, who often wondered editorially what lurked beneath the empty utterances and flashing grin. He was subtle enough to avoid provoking the masses, but he simple couldn't stomach the vacuous presence that presented as mayor of Hardlyville.

Ask the mayor for a political favor? Receive a smile and "honesty is the best policy" response. Say what one might respond? "The sun'll come up tomorrow" was a typical second response, leaked from between gleaming teeth. This was as specific as the mayor could seem to get.

Ask the mayor what he thought about abortion rights? "A hole is only as deep as you dig it" he might respond. Animal rights? "A caged lion is worth two in the wild." Human rights? "Slick as a baby's butt" was a common fallback smile for the mayor. How could he get in trouble for having no opinions and a million dollar grin? Who could possibly vote against such a harmless and shallow thinker? Pierce Arrow, for one.

Holly Howell accepted a dare from Sheriff Sephus, during one of their recovery sessions after a particularly robust workout, that she could get Mayor to say something substantial. She would even wear a wire to validate her success. Shortly thereafter, she strode into the mayor's small office in City Hall, past his surprised secretary, and fronted his desk. She reached beneath her sweater and freed an ample orb from its container to present to his honor.

"What you see is what you get," he chirped, smiling all the while.

"Does his honor like what he sees?" she followed up.

"Beauty is in the eye of the beholder," he grinned.

"Would you like to hold instead of behold?" Holly gently offered, leaning forward over his desk.

This set the mayor to stammering about "an eye for an eye" and "a breast for a breast." Holly, thinking she was making progress, quickly pulled her other one out to present, both perched lovely and lonely, just inches from his honor's nose. Mayor just as quickly dove his nose into that Garden of Eden between her matching pair, inhaling deeply, before retreating to the cavity beneath his desk with a timid "life is no more than a dangling participle." Holly had never heard that one before, so she claimed a minor success before re-stuffing and strutting out.

Mayor's only goal in life was to offend no one. He determined that any opinion, reasoned or not, would not play well with at least someone, so he had none. Likewise, anything short of a grin, no matter how cheesy, would likely rub someone the wrong way. So he spouted and smiled on into the eternity of every day's end.

That was the way Mayor played poker as well. He rarely passed on any hand during the marathon weekend sessions but folded directly upon review of down cards, losing only his ante. This made him one of the boys, cost him little, and fed the general pot to the benefit of everyone else. He once rolled two aces to go with two aces down to minimize the losses of others through early disclosure. But when Banker Bud winced slightly, Mayor swore to himself to never win another hand, even if he had to hide cards.

Mayor's keen sense of civility and uselessness seemed to sell well to most Hardlyvillians.

Thus it was that into these four sets of hands, Hardlyville's future was placed. What they contributed was rarely discernible but reasonably sterile. A few hoped that a next generation of leadership would emerge to provide more progressive direction, but most were happy to salute a harmless group of incompetents as such and do their own thing.

As Ms. Rosebeam once observed, "At least we don't have to worry about any Ides of March with this crew in charge." Dill wanted to know when the march was to take place and what the charge was, as he wished to participate.

SWINE BRANCH

While Lucas and Sheriff Sephus had touched on water and waste and the incapacity of the former to accommodate the latter without going sour in their far-ranging, behind-bars discussion of several months past, it had seemed inconsequential at the time. Religion, philandering, public inefficiency, and forgiveness clearly stole the headlines of that exchange. That both cared deeply about the pure, clean waters of Skunk Creek was clearly a common passion. Beyond that, they shared little but seemed to grow in begrudging mutual respect as days and weeks passed.

Sheriff did buy Lucas the promised beer, and forgiveness and lust ruled the roost at Lucas's place in this era of fresh beginnings. Lucas drank a little less beer, and the legend of Sheriff Sephus as lover grew exponentially. He even had to leave town for a week to recharge his batteries. Gaining a few extra pounds did not dent demand and only stretched supply. He loved free market capitalism. The sheriff's conference room became the place to be. Young Holly longed for matrimony, but that was the furthest thing from Sheriff Sephus's mind. Instead, she settled for less, which was generally more with the good sheriff.

On the east side of Skunk Creek was a small, indistinctive branch of flowing water, which generally ran low during summer months but plumped up with seasonal rains. Its headwaters extended into rough hills to the east beyond, and no one from Hardlyville paid much attention until it began to carry green, slimy mucus into Skunk Creek proper after a heavy downpour or two. Lucas took particular note one beautiful spring morning when his new Japanese top water, for which had secretly dished out twenty-five hard-earned dollars, unbeknownst to Lettie, got so stuck in gunk he had to cut line and jump in the mess to free it. He reported the aberration to now friend Sheriff Sephus. Though Lucas didn't seem to be drunk as much these days, his credibility as a reporter had long ago been tarnished. Sheriff just filed it away without substantiating.

Lucas had taken to float fishing his old favorite stretch of creek alongside that cursed gravel bar again. Some days Lucas even doubted that what he'd seen had been real. Sheriff Sephus reinforced that doubt at every opportunity. Though Sheriff had indeed noted several missing person bulletins crossing the wires over time, none fit Lucas's tall tale exactly or seemed worthy of digging into. It was just too crazy, what drunken Lucas had dreamed up, and the cell phone with his duly confessed forgeries had long since disappeared from the evidence drawer. What good is evidence when the provider discredits it himself? reasoned Sheriff Sephus. "Shit, brothers." Amen.

Sheriff had noticed an unusual increase in construction material traffic, always heading east. He presumed someone was building something big out there somewhere, but it probably wouldn't boost the staid Hardlyville economy one iota. Hardlyville was Hardlyville and would forever be—mired in the past, suspicious of the future, inbred, and home grown. And damn proud of it. The Hardlyville Hounds would occasionally thump a rival town in basketball, and that was about as exciting as it would get.

Unbeknownst to Sheriff Sephus and Lucas, the machinations of power, money, and influence were contriving against them and their precious Skunk Creek.

The state board responsible for keeping water clean was no more than a toothless hag. It had no real authority, and its record of rule making and enforcement was downright ugly. That was the way state legislators wanted it, and that was the way it would stay. How else could they bow and scrape to their constituents' every whim and fancy? Old Dave down in Bundyfunk wants a permit to dump sour mash from his still into a sinkhole. Well, give it to him. One more vote counted to the good and a nice contribution as well. Young Rickie wants to fence his herd of cattle in the headwaters of Turkey Creek so they can keep themselves clean and presentable for market? Why not? He'd do it anyway, permit or not. Fine him for fouling a beautiful creek? Why bother? He'd never pay. John Poe's septic tank hasn't been cleaned or repaired for decades? Who cares? Just means his shit and that of his wife and eight kids goes downstream.

And who in them hills even knows what a sinkhole is? Who understands that what gets put in one eventually shows up in someone else's well or bath water? Who understands that karst topography is not the name of an Eastern European immigrant or a new-fangled medical diagnostic machine invented by Homer Karst, Hardlyville's resident Doc? Who could ever imagine that the innards of the Ozarks are like Swiss cheese, full of holes and drainages that spread water to and fro, that sinkholes and springs and the like provide entry points to the system and share the wealth of every deposit, no matter how foul or toxic? Some get it and are held suspect as academics, liberals, do-gooders, and environmental meddlers. Some get it but value money above theory, no matter how sound and proven. Most don't give a shit where theirs or that of their livestock ends up.

The new chairman of the State Oversight Board (SOB) is case in point. He lives in a big house, big city, and gives big bucks to select elected officials, one of whom represents the district in which Hardlyville lies. Why? Seems the herd of show horses he raises and sells to wealthy patrons of the national horse scene love to frolic, unfenced, in the flowing waters of the lower Skunk, just above its juncture with the big waters. Wouldn't want a state rule against destruction of critical riparian corridors to stifle a little horseplay, would we? And while states' rights trump national rights in his humble view, individual freedoms reign supreme, including those ascribed to expensive horses.

He always wanted to chair something big, and SOB was the perfect portfolio, all of the state's precious waters. The state's favor dispensing governor was happy to oblige, and even though the significant contribution to his reelection campaign preceded the appointment, all was above board and within the ethical rules of a "pay to play" political system.

It also seems powerful chairmen of toothless regulatory bodies are susceptible to cash bribes. And this is where Sheriff Sephus, his buddy Lucas, and their Skunk Creek loving brethren get screwed, as do successive generations of their ilk.

The clandestine meeting took place over drinks and dinner. Many drinks and dinner. The guest of honor was the new chairman, and the facilitator was a lobbyist for Big Pork, and we're not talking Sheriff Sephus here. Seems his internationally prominent client was intent on putting a pork chop on every table and was running out of places to raise the beasts that provided them. Between increased demand and enhanced regulation in some states, the client was desperately looking for places off the beaten path to develop.

They also needed access to water in large quantities. Of course, their investments in new technologies over the decades assured the protection of such waters from degradation. They could even cram up to 10,000 swine into a confined breeding area for months and years without sullying a drop. Finally, they could deliver and spread hog shit as free fertilizer for local farmers throughout the region. How egalitarian can you get?

Build big lagoons for swine waste, make them safe for twenty-five-year flood levels so no breach can possibly occur, at least in our lifetime. Sure the transport in and out will kick up a little dust. Just spray it down from time to time. Water from the stream will trickle back in the stream, recharging the flow. An efficient closed-loop system in the interest of feeding families at home and around the world. And the smell of hog poop? Absorbed in the mellifluous scents of wooded Ozark wilds. Have to be at ground zero to even catch a whiff.

This guy can really talk, marveled New Chairman.

Land was cheap in one previously untapped corner of the Ozarks. Chicken farmers had yet to lay claim to it, and fresh water was plentiful there. The problem was the SOB had not been overly supportive of prior efforts to expand the Big Pork realm beyond existing jurisdictions. Regulations allowed it, but rule making and permitting were more discretionary, and prior water body regulators had been stingy with their approval.

All that could change with new entrepreneurial leadership at the top. New Chairman was impressed and particularly flattered. That said, he wondered aloud if hog lovers might have a soft spot in their hearts for simple show horses. New Chairman was in the process of setting up a unique national foundation for promotion of the noble sport and was seeking a significant founding and naming contribution. Significant, he explained, carried six figures behind the dollar sign. Hog Farmers of the Ozarks for their Show Horse Brethren (HFOSHB) had a nice ring to it and would look good on an inaugural naming plaque. He could personally assure the integrity of funds application as his young wife of two years, an exquisite show horsewoman in her own right, would serve as president of the foundation and have final approval over everything. All that was needed at this critical juncture was that one big, launching gift. What did Big Pork think?

"Shouldn't be a problem" was the answer New Chairman was looking for. The rest was up to him.

"Oh," Big Pork Lobbyist concluded, "we would like to keep this quiet. We're still in the process of assembling acreage and moving construction materials onto the prospective site. We even have a few hundred sows in place, kind of wandering about to get their bearings. A government guaranteed loan has been secured, subject to regulatory approval. A nearby settlement of some loony, reclusive religious sect is providing cheap and steady labor. We pay them well, charge no rent, stay out of their antics and rituals, which sometimes get a little loud and racy according to our site manager, throw them an occasional hog or two, and all is well. All of the pieces are in place to get up and running before any of those crazy tree-huggers and water quality wing nuts can stir things up with the locals. Once in place, can't displace. A stone set is a foundation laid. Not to sound presumptuous, but we knew we could count on your support, Mr. New Chairman, all along. That's why we didn't wait."

"Get your paperwork in, and we'll flush it through at next quarterly board meeting," Mr. New Chairman assured Big Pork Lobbyist. "Send your contribution in several smaller checks from nondescript donors to my office. Pleasure doing business with those who know how. By the way, does project have a name yet?" New Chairman asked.

"How about Skunk Creek Ranch?" was the response. "It sits in that watershed and sounds a little better than Swine Creek" drew a laugh from New Chairman.

The chair gaveled the SOB meeting to order. He promised early adjournment, owing to the holiday season and lack of substantive issues to discuss.

The state rulemaking agency was recommending approval of all submitted proposals except one, Skunk Creek Ranch. They had some reservations about the potential impact on water quality in upper Skunk Creek, a relatively well-preserved tributary of big waters downstream. Seemed that a large spring branch flowed through the proposed site for the ranch east of and then into Skunk Creek, and some felt the watershed could be at risk for potential degradation. They questioned why this reach into decidedly non-agricultural land, at least in a large farm configuration, made sense for state waters. They had raised many questions with the proposal submitter and not received much in the way of relevant responses. There was not even an environmental impact statement, which, while not legally required due to recent state legislative action, they deemed as critical to fully assessing the environmental risk. They recommended that the board table the Skunk Creek Ranch proposal until next quarterly meeting and review of additional data. New Chairman reiterated that he wanted all facts and options on the table. Thus the lengthy, if somewhat misplaced, concerns of some deserved airing.

The board moved seamlessly through the agenda until item number seven, Skunk Creek Ranch. Following the agency official's presentation, several spoke against the project on vague general grounds. No one was present from Hardlyville. No one in town even knew about the game-changing proposal.

New Chairman asked the board whether they were there to protect clean water and encourage economic development by responsible and resourceful entrepreneurs in the poorest parts of the state or to just continue to serve as another inefficient government bureaucracy, controlled by fringe environmental groups with no interest in the welfare of those citizens who would benefit most. He asked if anyone was present from Hardlyville, the principal village near Skunk Creek, to share the community's view. When no one stood, he concluded that they must have no objection or they would speak up today. He added that, as a property owner along lower Skunk Creek, he and his wife welcomed the quantifiable economic development impact on the region and were grateful that many long-suffering souls could now share in the fruits of the free enterprise system. He invited other board members to share their views or concerns, knowing that state representatives and state senators from their home base had been contacted by Big Pork long ago with pledges of support, significant contributions, and words of assurance about the importance of pig farming to economic development in the state.

One board member politely asked why Skunk Creek, of all places—why there, why now? She did not expect an answer and did not receive one. The busy members of this board did not have time for rhetorical questions. The Chairman, hearing no further questions or concerns, called for the vote. The board was unanimously in favor of issuing a permit for Skunk Creek Ranch to operate an industrial pig farm for up to 10,000 of the creatures on a tributary of Skunk Creek.

That Skunk Creek Ranch had been built, bought, and paid for before rubber stamp SOB approval was not lost on some in attendance.

GRISLY, AGAIN

This was even worse than the other, if such was possible. Lucas was again in the wrong place at the wrong time. Except this time, he was not alone. Cousin Jimmy Jones was with him. It was early morning, summer top water time, just over a year later, same stretch of river, different gravel bar above the stream confluence with "putrid creek branch," as Lucas had taken to calling it. He and Jimmy were fishing upstream to avoid its spew and stench. Green gunk was contained by low flow this time of year.

The screams startled them. They quickly pulled ashore and slipped into the facing upstream woods, in the direction of the piercing shrieks, which soon clarified as pleas for mercy. A dastardly band of four men stood over two unclad couples, cowering in front of them, tents rent asunder in the background, camping equipment scattered about.

Lucas and Jimmy watched in horror as the rapes began.

Lucas immediately sent Jimmy scrambling downstream for the old .22 they always carried in the canoe for moccasins and, on return, back down again to paddle in for help. He was too far away for the accuracy that would be needed to stop at least one or two of the heathens, so he began to crawl slowly forward, carefully and quietly, avoiding notice.

As the evil men rested and laughed, an apparition emerged from the rising sun. A scantily-clad lady with a long, graying ponytail loped into the scene and began taunting the captives. She took great pleasure in stripping naked and jumping over each of the young men, screaming something to the sky. With great fanfare, she pronounced them useless to the human race, sinners and fornicators of the worst kind, and in dire need of cleansing. She then reached behind her to grab a gun from one of her men, she as naked and cold as its extended barrel. Lucas was far enough away to have to fill in the blanks, but her message was obvious.

Again, each of the young ones appeared to beg for mercy, and as if on cue, one of the men grabbed a hunting knife, stepped behind a young lady, who appeared to be no more than twenty years old, jerked her head back to expose her throat, and cut it wide open with one stroke. The sudden death gurgle sent the remaining victims into shock and disbelief. Their high-pitched screams spoke to terror, raw terror.

"Who's next?" boss woman shouted with glee before pointing to the second young lady. She claimed to still hold out hope for at least one rise among the boys.

Lucas could take no more. He knew he would die, but to do nothing carried far greater pain into the future. As he processed the hopelessness of the situation, he rose and fired at the little prick raising a bloody knife to a second throat, striking him in the side of head and delivering instant death. A second shot dropped another before return fire clipped his left arm and sent him spinning back into woods.

"Get him!" the lady from hell screamed as her remaining two boys foolishly rushed directly at Lucas, allowing him to stop another. Three shots, three dead soldiers. Easy as squirrels on a limb from a hundred yards out.

The Demon Lady quickly changed her tone and strategy, as the stunned kids looked on in disbelief. She shouted to her one left standing to head upstream with her to additional cover and a sentry, who was running toward them. All three quickly disappeared in the thick underbrush and could be heard thrashing through in full retreat. Lucas warily walked toward the survivors and their fallen float mate. Blood dripped from his wound as he freed them from the ropes and urged them to quickly reclothe. They would launch their own canoes and head downstream with the lifeless cargo, away from the mayhem, putting as much time and space between them and the hounds of hell as they could. Lucas scanned the tragic scene, knowing it would likely be scrubbed clean before he could get the sheriff there. At least there were others with him who could attest to what went down.

"Who were these evil ones?" Lucas asked out loud. The young survivors could only moan and sob and paddle like the daylights.

Sheriff Sephus, Cousin Jimmy, and several townsfolk were waiting at the Skunk Creek Bridge, just beyond town, trying to figure out themselves what to do next. Jimmy had spilled all to the sheriff as fast as he could talk, and after prior context, Sheriff took him at his horrid word. Should they paddle a small armada upstream to try and save Lucas and the captive strangers? Should they drive up to the AA put-in and float down? Should they try a difficult cross-country trek through hostile terrain? Could Jimmy even find Lucas's secret put-in that would save them hours? His shocked and baffled demeanor screamed NO. There was a reason most who floated the fifteen miles of isolated Skunk Creek chose to camp out at least a night. There was no well-known, easy way in and out between. Or they could just wait and hope for the best.

Lettie was there and beside herself. Her fresh beginning with Lucas had bound them closer than ever and had recently yielded a new beginning in her belly, which protruded only slightly, even at this stage of development. She urged the sheriff to take action, whatever that might be, beyond wait and hope.

Then, slowly into sight, came two canoes. Lucas with a screaming young lady, who hadn't stopped screaming since he met her, and the two young men paddling mechanically beneath frozen stares. All were in one state of shock or another. Lucas bled from a bullet wound but was alive, thank God, alive, prayed Lettie. The towel-covered body of the young victim rested mid thwart in Lucas's canoe. He had not told his bow mate for fear she would abandon ship. She had not looked back once.

"They killed her!" she screamed over and over again. "Cut her throat wide open" slipped out occasionally.

Pierce Arrow took photos and copious notes for the *Hellbender*, thankful there was little blood left to record. Undertaker Bob removed the stiff body. Pastor Pat prayed over it. Doc Karst tended to Lucas's wound, while Lettie held his good hand and sobbed silently. Doc's wife and the town nurse gently led the young woman to the town clinic and began to treat her wounds. Doc's wife held her close and would most of the night. One of the young men finally spoke, allowing that Lucas had saved them from certain death and shot three of the bad guys in the process. Lucas was a genuine hero, and this two-bit town in the middle of nowhere better goddamn say it. He then broke into tears. Lettie squeezed Lucas's good hand again.

Sheriff Sephus asked Lucas who done it. Lucas said he didn't know them, but there were four heavily-armed, trash-talking demons, led on by a surreal jumping and leaping lady with a near-gray ponytail flying fore and aft and screaming out the name of the Sacred Mother amidst charges of fornication and sex with the devil, as best he could hear. He had never seen anything so bizarre, frightening, or demonic in his entire life. Or as cruel. She was possessed or possessing, and they were her minions. Cousin Jimmy just stood by with his head bobbing up and down. Lucas would tell the sheriff more in closed session.

"It was her eyes," sobbed one of the young men. "They were green or yellow or orange and glowing like embers in a fire. She looked right through me to my soul and grabbed it by the balls. Sorry," he muttered.

"It's okay," assured the sheriff.

It was clear everyone needed space and time. Sheriff found where the young floaters were from, a university town hours away. Given the late hour and knowledge that they were not due back for another day, Sheriff asked them to stay the night with neighbors for food and moral support. Sheriff would call their parents to report in if they would provide phone numbers. Doc would provide drugs to sleep, and after they told their story tomorrow morning, Sheriff would get them home, subject to recall to help catch those sorry bastards. And the Devil Woman. All agreed and hugged Lucas tightly before leaving.

After his brief interview, Sheriff Sephus leaned against the hood of Lettie's small car. She breathed a sigh of relief that he hadn't sat. He would likely have left his mark. He slipped into deep thought for a quiet moment.

"What you thinking?" had been Lucas's question. "On to something?"

"Might be," was Sheriff's soft response. His "shit, brothers" was considerably less constrained. He said he thought he had met the women with the slightly-gray ponytail once several years past. The yellow, piercing eyes and wild-ass ways described by the survivors, and confirmed by Lucas from a distance, were not easily forgotten.

All leaned in to hear more.

"Met her in the gas station, having coffee," he recalled. "She presented as an attractive, well-constructed, middle-aged woman on a mission. She saw my badge and confidently sidled up, wanting to know what Hardlyville was all about. Said she was looking for a place to relocate with her family and thought she had roots in the area. Couldn't recall a name to put with the claim, however. She was going to spend a few days checking us out. Liked what she was seeing so far."

Sheriff confessed that he didn't. She had the strangest-looking eyes, though partially hidden by sunglasses, he'd ever seen.

"I asked about her family," Sheriff continued, "about children and all, and got nothing more than a vague affirmative. Saw her several times that week, just nosing around, before she stopped by the office to advise that she was leaving next morning to check out another place. Not enough going on here for her crew.

"She said she had appreciated the hospitality, though, and had discovered a lot of interesting things, including one about me. Always curious, I inquired as to what that might be. She said she heard from several young ladies that I had something on which they placed great value.

"The lady flipped a fifty on my desk and said she would like to check it out right then and there. I handed it back and indicated that I generally did not charge for services, but that the rest of my morning was relatively unencumbered, if she wished to join me in the conference room out back. She nodded, left the fifty behind, and led me by the hand to my oversized conference chair. She quickly stripped off every last piece of her clothing, except a red St. Louis Cardinals baseball cap perched high on her head. It was then that I felt the full brunt of those piercing, yellow eyes as she stared right through my stained khaki pants crotch.

"It didn't take long for her to get worked up. The wildness in her eyes encompassed her body as she began to shake and shiver and spit and curse out unintelligible words and phrases, eyes ablaze like a lit up jack-o'-lantern. Frankly, I never seen anything like it."

There was a gasp or two and a lot of head shaking going on in response to Sheriff's descriptive.

"Funny thing," Sheriff said, "she never once calmed down. She finally threw off her Cardinal hat, freeing a long, braided, slightly-graying ponytail that whacked me in the face. She glared yellow sparks and just kept going.

"And boys, she had more hair on her than I ever seed. Couldn't rightly tell whether she was human or beast. When her abnormality really hit me was when she turned around to reclothe at the end. Her mess was way worse out back. And that wasn't all," Sheriff Sephus continued. "Staring back at me from her behind was two red eyes, tattooed one to each cheek along where all that brush began to thin out. Like she was watching every move I was making.

"This she-thing was like an animal all right, no two ways about it. Shit, brothers, she was downright insatiable," mused Sheriff Sephus. Lucas commented on another big word from the sheriff and wondered what it meant. "An otherworldly appetite" was as close as he could come.

Yep, Sheriff Sephus Adonis was pretty sure he had seen that evil lady before.

REDEMPTION

Her voice carried an otherworldly tone. She screamed for redemption. She chastised for failure. The Sacred Mother can die for us, but we can't even redeem our sorry souls by carrying out a simple sacrifice for her. We are failures of the highest order. Her graying ponytail waived wildly behind her. She shook a tattered *Bible* with blood stains in one hand and reached with the other into a bucket to pull out a snake—copper colored with black-and-tan hourglass markings on its back, mouth agape, and fangs showing. She stared it down six inches from her beaked nose, then shook it wildly as partisans raised their voices in rapture and strange guttural sounds of praise.

She lamented the loss of two brothers and the critical wounding of another, who lay on a cot just beneath her exhortations. She challenged her followers to even the score, noting that they had "taken three of ours to one of theirs." That one, and her sorry excuse for a life as an underaged, fornicating sinner, was not adequate sacrifice for the losses of their own.

"We must seek redemption through more sinner's blood, shed for the Sacred Mother."

The remaining thirty or so congregants—men, women, and children—roared their approval.

She wanted to know who would begin the sacrifice tonight. A burly young man rushed the makeshift stage, wife in tow, lifted her dress to reveal her nakedness, and plunged into her from above, pumping with purpose and vengeance. His culmination drew more mutters of support as others followed suit. She gazed on with approval, replaced the copperhead into the bucket, and called for a restoration of order once active ritual participants were spent.

Her charge tonight was for more blood. Customary annual sacrifice of sinful heathens would not suffice going forward. They had followed that course in previous years and other remote locales, always moving on to protect the flock from prying secular authorities. But it was time to get even. The Sacred Mother would reward their failure of this week with more opportunities for redemption.

"No longer is one eye for one eye enough," she whispered. "We must take two, three, and four to atone for our failures, to redeem ourselves in the heart of the Sacred Mother. She has told me this," she finished, "and I share it with you tonight. We must balance the Holy Ledger if we are to suckle with the Sacred Mother in gardens of glory."

Congregants knelt in prayer before retreating into ramshackle cabins, tents, and temporary shelters for more redemptive coupling, always man atop woman, as in the holy word. With one exception.

She always had her pick for Saturday Sacrifice and Communion. Tonight it was a young one who had pleased her deeply not long ago. And she would be on top, as always. She would sit astride in honor of her place of ascendancy. Howls, guttural growls, and moans would be heard throughout the long night, gray ponytail thrashing in praise and glory, the sacred community of servants drawn together in love and lust.

No one knew from whence she came in the beginning as a wild, young thing without home or company, singular in her sleek beauty, passion, and ferocity. No one cared. Her Gospel of the Sacred Mother and primitive pleasure, greased with the sacrificial blood of others to atone for their sins and redeem a flock of fallen believers, resonated with this group of castaways searching for no more than to be left alone. She aged as she began, above and beyond the rest in ethereal and mythical trappings. That it was said she occasionally bedded cougars and wolves in their caves and dens only added to her mystique and lent power through association. They followed her through generations and relocations, always one step ahead of law and order. They followed even today, though none knew her beyond couplings and charisma. This lady of the night ruled their every thought and emotion. She would lead them on yet another foray into the belly of the heathen for redemption and retribution before moving on to safer space in another remote locale and another cycle of holy fulfillment.

INTERVIEWS

Seemed like bad news descended on Hardlyville all at once.
First, it was the large-scale hog farm approved unanimously by the State Oversight Board on a feeder creek to the
Skunk out east of town. Townsfolk knew why it was leaking green
goo once they learned there were already hogs on the premises.
Skunk Creek Ranch to boot. What an insult, and how devious.
They never even had a chance to object. Pierce Arrow was
particularly incensed and wrote an editorial in the *Hellbender*
so brilliant and biting that the state's largest papers ran it. There
seemed nothing legal they could do about it right now but keep
a wary eye out for what was to come.

And then there was the matter of the interviews. Two young
males and one female, survivors of a diabolical attack, and their
rescuer Lucas Jones. Sheriff Sephus asked Lucas to sit in on all
interviews, given his perspective from a distance.

They started with the young lady, who was desperate to get
home and in a very fragile state. The sheriff began gently as she
burst into tears. She could only talk about the blood gushing from
her best friend's severed neck and how she was next. She had
felt the bloody hands grab her long hair and jerk her head back

before the pop of a single shot and gurgling death sounded from just behind. The voice of God, she had wondered, welcoming her to his heavenly kingdom? And then the strange, smelly body falling forward on her and a dead man's head oozing matter from a small hole. She simply couldn't remember another thing. Every time Sheriff raised a line of questioning, she burst into tears and repeated her gruesome tale. After forty-five minutes, the sheriff gave up and released her to her parents, who had driven in early that morning. She hugged her boyfriend and Lucas, and prepared to leave Hardlyville forever, she hoped.

Boyfriend was next so he could ride back with them and was not much better. He did remember hearing strange noises just before dawn and yelling out to his buddy in the adjoining tent about the big bear outside. As he dozed back off, the tent was rent asunder by long knives. He and she were ordered by two scraggly excuses for men to remove their clothes and prepare for a good sin-scrubbin', forgiveness-givin' cleansin'. He had instinctively jumped on her attacker and only vaguely remembered coming to at some point later, blood dripping from the place he had been clubbed, and his girlfriend bound by rope, moaning softly. Nothing after that seems to have registered. Could he remember any faces or a lady with strange eyes and a long ponytail? Not really, he said, not really. Must have been the blow that took away the later moments. Sheriff patted him softly on the shoulder and told him he had been brave.

"Take care of that young lady," he whispered. The young man hugged Lucas too.

Last up was the date of the deceased. He was able to recount more clearly what had happened. He started from the beginning. The courting couple were good friends. He and the dead girl were loners, pretty good students, and pretty independent. All were seniors with career plans in place.

"They fixed us up for first date. Make it a memory. Float beautiful Skunk Creek in the Ozarks. It's a bit of a drive, but we have the canoes and gear. 'You must be shitting me,' I told my laughing best friend. 'First date in the wilds of the Ozarks? First date camping out on a river? Well, if she's okay with it.'

"So, we did it. Headed out over a long weekend. He knew about it from a cousin who lived nearby and said Skunk Creek rocked. Check out the map, take two vehicles with racks, leave one front and back, and party on. He was experienced. I wasn't but learned how easy it was quickly. Girls were along for the ride.

"We left the pickup vehicle beneath your bridge here late morning and drove up to the AA put-in. What is it, fifteen miles or so?" Sheriff nodded. "Beautiful water, not a soul in sight, spectacular set of gravel bars. Settled into one about six with camp set up, steaks, and a couple more beers. Probably about halfway home, my friend noted. But a world away as well. We were all pretty loose when we hit the sleeping bags late and didn't notice much. Suppose they could have been watching then, but certainly no overt signs or sounds.

"First thing I remember next morning was my friend hollering out something about a bear and laughing, probably just before sunrise. I nodded back off, then all hell broke loose. Knives ripped through tent canvas amidst growls and promises to make us pay for our sins, right then and there."

Sheriff interrupted to raise the delicate question of whether they had done anything that religious fanatics might count as sins the night before.

"Can't speak for my friends. They have been dating for a couple of years and set their tent on the other side of the campfire. As for us, no way. First date, out in the wilds, a little kissy face and touching, but no more."

Sheriff nodded thanks.

"Anyway, there were two guys, both big and shirtless, smelling of sweat and urine, pulling us out of our tent, telling us what they were going to do to both of us to cleanse our filthy souls. Most of their words started with F.

"They ordered us to remove our clothes and get 'birth naked,' as they called it. I could see a similar exercise playing out across the way. I have never been so frightened in my life and raised my screams with the rest. They tied my hands behind my back to my ankles, so I was totally immobile, and planted my knees so deep in gravel that I could see the blood begin to run. They were in such a hurry across the way to get at the girl, they forgot to truss up my friend, who threw himself on one of the attackers. A harsh blow to his head ended his gallant effort. I'll spare you all the details, but fear gave way to acceptance and a simple desire that it all be over, whatever form that took. Soon there were no more screams to lift. One kept whispering to me that I'd get mine but not before she blessed me first. I hadn't seen a she yet, but that soon changed.

"When they finished with the girls, they lined us all up in a row, execution style, squinting directly into the rising sun. The beasts reclothed and even grabbed our own camp chairs and a couple of beers in preparation for Act Two. Showtime, indeed.

"She walked straight out of the sun toward us, slowly and bathed in light. She wore a loose-fitting tunic, no shoes, and carried her authority with almost holy grandeur. She leaned into my face and spit out the word sinner, again and again. She asked if I had fornicated last night. When I shook my head no, she smiled broadly to reveal oversized, stained teeth and whispered into my ear that I was a lousy liar.

"It was then that the evil, yellow eyes fully registered. I thought it was the sun's glare at first, but when they shone in the shadow of her face, I saw a beast of prey. She swung around to face my friend, intentionally slapping me with her long, graying ponytail. She read him the same riot act."

Sheriff Sephus suggested to Lucas that this was about when he and Jimmy showed up, according to his prior testimony. Lucas nodded in the affirmative.

"She crouched like a wild animal and began toying with us, her beer-drinking boys cheering her on and ridiculing our respective endowments. She then leapt skyward, ripped off her tunic, and began to strut her naked body around us, taunting us as useless to her and the entire human race.

"I passed out from the sight and the smell. I awoke to her backside, and believe this if you can, two red eyes staring at me from the hairy fringes. Tattoos, I guess."

The sheriff and Lucas exchanged a knowing look.

"She then handed one of her boys a rusty, long knife and nodded toward my date with a smile. You saw what happened next. He slipped behind her, grabbed her hair, jerked her head back, and cut her throat. He then moved to my friend's girl-friend and began the same process, as if he were working a production line.

"That's when a shot rang out, and you saved our lives," he nodded to Lucas with tears dripping down his cheeks. "You dropped another and then another as she and one more melted into the woods upstream. The rest is one big blur.

"I apologize for all the graphic detail, but this simply was not just another random act of violence and brutality. This was evil incarnate, with a dose of the supernatural thrown in, and you need to know the craziness you are up against."

"It was just as I seen it," confirmed Lucas.

Sheriff thanked the boy and promised him he would find them. Evil will be faced, and justice will be served. The boy promised he was capable of driving home and headed to the take-out site on foot, to go back and bury his new friend.

"Shit, brothers," Sheriff Sephus Adonis muttered to Lucas, then repeated it for good measure.

"Sheriff, one question if I may. You never mentioned her stench."

He nodded and responded that he remembered having a horrible cold that day and couldn't have smelled shit if it had been caked on his upper lip.

"It's her all right," he confirmed to Lucas, "and now we need to find her."

LOOKIN' FOR LEADS

Sheriff Sephus immediately sent a small party of hastily appointed deputies with Lucas to the crime scene gravel bar via Lucas's secret put-in. All were blindfolded, except Lucas, his standard requirement. Seems an old girlfriend of Lucas's used to take him up there to dally in high school. Hard to get to, but owned by her daddy and cut the float in half. Even after they broke up, she allowed Lucas access through a series of locked gates on the promise he wouldn't share with no one else. Lucas was many things but not one to break a promise.

The search party found what they expected. Nothing. No blood. No guts. No campfire or campsite. No knives. No bullets. No sign of life. No sign of death. A bird or two singing, creek running, but no. Nothing. Like before. Gravel bar scrubbed clean beyond natural, beautiful creek flowing by, life as it should be. Except, life gone.

Sheriff Sephus put out an APB for an aging but well-built lady—had to pick those words carefully to get it posted—with a graying ponytail. He also got what he expected. Nothing. Nothing.

Sheriff Sephus decided to shift gears. There were two really bad things going on in the neighborhood, he reasoned. Brutal murder, probably plural, and a large-scale hog farm. When evil begets evil, there is usually a connection. Thought he remembered that or something like it from the *Bible*. So leave one dead-end and seek another. Maybe all dead-ends merge and become live. That sounded Biblical as well. Sheriff was simple but smart that way.

He asked Lucas to visit the hog farm with him. A courtesy call, of sorts. Lucas asked if he could take his weapons on this one. Sheriff said no, and that they would take Lucas's pickup to avoid undue attention.

Sheriff got the address from the State Oversight Board public minutes but didn't recognize the access road. Had to drive plumb around the east side of the county to connect to it.

"No wonder we never seen it coming," he muttered to Lucas.

One dirt track led to another but finally ran into a small herd of swine, rooting around in a field just beyond a small stream.

"Has to be close," noted Sheriff Sephus.

"Should have brought my deer rifle," observed Lucas.

"A GPS would have been more useful," the sheriff responded with a slight grin.

They followed a hog path over yet another hill and spilled down into a major contradiction in terrain and development. Skunk Creek Ranch lay out beneath them in all of its modern glory. The small valley was lush, with irrigated fields, and a small creek had been dammed into a two- or three-acre lake with a dock and several canoes. Lo and behold, there were even a couple of apparently bare-breasted young ladies lolling in the sun. Lucas pulled out his hunting binoculars and cancelled "apparently" on the spot. Sheriff Sephus's trademark "shit, brothers" did not begin to do justice to what lay below. Lucas was more dumbfounded than usual.

"Where's the pigs?" was all he could mumble.

He drove down the hog track to a large, newly constructed ranch house where an elderly gentleman in jeans awaited their arrival. He wore a pistol around his waist. Sheriff introduced himself and Lucas and stated the purpose of their call as "getting to know the new neighbors." They were invited inside for a soda pop after their long drive. Several scraggly-looking young ladies were cleaning the comfortable surroundings, which were neither opulent nor sparse. The young ladies out back waved, tops securely back in place.

The gentleman welcomed them to Skunk Creek Ranch and proudly showed them around the premises, which he referred to as the caretaker's house. That would make him the caretaker, he confirmed. The rest of the staff were out overseeing operations. He didn't mention what the two young ladies out back did for a living.

He led them to a large topo map, inscribed with clearly delineated sharpie markings. He oriented them to the current location, then upstream to a spring issuing from solid rock. It fed the lake, leaking into a small branch, then went downstream at least a mile to livestock barns, feed silos, the water treatment plant, waste lagoons with reinforced concrete lining and built to twenty-five-year flood plain specifications, and a fertilizer plant where hog waste not spread on adjoining fields would be baked and bagged for distribution to farmers throughout the region. For free.

Their host went to great lengths in explaining the closed-loop water handling system, which assured that folks like Hardlyville residents would never see their precious Skunk Creek waters sullied. Water from the branch is piped through shallow barn pits into a waste lagoon, then recycled into sprinkling systems that run off to replenish the waste lagoon, supplemented by deep well water, which is introduced during drought or dry months.

All water is treated at some point in the loop. Comes out clean enough to drink.

Say what? Lucas's head was spinning and screaming bullshit from every corner of his mind. Made his hair hurt. *Is that why we get green goo with every heavy rain, squirting out of this branch into the Skunk?* he wanted to ask. *Closed-loop water handling system? Clean enough to drink? For pigs?* Sheriff Sephus could feel Lucas fuming and kicked his shin hard. Lucas jumped but got the message. This was not the time.

Their host proudly announced that the new chairman of the State Oversight Board, which had recently "permitted" the ranch and farming facility, would be arriving the next day for an extensive tour and several days of operations observation. Even Lucas could reduce State Oversight Board to SOB. This equation made sense in his simple mind.

Sheriff asked how long it had taken to construct such a complex undertaking.

"About two years, but we proceeded ahead of licensing so we could hit the ground running. There was no doubt that approval would be forthcoming for a project of such environmental integrity and local economic development potential. We pay taxes in both states, and no state legislator in his right mind could say no to this."

He was right about that, Sheriff nodded.

"Who does all the work, slopping and feeding pigs, moving them around, shoveling up after them?" Sheriff Sephus asked.

"Well, we got lucky on that," their host announced. "There's this modest compound of religious folk less than a mile away from operations who need the work."

Bingo, thought Sheriff Sephus.

"They live in a box canyon back there, with a couple of caves and a large spring complex for water, at least that's how the young cleaning ladies you met describe it. Even has its own small, natural rock amphitheater, they claim, perfect for their rituals and services. They seem nice enough folks, don't mind dirty work or smell of the pigs, and always show up on time. They do get a little rowdy on Saturday nights, which is apparently their time of worship. We can hear them carrying on for hours, if the wind is right. Wanted to stop by sometime but never got an invite. We pay them well and give them their own small herd of pigs to wander at will. You may have run into the herd driving up. As I said, those two young'uns cleaning house belong to their clan."

"The one's swimming as well?" asked Lucas.

"No, those are aides to the chairman, who he asked be allowed to accompany him on his visit—note taking, dictation, photography, and such. Cute little things, aren't they," their host smiled.

Yes, and they was proudly showing them right at us as we drove up, thought Lucas.

"How many pigs you feeding these days?" Sheriff Sephus inquired.

"About thirty-five hundred," their host responded, "but we can accommodate up to three times that number at full capacity. We are developing a dirt road network to handle traffic out east of here, so again, your fine community won't even notice."

"Well, you've been very kind, sir. Never did catch your name," Sheriff observed.

"Norm. Norm Seaton."

Sheriff introduced Lucas Jones as his deputy and himself as Sheriff Sephus Adonis. Norm asked if he could return the visit someday. Said he would like to meet with the community to share a presentation similar to what they just heard.

"Want to assure them that we're good neighbors and wear the name of Skunk Creek Farm with pride and deep affection for its namesake."

Lucas thought he was going to puke on the spot. Instead, he waved goodbye to the pretty young ladies and moved out.

The two ladies cleaning the place took note of the names. Will need to report this back to her, one whispered to the other.

Sheriff and Lucas were quiet as they retraced the long trek back.

"Never heard such bullshit," Lucas finally confided.

"Yep," Sheriff Sephus agreed.

"Think I know where she roams," added the sheriff. Lucas looked puzzled. "Our wild woman with the graying ponytail," confirmed the sheriff.

"That group of religious hippies?" asked Lucas.

"They ain't no hippies, if she is their high priestess," said the sheriff. "Let's see," he continued. "This is Friday, ain't it? Reckon we ought to sneak up her way about dusk tomorrow night and see if she shows."

"Bound to be difficult and dangerous, Sheriff," Lucas noted.

"Yep. Let's go back and study that topo map to see if we can make it less so," Sheriff Sephus challenged.

"Just you and me, Sheriff?" Lucas asked.

"No. Think I'll ask Pierce Arrow to join us," Sheriff responded. "Could be important to have someone along to write it all down."

"What if he vomits again?" asked Lucas.

"Well, if there's that much blood around, we're all in trouble. Better not let Lettie know what we're up to, Lucas. She'll worry that little bald spot raw," slipped out before Sheriff could swallow the words. Fortunately, Lucas didn't hear. Sheriff wouldn't hurt him for anything. Not like that.

INTO THE LAIR

Sheriff spread a topo map atop his conference room table, Lucas and Pierce on either side. He quickly spied a good site candidate on the map, about where it should be. A box canyon was clearly delineated, with a spring site equally as obvious. More difficult to pick out was a natural amphitheater, but there was plenty of static on the map to support that theory. Thick woods all about was also a logical conclusion. A natural compound, hidden from the world.

The problem was clearly going to be access. The dirt track ended at the head of box canyon, but it was hard to track back. They could probably enter off County Highway 52, but it was hard to be sure. Couldn't come that way, anyhow, unless invited, which they were not. Lucas noticed that the spring seemed to disappear, then resurface in a parallel mini-watershed to the Skunk Creek Ranch branch before joining it downstream. It also seemed to border his ex-girlfriend's father's property line to the east. Might be able to borrow a couple of horses from Cousin Jimmy, unload them on that property, and ride them up the spring mini-watershed to get within walk-in, striking distance under cover of darkness. An obvious, but unsaid, corollary consideration was accommodation of Sheriff Sephus's physical limitations.

Sheriff nodded approval of Lucas's access plan and asked him to approach Cousin Jimmy in strict confidence. The plan would be to load Jimmy's horses midafternoon tomorrow and arrive at said launch site about four. Shouldn't take more than a couple of hours to ride in, and with walking time allotted to favor Sheriff Sephus's girth, could arrive at the compound as early as nine, well after sunset.

"We could watch a while, see if the lady with the graying ponytail shows, make a positive ID, then hustle back to issue a warrant for the bitch's arrest to be served on Sunday. Long day, dangerous circumstances, but worth the risk."

All agreed.

A steady rain began to fall about noon the next day, and Sheriff Sephus gave some thought to postponing. It would gum up already challenging logistics, and who knows how weather affects their ritual. May even cancel showtime. Talk about a wasted trip. Ironically, it was Pierce Arrow who stepped in to insist on going forward with the plan. Said it was too important to the safety of the community, and who had ever heard of crazy folks being afraid of a little rain? Lucas concurred with Pierce's assessment, and together they shamed Sheriff into moving forward. Sheriff Sephus wondered if Pierce had a deadline to hit for the *Hellbender* and nothing to work with but this crazy outing. Still, Sheriff soldiered on.

They pulled into Cousin Jimmy's large field, where he awaited them with three horses. Sheriff looked the other way when he saw Cousin Jimmy's healthy pot patch growing tall in a corner next to the woods. Jimmy noticed his glance and muttered a quiet something about more weeds. Sheriff shrugged. No arrests today, he assured Jimmy, but cautioned him to grow a little more cover in his field. Jimmy nodded with gratitude. They saddled and loaded the horses into Jimmy's horse trailer and drove quickly away, Cousin Jimmy wishing them well and promising to send in the State Highway Patrol if they were not back by dawn. That was where Sheriff Sephus had his strongest set of contacts.

They drove to Lucas's ex-girlfriend's father's property, unloaded and mounted the horses, and rode quietly up the spring branch watershed. The path was sloppy from all the rain, and progress was slow. There was an ominous feel to the moment and the task at hand. Lucas led and Sheriff followed, for a change. Pierce was taking notes as he rode. Oh, what a story lurked ahead. A journalist's dream. He was already writing it in his mind.

They went as far as Lucas was comfortable by horse, tethered them, and began to walk through the mud and muck of the source spring's runoff and continuing rain. Sheriff Sephus labored mightily through the dark and the slime. *Fitting metaphor*, he thought.

The shouts and screams were vague, then grew into what seemed to be a sense of joy. It had not rained on this parade. They had discussed the possibility of sentries and were quiet and alert as they crept through heavy cover, the crescendo growing with exponential fervor.

"Sacred Mother" was the first real sound they could discern. Then "blood." Then "sacrifice." Then "redemption." The loaded words rolled out of the box canyon like a tornado. They ducked, in fear of being sucked into an unholy vortex.

There was a small grove of trees ahead. They slipped in there and walked, tree by tree, toward the sounds of voices ahead. There was still no light in the dank, dark sky that enveloped all, rain dripping all along. Even the smells were sour and sordid.

Then a light flickered into a large fire, despite the rain. Someone had started a bonfire. They slid around, jumping the light's outer arc, still under tree cover, toward a small rock promontory that might afford them a broader view. They peeked over to a small mass of shaking humanity, gyrating in fits and spurts to the gestures of their leader, who was covered from head to toe in black burlap. It was a frenzy none had ever witnessed before.

The leader soon revealed herself, casting the burlap aside and swinging her long, braided ponytail in a violent circle. Pierce recorded that he thought her head would spin off. It's her, Sheriff Sephus nodded to Lucas, who watched her live and in person for a second time. She quieted the crowd with palms down, reached into her bucket of snakes, and pulled one forth, hissing in fury—both she and the snake.

"Holy shit," muttered Lucas, "it's a copperhead."

"Quiet," said Sheriff.

It was then Lucas noticed the metal cage to her right—empty, but foreboding. Something bad is going to happen in there, he just knew it. All of this was set in a natural amphitheater, a small stage alit with fire and her fury, audience just below, looking up. She was scantily clothed in the skin of a wolf, which shifted and moved with her every gyration, revealing her nakedness in strobe bursts. She laid the snake at her feet, where, like the others, it stared on with rapt attention.

Her sermon carried on for more than two hours, punctuated periodically with calls for sacrifice, when, as if on cue, a couple would mount the stage and each other until he grunted his pleasure and they returned below to weave with the crowd. She spewed hate and vitriol between these calls for coupling, mixing pain with pleasure in a master's brew.

Sheriff wanted to leave. They had what he was looking for, a positive ID—from flashing, yellow eyes to glimpses of at least one red-eyed butt cheek, if not both. No way Pierce was going to leave this story of the century behind, and Lucas was too mesmerized to pay any note to Sheriff Sephus. Pierce scribbled in his small pocket notebook as fast as he could write. It was good they stayed, at least in one sense.

Just when it seemed she could hate no more, she mouthed the names of Deputy Lucas Jones and Sheriff Sephus Adonis. Both listened in stunned silence as she delivered their death sentences to the reenergized crowd below. They had been identified just yesterday, snooping around the hog ranch, by loyal servants who cleaned the ranch house. Jones was the one who had murdered her boys and their brothers. Sheriff was a fat shit-for-brains, whom she had seduced long ago, only to find him lacking in every pleasuring grace. Even Sheriff winced at that one. It was time that both died to repent for their sins and redeem the flock's purity. It was also time to punish the townsfolk for sponsoring and supporting their sinful ways. A few of their children will be sacrificed as well.

"We must even the Holy Ledger," she screamed.

She asked for volunteers to lead the sacrificial run and, of course, every hand in the crowd, including women and children, was raised. She beamed her gratitude.

First, she must commune with brother cougar to formulate a holy plan.

"All will gather for a special Sabbath service tomorrow at dusk for implementation."

With that, she stepped stage right and into the cage Lucas had seen. She screeched an unholy scream, at which point a large male cougar bounded across the stage and into the cage with her. She stroked it for a few minutes behind the closed cage door before emerging with the beast to exit into the dark behind the stage, crowd in a frenzy, Lucas with his mouth agape.

"Let's get out of here," whispered a clearly shaken Sheriff, and this time they did as the crowd broke into orgiastic rhythms and frenzy.

Lucas led as they descended from the rock lookout. His foot slipped into a crevice, cracking at the ankle before he could redistribute his weight. All heard the shot-like retort and grimaced helplessly as Lucas bit his hand to stifle a scream. He settled on the ground to assess the damage and could only shake his head and bite deeper. Sheriff and Pierce sat in stunned silence.

"You must go on," he urged between gasps. "Our town, our friends, our families are in grave danger from these lunatics."

"We can't leave you," moaned Pierce. "We'll carry you to the horses and ride you home to Lettie. There will still be time to deal with this coven of evil."

Pierce registered that phrase in the back of his mind, as every good writer would, despite the monumental distractions.

"No, Pierce, you must go on without me. There are more precious lives at stake than just mine."

Lucas nodded to Sheriff Sephus, who nodded back in the affirmative.

"Look, I'm a country boy and can survive most anything on instinct alone. I'll root around in these rocks until I find a hole to curl up in. Fly home and bring back the friggin' Texas Rangers or Butch and Sundance or Billy Jack to destroy these brainwashed vermin before it is too late."

Sheriff Sephus nodded again.

"Lucas is right, Pierce. It isn't pretty, but the choice is clear. There is too much at risk."

Sheriff patted Lucas's shoulder and threw his large, tent-like poncho over him.

"Love you, bro. See you tomorrow night," was all he said as he grabbed Pierce by the arm and led him quietly away.

"Tell Lettie I love her more than anything," Lucas whispered.

Lucas began to burrow beneath a large rock, as he had occasionally done in waiting for a deer to kill each fall. Never in such pain, however. He pulled off his boot to relieve the pressure and allow the swell. He stuffed the dirty sock in his mouth to stifle the screams that accompanied every cycle of pain. He passed out from it occasionally, but was soon awakened by it again. Rain continued to drip. He had never felt like this before in his life and passed Lettie's face and touch through his mind to slip away to.

Lucas heard a rustle nearby on his left. Then a slap and the rip of clothing.

"Yes, you will spread your legs for me right here and right now, no matter what your husband says."

"Okay," was the frightened reply.

It was surrealistic for Lucas to be lying a few feet away from forced sex in the woods and rain, with a dirty sock in his mouth and a scream in his throat, unable to help this damsel in distress.

A few grunts later, he heard them rise and turn toward him. She stepped first and screamed at the ensuing contact.

"It's him!" she screamed. "The Lucas one!"

She was the housekeeper at the ranch. The man followed behind her, dragging Lucas to his good foot, and seeing the twisted one dangling, kicked it straight on, causing Lucas to go black.

THE PLEASURE PRINCIPLE

The rapist turned dark hero dragged Lucas's large frame behind him through rocks and brush, bellowing for all to return to the amphitheater, regardless of their state of sleep or dress. The small housekeeper trailed timidly behind at his order to provide a positive ID and verify what he said—or face her husband as an adulterer. The crowd drifted in from all corners, in various forms of disarray, as he dumped Lucas on stage and kicked him back to consciousness. Lucas had never felt such pain in his life and tried to lie still to absorb it.

"Look what the cat dragged in," he screamed. "The infidel himself."

A discernible buzz arose from those assembled. He pushed the housekeeper forward, dress torn above her now visible bra.

"Who is this?" he demanded of her in the same tone he had earlier ordered her to have sex with him.

"It is the Lucas one," she confirmed.

"This would be the same Lucas one who murdered our brothers in cold blood and just attacked you with intent to rape?" he thundered.

"Yes," she replied softly.

"This would be the same Lucas one I pulled off your helpless body as he sought to penetrate you while clawing at your breasts?"

He pull one from its cup to reveal the large scratch he himself had just inflicted.

"Yes," she whispered.

"This would be the same Lucas one whose ankle I snapped to prevent his escape?"

"Yes, yes," she repeated.

"This would be the same Lucas one whose spawn is dripping down your leg?" he screamed as he raised her dress.

"Yes," she cried.

"Case closed!" he thundered.

Her husband leapt to the stage, demanding revenge for the desecration of his helpless wife. Someone threw him a hunting knife, which he pulled from its sheath and lunged for Lucas, the crowd roaring its approval.

"No!" bellowed a big man, leaping up to tackle him. "No!" he roared again as he disarmed the angry husband and pushed him back into the crowd.

This was obviously a man of some authority, as he loudly established that the infidel belonged to their grand mistress. He kicked Lucas twice, then dragged him to the cage stage right and slammed and locked the cage door. He patted the dark hero a thank you on his back and hugged the young housekeeper victim before facing the unruly crowd.

"I will stand watch over the infidel until she returns from brother cougar's lair. I'm sure she will have fresh ideas on how to save this sorry soul and will include us all in them."

"When might that be?" was raised from the floor.

"Who knows?" he responded. "When they get together, time is only conceptual."

Lucas rolled in and out of being alive. Dawn did nothing to ease his pain.

He hoped Sheriff and Pierce had made it back and would be headed in to take this lady out, but that was beyond him now. He would die. *How shall I choose to go that will honor Lettie, my sheriff, and my town?*

Lucas knew what she would do with him. She would ridicule, accuse, cajole, and curse him in the name of her God. Then she would sexually taunt and abuse him in front of her disciples. Then she would kill him. Knife or pistol. He had seen her show before.

As Lucas lay fermenting in pain, dread, and droll anticipation, the glimmer of an idea seeped into his stream of semiconsciousness. There was one option beyond the meek acceptance of death. He could choose to pleasure Her Evilness. To live outside of fear and disgust. To treat her like a lover. Sheriff Sephus's prior experience with the She Devil, as unpleasant as it had been, confirmed one thing. She had earthly longings and physical reactions beyond her otherworldly trappings.

Lucas honed every ounce of focus and mental energy into his conclusion. He would become the fornicator of her followers' accusations and leave her squirming for more. He would will himself hard, beyond the gross and fetid distractions, and put it to her as no one had ever done. He would make himself indispensable to her carnal cravings. He would make her scream for more. Lettie would understand and forgive. He would overdose the demon with her own sick medicine. He would take her to the top, then bring her down slowly before lifting her again. He would be her wild animal of the night. He would bite and claw. He would prove her to be no more than the lust-filled lady she is. He would rip off her supernatural cloak of invincibility and publicly caress her vulnerabilities. He would be everyman to her everywoman's needs. He would attack her dank, smelly garden of evil with all he had. He would buy every second of time he could for the good guys to arrive. Then Lucas passed out at the thought of it all.

She limped back into camp a little after noon. She was covered with ticks and fleas, nips and scratches, and what remained of her wolf skin. She liked for her people to see her like this, as it polished her halo of power and potency. Self-inflicted or not, they would never know.

All waited quietly to see how she would react to the capture of the infidel. They led her to the cage without a word, where her faithful attendant stood watch. They saw her wicked grin broaden beyond the seams of her leathery face. They saw her spit on the still form through the cage bars. They watched her gloat a minute more before shedding all and walking back to the cold spring to bathe and ponder the night's activities from deep within the catacomb of caves and tiny passages. She would emerge at dusk to preside over the cleansing death of the infidel and share her plans for further sacrifice in the interest of redemption for all.

A LITTLE NIGHT MUSIC, PLEASE

Sheriff Sephus Adonis and Pierce Arrow were on their horses and headed to the trailer within two hours of leaving Lucas, trailing his horse behind. Pierce still didn't like it, but Sheriff was a man possessed, pushing his bulging carcass through the woods and rain like a wounded bull in a bramble thicket. Pierce liked the feel of that one and tucked it away for future application. Neither were accomplished riders, but both whipped their ponies into a bone-jarring gallop, hanging on for dear life and Lucas. They loaded the horses quickly and were back in Sheriff's conference room before dawn.

Sheriff Sephus called the Regional Highway Patrol Head-quarters in both Missouri and Arkansas and demanded immediate access to their supervisors. An emergency of epic proportions was unfolding along their shared Ozarkian border, and time was not on their side. One deputy was down, possibly in a hostage situation, and an entire town, Hardlyville, at risk of an immediate terrorist attack focused on young children. This concise descriptive got the attention it deserved, and Sheriff was soon on the line with those who could make things happen. Quickly.

By noon, the leaders of their respective Highway Patrols were seated in Sheriff Sephus's famous conference room, listening to Pierce Arrow's blood-curdling notes. Why had Sheriff waited so long to call in help? Because he didn't have the facts until late last night, was his response.

"Now we know this. A looney-tune religious cult has murdered one, and probably three, young people over the past year, in the name of their perverted take on religion. They are planning to murder Deputy Lucas Jones—they may have him in their hands by now—and Sheriff Sephus himself. They are going to terrorize the small town of Hardlyville by kidnapping or killing several of its youngest children. And the whole scheme of attack will be laid out at dusk tonight in their evil den of iniquity."

The officers shook their heads in disbelief, then registered their recognition of the seriousness of it all. It was beyond time to plan a powerful response, and they set out with a sense of urgency and purpose.

Sheriff Sephus Adonis's conference room was still the place to be.

By midafternoon, a plan was in place to attack the evil coven, as Pierce Arrow insisted on calling it, utilizing the full set of resources available to both state institutions. Troopers would be marshaled and deployed from tiny Hardlyville immediately to trek into the vicinity of the compound by seven p.m. and would assume attack positions, as directed by Sheriff Sephus, by dusk. Sheriff and team leaders would ride horses part way, others would follow on foot. Three helicopters would be used in the raid scheduled for post dusk and were already in route to Hardlyville, avoiding targeted airspace. A command post would be established simultaneously at Skunk Creek Ranch, where Pierce Arrow would be given special dispensation to record everything as it unrolled.

Objective one would be to find or free Deputy Jones. Objective two would be to detain and arrest the lady with the graying ponytail. Objective three would be to detain and place under arrest every male and female member of the cult. All in that order.

Two helicopters would sweep in and bathe the purported amphitheater in spotlights, as perimeter troopers attacked from behind. All gunfire would be directed in the air unless fired on first, then focus would be on active shooters. A third helicopter would ferry raid leadership to the ranch under the cover of darkness for establishment of the command post. Respective state governors would be advised of the raid five minutes before launch. Confidentiality and speed were critical to success, and all trooper movements would be classified as a drill. Post-attack communications would run through Pierce Arrow, under the supervision of the respective state commanders.

"Ready, aim, fire," quipped Sheriff Sephus as he exited the conference room with one "shit, brothers" in honor of his friend Lucas, for whom he feared deeply.

Dusk deepened over a remote corner of the Ozarks as the plan swiftly unfolded. The rain had ceased, and a new moon gleamed in a corner of the sky. Peace would be fleeting. Sheriff Sephus and his front guard of highway patrol troops, all camoed up, were arrayed behind the rapt crowd—far enough removed to avoid detection, close enough to view and hear the spectacle. They had encountered no sentries, to Sheriff's amazement and relief. It had been agreed that Sheriff would signal the first move. He was torn between going now and waiting for a moment of greater distraction. Plus, there was the unfortunate fact that poor Lucas had been captured and encaged like an animal. And it was clear that a caged Lucas was the main event tonight. Sheriff would wait to move in.

She emerged in total darkness. The place was packed and still. No one in the compound would miss this one, including previously posted sentries. She lit a small fire that had been set at the front of the stage and stacked wood on it slowly and deliberately.

Lucas lay still in the cage, steeling himself for what lay ahead. His strategy was simple and in sync with hers, oddly enough, at least tonight. Pleasure as and beyond principle. Pleasure as and within her holy writ. Pleasure your neighbor as they would pleasure you. Thou shalt not only covet pleasure, but revel in it.

She growled her agenda through large, clenched teeth. Redemption through pleasure, redemption through sacrifice, redemption to the Sacred Mother through blood and revenge, redemption tonight, through each and all. No sermon tonight, only redemption. And a plan, a plan, to spread redemption beyond them to everyone.

She started with the plan, which was focused on the young children of Hardlyville. Random, swift, and brutally redemptive, it would require one afternoon from five fearless members of the Movement.

"The rest of you will be equally critical, as you organize and move to a new home just before the righteous strike. It is time for that again. Moves invigorate our community of redeemers, restore our purpose, and spread our touch."

She had secured, long ago, a remote parcel of equal beauty and remoteness in Western Tennessee.

"It will serve as our new home, as well as that of the three young ones we will remove after their school next week and raise as our own. They will fill the void of our loss. They will balance the ledger. Their sacrifice will share our loss. I will meet with the group captains after tonight's festivities to detail responsibilities and mundane logistics."

Sheriff cringed at the simplicity and brutality of her edict. They must be stopped.

She turned her attention to Lucas.

"The task at hand is to milk the infidel and prepare him for salvation through the Sacred Mother before avenging the loss of our brothers at his hand."

95

She laid a long knife and long-barreled pistol on a stool behind her. She begged support from the community as she undertook her challenge for the evening, and then began to gyrate slowly and sensually as she moved toward cage and captive.

Lucas shut down all systems related to pain, feeling, and sense, and rose on one leg to greet her advance. She wore a loose-fitting tunic of light camouflage, then shed it to reveal her nakedness in profile behind the dying embers. She threw open the cage door and challenged Lucas to come out and make her whole in the interest of his salvation. He limped forward and kissed her on the lips with purpose and passion. She leaned back in stunned surprise, then allowed herself to reengage. His energy enticed the most callous of her feelings, and her animal core roared its approval.

Sheriff Sephus cringed again, with a "shit, brothers" whispered to Lucas for good luck. He couldn't believe what was playing out before him, but thought he had a remote sense of the purpose in Lucas's aggression. He knew it was too risky to move in now, with her naked, armed, and dangerous.

Lucas focused on erection, playing tapes of Lettie in her naked beauty and glory in constant rewind in his mind. He must bring the She Devil to ecstasy or all was lost. Surprise was his only advantage at this point. She growled her approval as she stripped him bare and stared at his handiwork. She smiled an evil leer and pushed him on his back. Twenty minutes later, she was roaring and screaming. Lucas kept his focus and purpose in getting her there. He could feel nothing from his ankle to his groin, but he stayed the course in desperation.

Pleasure, not redemption or salvation, was all that was on her radar now, and her people shared her euphoria. He had captured the animal within her, redirecting from murder and mayhem to lust and larceny. She would steal his seed and milk him dry. She would return to dispense with him only after she had used him up. Lucas pumped gamely on, obsessed with hanging on to what was rightly his and not wasting it in a bottomless pit of evil. Deflation would be a game ender, and he knew it.

A distant hum beyond her immediate sense of alarm became a present roar before she could place the noise. Her people feared not what she didn't acknowledge.

Two helicopters, beaming bright light on the stage, changed all that. Sheriff Sephus screamed to move out and fired into the sky.

"Black helicopters have come to take away our freedoms," one soul shouted.

Another pulled a pistol and began to fire at lit targets. Return fire from behind quickly dropped him. Men in uniform were closing the circle of congregants. Helicopters turned lights on and off to lesson targetability. The strobe effect hastened panic on the ground.

Only she grasped the whole story. She leaned into Lucas with a vicious kiss before biting deeply into his tongue. This broke his focus into pieces of pain, and Lucas popped. She screeched in victory, rode him to empty, and climbed off, trailing a high-pitched wail behind her. She had won this battle of wills and could move forward to avenge. She turned away for a moment, then back with the long-barreled pistol in hand. She aimed down at Lucas and fired, point-blank.

Sheriff Sephus watched in horror as Lucas jerked, then lay silently on the ground. He heard her cackle loudly above the din and chaos, then watched her turn and lope away.

Sheriff plowed his way toward Lucas, knocking bodies, large and small, aside. He knelt beside him and cradled his head softly in his ample lap. He begged Lucas to fight through this, to hang on with whatever he had left. Lucas's eyes remained closed. Sheriff Sephus screamed for help to God and whomever else could hear him. He cursed himself for waiting to move in.

Meanwhile, over at the ranch, thousands of porkers oinked their confusion in unison as a third helicopter swept in, with lights ablaze, to establish the command post. Their confusion was nothing compared to the dismay in the ranch hot tub. A copter landing caught New Chairman of the State Oversight Board therein with his two young, female assistants, all naked as the day they were born. Pierce Arrow was snapping pictures as fast as he could pull the trigger.

New Chairman's first mistake had been to extend his tour of operations to a week because they were all learning so much about hog farming. His second was to rut like a boar that week with two sows half his age. Now Pierce had it all on record.

"You can't do this to me!" screamed New Chair, trying to find something to cover up with other than his nude assistants, who were too stoned to worry about much of anything. One even offered a toke to Pierce, who politely and regretfully turned her down beneath the watchful gaze of the two state highway patrol leaders. After all, this was now an official command post. Arrests for possession of pot and public indecency followed. The assistants seemed not disturbed nor particularly anxious to reclothe on such a hot night.

Finally, clad in a towel, New Chairman explained the great misunderstanding that had occurred. The highway patrol leaders were engaged in much more important deliberations—following radio transmissions, orders to fire, and casualty reports. The perimeter of the compound had been secured, the deputy hostage was down and in grave condition, and the lady with the gray ponytail had simply disappeared. There looked to be about a dozen sect members wounded, one fatally. Patrol injuries were insignificant. The raid could not be deemed a success at this point.

Two patrolmen accompanied New Chairman to his room for clothes, only to be asked to remain outside.

"Something to hide?" one asked.

"No, just painfully shy," New Chair responded.

"Couldn't have guessed," they laughed and entered his room to find stacks of one hundred dollar bills and several large bags of marijuana strewn on the bed and about the room. Handcuffs and ropes dangled from the headboard.

New Chair demanded to see their search warrant, which was a bad mistake in that they had one in anticipation of needing to gather evidence at the ranch. New Chairman sat on the edge of bed and cried as they began to catalogue evidence that would ultimately land him in jail for two years.

The troopers divided the captives into groups of men, women, children, and wounded. Women and children were allowed to return to their respective lodgings but required to remain on premises until advised otherwise. Several troopers were assigned watch duty.

The wounded were treated at the ranch command center and, short the single fatality, were placed under armed guard until charges against them could be filed. All would be charged with conspiracy to terrorize, many with more specific offenses. Pierce Arrow's coven of evil would be dismantled.

For Lucas, it was too late. Too much blood had pulsed out on the stage of his final performance. He stopped breathing in Sheriff Sephus Adonis's arms, Sheriff's tears dripping on his matted hair. Of all the things Sheriff had foreseen in his life, this was not one of them. He held Lucas close until troopers convinced him to let go. He held him like he might hold a son, if he were ever to have one.

There was no sign of the lady with the graying ponytail. She had simply disappeared stage rear, clad only in a tattered wolf skin.

JUST SAY NO

Sheriff awoke Lettie before dawn. She sobbed before even knowing why. Her emotions were out of control, being pregnant and all. He could only look at her through his tears, no words would come. Finally, she screamed "NO!" over and over and over again. Sheriff took her trembling body in his arms and whispered that Lucas had died brave, that he gave his life for the children of the community.

Lucas Jones was memorialized as the greatest hero in Hardlyville's history. Pastor Pat presided over his open casket in a church that could barely accommodate half who wanted to pay respects. Pastor Pat focused on Lucas's love of Lettie and his children with many Biblical references, always returning to *John*, Chapter 3, Verse 16. No, Lucas was neither God nor His Holy Son, but Lucas's love of his children, and all the young ones in Hardlyville, was abiding. He had given his life for them. Pastor Pat labored with connecting the dots, but no one cared. All felt indebted to Lucas Jones for his sacrifice, though none knew of its final form. Neither Sheriff Sephus nor Pierce Arrow felt that sharing Lucas's final thrusts at life were relevant to the task at hand. In the end, Lucas had given it all for our community's children, they reasoned.

Lettie sat sniffling in the front row next to her children, belly bulging expectantly. Cousin Jimmy sat right next to her, his periodic sobs echoing clear to the crowd huddled in the dripping rain outside. Most accompanied Lucas on his final journey to the Hardlyville Cemetery, where he was placed in the ground not far from town founder Thomas Hardly. Pastor Pat dawdled through his graveside ritual. Never the fiery preacher, he still held the crowd at rapt attention.

Lettie finally sped him along by leading her children to the fresh turned dirt covering their father to lay daisies on it. Cousin Jimmy buried his face in the muck, mourning the loss of his only real hero, until he passed out from lack of oxygen. Sheriff Sephus gently pulled him up and wiped his face clean with his shirt tail. Pierce Arrow dripped tears on the obituary notes he was keeping beneath his umbrella.

Finally, Pastor Pat relinquished his pedestal with a vibrant "Amen." Most lingered beyond his adjournment, despite the drizzle.

Nothing could assuage shared pain except time. Lettie and her children were taken into a warm and protective community embrace, and she named her new son Lucas, just like his Dad, on his arrival several months later.

Pierce Arrow was nominated for and received one of those Pulitzer Prize things for his coverage of "The Coven of Evil." The *Daily Hellbender* attained national recognition, including an immediate quadrupling of subscribers. Pierce had to farm out printing and distribution, adding jobs to the Hardlyville roster. His focus on writing and reporting allowed him to do what he was born and raised to. And then there was the book. In time, he told himself. Let it all settle in for better perspective.

One day a liberal big-city newspaper came calling in Hardlyville. They had a proposition for Pierce. They wanted to hire him to manage their editorial page and offered him a big salary to move to an urban home base. They also threw in an offer to purchase the *Daily Hellbender* for five hundred thousand dollars cash, up front, promising that he would continue to retain editorial control over it as well.

Pierce just said no. Why would he return to what he had run away from ten years past? He was older, and he was sure city beats hadn't gotten any sweeter. No, he didn't need that kind of money to live in Hardlyville. And he was kind of becoming intrigued with taking on Big Pork in the name of saving Skunk Creek. A crusading editor of sorts.

He was confident it was only a matter of time before something nasty slipped out downstream from Skunk Creek Ranch and sullied these special waters, far beyond the green goo that continued to show up periodically at the juncture of the Skunk and Swine Branch, as Pierce had dubbed it. He also believed that, despite their conservative natures, Hardlyville citizens would rally behind his pleas to "Save the Skunk."

"This is a cause worth fighting for, beyond politics," he wrote. "It is our own backyard, our own water table, our own well source, our own baths and showers. This is a battle that can be won in the court of public opinion and will ultimately lead to the removal of the soon-to-be ten thousand head of swine from a locale they never should have been in. Never. Ever."

No, he was where he needed to be.

About that same time, Hardlyville's representative in the US Congress, one Larry Larrsnist, stopped in to hold a town hall meeting in anticipation of being reelected in the fall. Nothing Scotch-Irish here. Larrsnist was of Swedish descent, his line immigrating through Pennsylvania then Tennessee to the Ozarks several generations past. He was the perfect US Congressman in most Hardlyvillains' view. His campaign slogan for four terms had neither deviated nor varied: "Just Say No." He billed himself as a "God-fearin', Good-listenin' Neighbor," who despite his limited vocabulary and education was just who honest folks needed to represent their interest in Sin City East, which was even worse than Sin City West. Though few from Hardlyville had been to either Las Vegas or Washington, DC, they took his word for it and him for his word. Congressman Larrsnist's sole objective in life was to vote "No" more times than he had the year before in office, recognizing that such consistent and linear accomplishment earned him affection and trust at home. He had been successful, though on several occasions he had to offer crazy bills from the floor so he could vote against himself and pump his numbers. His most famous moment, one that got him mentioned in *USA TODAY*, was when he introduced legislation on the last day of the session to protect the Skunk Creek Sculpin, sought to fund it with a creek use tax in a separate bill, and to establish the Skunk Creek National Drainage Area in a third.

Of course there was not, nor had ever been, a Skunk Creek Sculpin listed in the annals of US Fish and Wildlife recorded history, never had been a federally mandated creek tax or a national drainage area on legislative record, but he was two "No" votes short of his previous year's total. With one brilliant legislative maneuver, he managed to leapfrog into a new "No" record by voting against each of his three submissions. Yes, Larry ran as a Republican, though many in his party of choice preferred that he not. He didn't even vote party line that much, just "NO," fulfilling campaign promises and coffers.

He was greeted warmly in the Hardlyville High School gym by a large and fawning crowd, who listened more or less attentively over several hours to his laundry list of "Nos" from A-Z—from no alimony because divorce is bad to no nothing, aka zilch. He asked for questions from the floor, thinking he had worn them out and expecting none, when a solitary hand in the back extended. It was Pierce Arrow.

"Aw, shit," the congressman muttered under his breath.

Pierce extolled the content of the congressman's speech and his principles of negativism. He wished aloud that more of the congressman's colleagues would stand for something, even in the sense of being against it. He praised the congressman for leading the charge against this National Blueway poppycock and wondered what inane federal program would surface next for Congressman Larrsnist to do battle with. He hoped he had enough "Nos" in his quiver. Larrsnist nodded enthusiastically, beaming at Pierce Arrow's praise.

He then asked if the congressman was aware what was going on back east of Skunk Creek. The congressman looked puzzled. He asked him if he had ever heard of Skunk Creek Ranch. More puzzlement. He asked if he knew that Big Pork had railroaded a hog farm to accommodate up to ten thousand porkers in the Skunk Creek watershed through the State Oversight Board, and that the chairman thereof had been indicted for accepting bribes from Big Pork lobbyists to seal the deal.

"Hogs on Skunk Creek?" the congressmen shouted. "Hogs on Skunk Creek? Impossible, immoral, preposterous, and lunacy!" were among the words he spit out in disbelief. "The good citizens of Hardlyville deserve better than to wake up some morning to a flotilla of hog turds dribbling down Skunk Creek."

The crowd went crazy.

"Who committed this dastardly deed?" the congressman demanded, waving his arms as if to say "bring them on."

Pierce shared that ownership of the ranch itself was hard to track, but the international conglomerate, which owned the hogs and lent them to the ranch for raising, would probably be a name that registered. The thought of some "ferners" behind this sent the congressman into an apoplectic rant about their infringement upon the individual rights of all Hardlyvillains. He promised that he, Larry Larrsnist, would get to the bottom of this and personally intervene on behalf of his aggrieved constituents. It was time for another "NO," with a capital N. More cheering, even some backslapping in the crowd.

It was only then that Pierce noted the congressman's handlers waving frantically to get his attention. One finally dashed forward onto the gym stage and whispered something in his ear. The congressman gulped, caught his breath, and quickly apologized for having to leave. It had been brought to his attention that he was late for another town hall meeting up the road, and in all fairness, he must move along. Congressman Larry Larrsnist's handlers had waited one question too long. Them "ferners" were indeed a major donor to the congressman. Before the congressman could leave, Pierce shouted out the name of the international conglomerate so that all might hear, asking the congressman what he was going to do for the "infringed upon" citizens of Hardlyville.

"What can I do?" moaned the good congressman.

"Just say 'No,'" was Pierce's crisp reply. The congressmen looked around in desperation for more hands, different questions, as handlers tugged at his arm. Pierce Arrow repeated his question and answer with more authority.

"What are you going to do for us? Just say 'No.'"

There was an audible buzz among those remaining in the gym, as well as an implied expectation for response.

A clearly exasperated congressman launched into his economic development stump speech, feeding more murmur in the audience.

"What are you going to do, Congressman?" Pierce asked a third time. This time he got an answer that surprised even him in its clarity.

"I can't do nothing," the congressman lamented, claiming his hands were tied. "I can't 'Just Say No' to free enterprise and job creation. I can't 'Just Say No' to our finest corporate citizens, who take entrepreneurial risk in far flung corners of the Ozarks. I can't 'Just Say No' to the farmers who put pork chops on your table, chitlin's in the inner cities of America, and ship what's left to starving children overseas. This is America folks. I can't 'Just Say No'—"

"... to your biggest donors," Pierce finished for him.

It was then and there, in that moment in time, that Pierce Arrow decided to run for Congressman Larrsnist's seat in the House of Representatives.

The congressman was led from the quiet gym, waving frantically to the crowd, a crowd whom he used to own, a crowd with quiet doubts of their own now.

Pierce Arrow announced his candidacy for the seat in Congress currently held by Larry Larrsnist on the front page of the *Hellbender* next morning. He acknowledged it would be a long, uphill battle but that their little corner of the Ozarks deserved better than to be represented by one so beholden to Big Pork. He asked citizens to join him for a one-hour town meeting Saturday morning so that they might exchange views and together "Just Say No To Big Pork."

NEW BEGINNINGS

Lettie struggled to put one foot in front of the other every day as her new baby, Lucas, Jr., grew up and her heart grew heavier. Sheriff Sephus provided her with moral and financial support in honor of her husband, his friend. There was never a mention or acknowledgement of their one dalliance and none additional ever contemplated by either.

Their friendship grew, and Sheriff Sephus became a surrogate grandpa to her children. This relationship, grounded in sorrow, grew into mutual respect and platonic affection as the months passed. Sheriff particularly embraced little Lucas and showered him with touches of affection. Lettie slowly began to breathe of life deeply again.

One morning, Luther Lane, who cut the grass at the cemetery, came running down Main Street and into the sheriff's office. Sheriff need to come with him, quick. Sheriff drove the quarter mile to the cemetery with Luther jogging beside him, trying to explain what he had found while mowing this morning. Luther had a bad stutter that went to incomprehensible when he was flustered. Sheriff Sephus couldn't understand a word he said beyond "Lucas" and "grave."

Sheriff waddled down to Lucas's headstone, and there, on the ground next to it, was a live baby. It had been wrapped warmly in animal pelts and tucked into a basket of reeds and vines. It slept silently and peacefully.

"This is a new one," muttered the sheriff.

The baby stirred and twisted as Luther and Sheriff stood, mesmerized, above it. Long eyelashes began to bat as its eyes opened. Sheriff Sephus's own eyes bugged out, and his breathing quickened. Luther wanted to know if Sheriff was having "the big one." Sheriff leaned down without responding and stared deeply into the yellowy eyes set sleepily upon him.

"Shit, brothers," was all he could say.

He soon recomposed and ordered Luther to go and fetch Miss Lettie and Pierce Arrow as fast as he could. Sheriff sat down on the grass beneath which Lucas lay and looked in disbelief at what he knew to be Lucas's child.

Pierce arrived first as Lettie needed to round up someone to watch her passel of kids. His eyes bugged too, and he mimicked signs similar to those of the sheriff having a heart attack. Both men had seen those eyes before, Sheriff Sephus up close and personal, and both wondered aloud what lurked behind them.

Both also agreed they would need to tell Lettie the whole damn story of the night of Lucas's passing. They had glossed over gory details to spare her before, but in the end, this child was sort of hers, seeded by her own beloved Lucas. It was hers if she wanted, or perhaps could stomach it, after all was said and done.

The baby continued to lie peacefully, awake now, and cooing. Nourishment would soon be needed. Lettie was still in her milk. Maybe she would nurse it. Should they tell her before or after? Holy shit, the ethics of this dilemma were as turned and twisted as a sordid novel. They decided to take the little yellowy-eyed baby back to the sheriff's office and asked Luther, who didn't have a clue what was going on, to send Lettie there.

Lettie announced her arrival with a cheery, "What's up?" Their sober looks and quiet response of "not sure" spoke to seriousness.

Sheriff explained, "This here baby was discovered on Lucas's grave this morning by Luther Lane, without owner or identification."

"Why Lucas?"

They asked Lettie to sit down. The baby started to cry. Lettie immediately knew the sound of hunger and picked the tiny infant up, cradling it gently in her arms. Without hesitation, she unbuttoned the top of her blouse, removed an engorged breast, and inserted it into the baby's sucking mouth with a quiet "'scuse me, gents." Baby suckled contentedly for about fifteen minutes before slipping into a happy nap. No one said a word. Lettie tucked back in with another apology for her lack of modesty and gently placed the baby back into its rustic basket.

"Okay," she continued, "why Lucas's grave site? Why a lonely infant? Why, why, why?"

Sheriff Sephus told Lettie there was a long and strange story line in play here, and they would share it with her, all of it. He didn't know how she would take it, but she needed to know.

Sheriff noted that he had only told Lettie that Lucas was shot during the raid on a wicked religious sect that had vowed to kidnap Hardlyville's children in revenge for those members Lucas had killed in defense of the young floaters. There was considerably more to the story, and she had better take a deep breath.

Sheriff recounted, in detail, the scouting trip he, Pierce, and Lucas had taken the night before the raid. They had gathered enough evidence to bring in from outside two state patrols for assistance, but just beyond the compound, Lucas had fallen and broken his ankle. He insisted that they leave him behind and gather the troops for a raid the following night.

"The last words he uttered were to tell you he loved you more than anything, and that he would do anything to get back to you."

"He told me he might be out coon hunting with Cousin Jimmy that night," Lettie sobbed, "and not to worry if he didn't make it back. They would probably stay at Jimmy's and head out again the next night. Didn't want to wake the children or me."

"Well," Sheriff continued, "the sad fact is, he didn't make it back, but, in fact, he did try everything within his power to do so. I know because I arrived to see it all play out in tragic detail. Are you sure you want to hear?"

Lettie nodded yes.

"When I arrived with the state troopers, Lucas was lying in an animal cage on a wooden stage in front of the members of the sect. He had obviously been captured and beaten, in addition to the broken ankle.

"We watched in horror as the Demon Lady, who was their leader, laid out a plan to kidnap three of Hardlyville's youngest in revenge for their losses at Lucas's hand. She then turned her sights on Lucas. What happened next is not easy to explain or describe, but you deserve to know.

"As you probably recall from the floaters' tales, the Demon Lady is beyond cruel and weird—claiming mystical powers, preaching a gospel of hate and sex—and sporting a long, graying ponytail and a set of gleaming, yellow eyes. Pierce noted that he always thought she had colored contact lenses, but now he is not sure. He had even looked it up online and found a natural yellow-eyed condition attributed to lipochrome, 'wolf eyes,' very rare in humans. Pierce couldn't explain the gleam.

"Anyway, Demon Lady promised the crowd that she must milk Lucas's seed for his redemption before a proper sacrifice could take place. She would sex him, then kill him. Lucas, despite his pain and loyalty to you, knew he had to play this game if he was ever to see you again and to buy time for our rescue team to arrive. So he did."

Lettie's eyes blazed.

"You mean he screwed this witch in front of the assembled multitudes as a great act of sacrifice?" she hissed. "And you just sat there watching, Sheriff Sephus? Did you get your jollies off too, Sheriff? Did it turn you on, Sheriff?"

"It wasn't like that Lettie, not so simple. Your husband did everything in his power to survive, which included making the witch need him in a sexual way enough to keep him alive. I got to tell you, Lettie," Sheriff Sephus continued, "that I had the witch once, long ago, and the only appetite she has when engaged in sex is for more sex. She was insatiable."

Lettie blushed, with several trains of thought colliding in her brain, before nodding for him to continue.

"Lucas knew that if he could keep her entertained and screaming with pleasure until we could intervene, he might make it through the nightmare and back to you. He knew you would forgive him for the superficial and embrace him for the result. I frankly don't know how he did it. She went on and on, hissing and pawing, spewing and spitting, and he stayed right there with her, broken ankle and all. You have to know how awful she was as well. You heard what the young floater described—the eyes, the teeth, the hair all around, the smell of rot and fear."

Lettie let out a sob.

"When the highway patrol helicopters descended on the site, she knew the gig was up and inflicted great pain on Lucas, nearly biting his tongue in half. This apparently broke his spell of self-control, and he spurted, to her cries of glee and victory. She quickly jumped off Lucas, grabbed a gun, and shot him dead before vanishing in front of our eyes. His strategy was sound, he executed flawlessly, under the most difficult of circumstances, but he came up just short in the end. The pain I live with every day is what you suggested. Why didn't I order in the troopers sooner? I feared for Lucas's life under any scenario, and I made a bad call in the name of caution. I'm sorry to be so graphic, but you need to know, particularly given what lies sleeping in front of you."

Lettie's mind whirred. She asked if the sheriff was suggesting that this baby was Lucas's last gasp for life. That he had impregnated this Demon Lady, and that she had recently delivered. That she had hauled her sorry heathen ass back to Hardlyville to lay the baby on Lucas's bones and again vanished into the hinterlands.

"This baby is mine, courtesy of Lucas's last fling? How do you know, Sheriff Sephus? How do you know?"

"Did you see the baby's eyes while it nursed?" Pierce asked.

Lettie said she hadn't noticed, only that the baby was hungry and cuddled nicely in her arms.

"They are yellowy," whispered Sheriff Sephus. "This baby found on Lucas's grave has yellowy eyes. We can test all the DNA you want, but this here is the baby Lucas spawned with the Demon Lady, and she doesn't want it."

"Boy or girl?" asked Lettie.

"We'll find out at diaper change," he responded, "if you can call that down and twig contraption the baby is wearing a diaper."

"I don't know," Lettie mumbled as the baby began to stir. "What if the baby is like her, all crazy and evil and such?"

"What if the baby is like Lucas?" Pierce responded.

Lettie burst into tears at the confusion of it all.

The baby whimpered, and Lettie lifted it gently to the conference room table, asking Sheriff if he had any diapers in his office. To her surprise, he walked to the closet and pulled a half package out, with a box of wipes as well. He made no attempt to explain.

The diaper change revealed a baby girl, who looked just like any baby girl, except for the shining, yellowy eyes. She smiled and cooed at Lettie, as Lettie did back to her. Lettie reckoned she could take her home and care for her tonight, to buy time for thinking.

She thanked Sheriff Sephus and Pierce Arrow for their honesty and efforts. She would ponder the Lucas thing, to see what was left in her heart. She was a mess of emotion, guilt, and love. Both men hugged her, Pierce perhaps more deeply than Sheriff. He genuinely felt her pain, on so many levels, and could only gush admiration for what she was even considering.

Pierce's inaugural town hall meeting as a candidate for Congress had gone well. He said he was running against Big Pork, not because he wanted to be in Washington, DC, but because he wanted to rid the county of ten thousand pigs that never should have been granted permission to live there as neighbors in the first place.

"Skunk Creek and Hardlyville, as we know it, are at risk."

Pierce had done some research on Skunk Creek Ranch and wanted to share what he had found. Skunk Creek Ranch was not a ranch but an industrial pig farm—a confined animal feeding operation, a planned source of four million gallons of manure and waste water a year that had to go somewhere. Downstream was a logical conclusion. Hogs in the barn would defecate into shallow pits beneath, soon flushed by water into the settling basins and waste lagoon, before application to fields or baking into fertilizer. Not hard to imagine where it all went when it rained hard. Again, downstream.

Four million gallons of toxic waste was more than a community ten times as large as Hardlyville could produce in a year. And the twenty-five-year flood plain had been breached two times in the past twenty-five years. Guess that made it a twelve-and-a-half year flood plain. What had happened behind closed doors and large dollar signs spelled nothing but trouble for

Skunk Creek, and Pierce Arrow only wanted a chance to right a grievous wrong.

"Why bother now?" Pierce asked. "The damn thing is already up and running. That was my first thought," he admitted to all. "But ladies and gentleman, it is never too late to right a wrong. Never. Too. Late."

Pierce had their attention. His obvious intelligence, passion, and credibility with the crowd struck a chord. One raised hand asked if he was one of them liberals from back East. He professed to liking Pierce and the pieces he does in the *Hellbender*, but he couldn't stomach voting for a lefty. Lots of nods around the gym floor.

"I'm only a liberal if saying no to Big Pork and taking back our land and water from swindlers, corporate thieves, and pigs makes me one," Pierce responded to loud applause.

"What do you think about this health care mess?" another asked.

"Especially when you throw in medical pot as part of the package," queried another.

"Government funded dope for the unemployed? Don't want my kid going to jail for a little toke, but all these deadbeats using and me paying for it . . ." he trailed off angrily.

Dylan Thomas raised his hand and shouted something before Pierce could answer. Pierce excused the interruption and asked Ol' Dill to repeat. Ol' Dill was asking Pierce what he thought about this frontal lobing.

"Say what?" responded a baffled Pierce Arrow.

"Frontal lobing," repeated Ol' Dill. Said he heard about it on the radio. All this gas in the air making things hotter than Hades, cow shit and farts and such, they had said. Pierce gently redirected Dill to "global warming" and promised to answer both questioners at once.

"It is not important what I think," said Pierce. "I think what you think, if I am to effectively represent you in Washington. My job is to get you as much information as I can, encourage you to digest it, not spin it, and then represent your take as best I can. I think what you think and not what some party hack or deep-pocketed briber tells me to think."

This statement was well received too.

Pierce went on to describe his long-shot strategy. He would not ask for campaign contributions. He would not run political ads.

"I will travel the district at my own expense to listen to what people want from Washington. I will debate my opponent, Mr. Larry Larrsnist, on any topic, in any forum, under any format, and at any time. I will always be honest and civil, in agreement and disagreement. I will employ a vocabulary larger than the one word Larrsnist takes such pride in, except when it comes to his big spending buddies. I will use "NO" only in running Big Pork out of our backyard. I will not sell my vote to the highest bidder. And finally, if you elect me, I will not serve in Washington, DC, where I might be drawn into the culture of power and corruption. I will serve you from here and demand that the powers that be accommodate my participation in governance as your duly elected representative, whatever communicative form that might take."

His people listened in stunned agreement. When he asked them for ideas, they had none. They had just heard a vision they could embrace. They rose as one and walked forward to shake Pierce's hand and ask how they could help.

And help they did, fanning out across the district in their spare time to introduce their neighbor and spread his refreshing message. Pierce Arrow had some local name recognition due to the Pulitzer, but little beyond his editorial positions was known. His platoon of volunteer spokespeople soon became an army.

Larry Larrsnist hid in Washington, DC, the entire summer and into the fall, returning to the district only once to trail the coattails of a potential Tea Party presidential candidate and attend a fundraiser given in his honor by several corporate interests, lurking behind a mask of innocent bystanders. He would not debate this idiot Pierce Arrow, who was devoid of ideas and character. Besides, the congressman had important business to conduct in the nation's capital on behalf of his constituents.

Sheriff Sephus Adonis decided to go on a diet for the first time in his life. He figured that if he was going to serve as Pierce Arrow's campaign manager, he needed to put forth a more physically appealing public image. Didn't hurt the big stallion waiting list either.

Lettie simply fell in love with the little yellowy-eyed baby and took her on to be the youngest of her clan. She called her the sweetest, happiest baby she had ever raised, purring and smiling constantly between feedings and poops. Despite the gentle demeanor, she named her Vixen, in acknowledgement of her less than domesticated root stock. It was hard to explain to her older children the ties to their daddy, and she simply became Cousin Vixen, whose parents had passed on. They helped care for both Lucas Jr. and the slightly younger Vixen, easing Lettie's burden, if not her sense of loss.

Sheriff Sephus pitched in as well, and even Candidate Pierce Arrow started saving one night a week for Lettie's cooking. He was particularly fond of her squirrel and morel pie. Sheriff wondered if a courtship was brewing but couldn't bring himself to ask. Pierce had never been married that he knew of, and like the sheriff himself, may have passed the marrying age. Sheriff knew he could never give up the independence that came with solitude and finally convinced girlfriend Holly of the inevitability that she would have to wed another, if that was what she wanted in life. That she did so did not lesson her itch for a rendezvous every now and again, just the frequency thereof.

Cousin Jimmy mostly fished alone these days. Perhaps no one in all of Hardlyville missed Lucas more. He was stoned so much of the time that he lost his job and, shortly thereafter, pretty little Sally as his soul mate when he just couldn't meet her needs on a regular basis. Even Sheriff Sephus couldn't stand his descent and felt a need to intervene. He had always liked Jimmy but somehow grew closer to him through Lucas. They seemed to share familial traits.

So Sheriff arrested him. Sheriff Sephus hauled Cousin Jimmy into jail on charges of driving his truck stoned and locked him up for thirty days to have a conversation. It had worked with Lucas, and who knew, maybe Cousin Jimmy would see the light as well.

Pastor Pat prayed for all in his uninspiring but caring way. God told him to leave ministering to his favorite choir member's deepest needs to someone else, which he did after one more trip down memory lane and shared tears over sweet wine. She found solace and a new beginning with Slammin' Sam the Used Car Man, as his ad in the yellow pages read. Sam's wife had left him recently after catching him in the back seat of his Cadillac demo with his corporate assistant, both demonstrating an appalling lack of corporate modesty and apparel. Slammin' Sam too sang in the First Church choir, tenor to her alto, and was soon confessing his most recent sins of the flesh to Pastor Pat, who could only forgive, not forget.

Life began to begin again.

DEAD ENDS

Pierce Arrow's noble run for Congress ended as incongruently as it began. Born of passion and righteousness, it fell prey to corruption and scandal. Kiddie porn to be specific.

As Pierce and his band of merry warriors spread the word throughout the district, all word of mouth as promised, not one political ad, Congressman Larrsnist's large lead began to shrink. Candidate Arrow focused his attention on the two major towns that would likely determine the outcome, both previous bastions of support for Larrsnist. Most who he and his supporters spoke with were amazed and appalled that the citizens of Hardlyville could go to sleep one night in blissful innocence and awaken next morning to learn of ten thousand hog bottoms soon to be pointed downstream, unable to do anything about it. This was simply un-American, and it happened on Larrsnist's watch, even if the dirty deed—and this really was one, noted Cousin Jimmy—took place at the state level.

Pierce Arrow raised the specter that the same major donors who funded Larrsnist nationally ruled the legislative halls of state government as well. Their money was dirty and their methods secretive and evil, in both venues. Pierce spelled it out for anyone who would listen: B-I-G P-O-R-K. Pierce promised to take them on for his constituents in public, while Larrsnist counted their money behind closed doors.

Larry Larrsnist's benefactors began to take notice and were not pleased with his strategy. They told him to get his sorry ass back home with a message of economic development, jobs, and a pork chop on every table. Larrsnist's own private polling showed him behind in key traditional markets of support. He finally realized that his life as a public purveyor of "NO" was facing extinction. So he did what every God-fearing, vote-counting, man of the people might do. He set out to destroy Pierce Arrow, by whatever means necessary.

Enter Banker Bud and his secret trans-generational collection of pornography. Bud himself was hip deep in hog shit when it came to Skunk Creek Ranch. His father had been friends with the original property owner and when approached about buying the entire acreage initially said no. Banker Bud felt differently and said yes, under certain circumstances. He would acquire the property through a personally controlled shell corporation, licensed in the Dominican Republic.

Banker Bud's best, and perhaps only real, friend was president of a swine producer. They cavorted secretly together, Bud saying he was going to the American Bankers Association annual meeting, friend picking him up wherever that might be in his private jet and flying them to Las Vegas for a weekend of "run and gun," as he called it. It was really Banker Bud's only annual break out, and break out he did, with unsavory hired women, copious amounts of expensive food and drink, and private card games where even he couldn't cheat. He often lost large sums of the bank's cash reserves, which he repaid with performance bonuses. Everything was behind closed doors, and he was returned to the Banker Convention's end for his flight home, thoroughly sated and satisfied, and generally with a few classic photos to add to his collection.

It was on one of these extravaganzas that Banker Bud learned of his host's desire for land on which to build a large hog farm beyond the range of his current holdings. Seems a large international food producer was looking for a new place to raise pigs, up to ten thousand of them at a time. They would own the livestock, pay a lot to have the pigs raised, and guarantee their purchase. All the investors needed was a large facility and acreage with plenty of water. If ever there was a no-brainer way to earn a buck, this was it.

When Banker Bud described the parcel he currently had under contract—with springs, branches, and a small lake, in addition to substantial acreage—best friend yelled "yes." The two would be silent partners in the real estate, and best friend's company would manage the operation, as they had so many. Top dollar for the land lease and profit sharing with the company were all part of the deal. Banker Bud required absolute secrecy regarding his role in any of it. A shell Dominican Republic corporation would seed the investment and funnel funds to him.

They quickly had a handshake deal, with final consummation over a shared hooker's final act of pleasure. Banker Bud even collected a small "personal transaction fee" and made the development loan. Sweet deal, all the way around.

As election eve neared, with Pierce Arrow surging like a male goose in heat, Banker Bud received a call from his best friend. Pierce Arrow needed to be stopped, and that idiot Larry Larrsnist was incapable of doing it on his own. He had a big favor to ask. What could Banker Bud do to destroy this Arrow fellow and his pious claims of virtue? Big Pork would foot whatever cost was involved, including a nice personal assistance fee, and twist whatever arms needed a turn. Banker Bud asked for twenty-four hours to come up with a plan and get back to him. No longer than that, begged friend. Time was not on their side.

Banker Bud huddled with his collection of pornography and his customers' stacks of hundred dollar bills. He soon emerged inspired, as always. He had concocted a devious plan of attack that would crush Arrow, whom he had always disliked as condescending, and further endear himself to his best friend.

Among Banker Bud's more disturbing images was an album dating back to circa 1910, which included photos of several young children in extremely compromised positions, literally and figuratively. Wouldn't it be ironic if that album ended up buried in damn Arrow's desk at the *Hellbender*? And what if his good bud, Sheriff Sephus Adonis, was the one who stumbled onto it?

Banker Bud hated to part with such a critical component of his world-class collection, but this was a surefire way to bring down the self-righteous little prick, swiftly and surely. Maybe he could steal back the evidence once the public damage had been done. Their district could elect all manner of scoundrel to Congress, but no one would vote for a pervert, a purveyor of child pornography. Banker Bud smiled and put the details in place.

He called his porker friend, explained the scheme, and asked for his help as well. He would need his ranch manager to call Sheriff Sephus and arrange for a meeting in Hardlyville tomorrow. The manager would ask Sheriff Sephus to enter the *Hellbender* office in search of several photos Arrow had taken of the State Oversight Board Chair the evening of the raid. He would report that New Chairman's attorneys are claiming Skunk Creek Ranch entrapped the poor dude, plying him with liquor and drugs, and paying his assistants to bring him down with their careless acts of reckless abandon. They have issued a subpoena for all photographs taken that evening and have demanded presentation of such by close of business tomorrow.

Since Arrow is spending every waking and sleeping hour campaigning on the road and is virtually inaccessible, Sheriff will have to accede to the ranch manager's demand. The ranch manager will, in turn, lead the law directly to the planted stash of kiddie porn shots, feigning shock and demanding that the sheriff issue a warrant for Arrow's arrest before he actually abuses a young child, if he has not already done so.

Banker Bud and his best friend laughed out loud at the blubbering Sheriff having to arrest the editor in chief of the *Hardlyville Daily Hellbender* on charges of possession of child pornography. Might even have to roar into one of his campaign appearances, siren and lights ablaze, and cuff him on the spot. End campaign. Dead on arrival. Congressman Larrsnist with a new life to spread his gospel of "NO."

Banker Bud's scheme unfolded exactly as planned, and Pierce Arrow's quixotic campaign came to a dead end. Pierce was too shocked and stunned to do more than post bail. When shown the photos, he could only wince and deny. Ironically, a big-city cub photographer was given an anonymous tip as to what was going down, and his photograph of the downcast candidate for Congress and Pulitzer sinner appeared nationally.

Sheriff believed Pierce's denial and knew it was a set-up, once he had time to think it through. He reasoned that Big Pork had their curly tails all over it, but he couldn't begin to imagine who had come up with such ghastly photos or devious scheming. He kicked himself for believing the ranch manager and not remembering that Pierce never locked his office door. Something about his belief in community access to all public affairs. The door had been locked, which implicated someone who had planted the evidence, but no fingerprints, except Pierce's, were found anywhere in the office.

The county prosecutor eventually dropped the charges, as not a single link between Pierce Arrow and the photos, beyond their location, could ever be established. No fingerprints on the photos. No corroborating evidence. Pierce's testimony, confirmed by Sheriff, that he never locked the door. There simply was not enough evidence to go forward. But the damage was irreparable, and Dr. No was returned in a landslide.

Lettie was heartsick for Pierce. She comforted him as best she could, but Pierce was inconsolable. He thought about leaving town under cover of darkness but was talked out it by Sheriff and Lettie. There was even a thought about shutting down the *Hellbender*, but this time the entire community rallied to Pierce Arrow's side. There was not a soul in town who believed that Pierce trafficked in child pornography. If indeed Big Pork was the culprit, they likely had a Hardlyville insider involved in the setup. No one could have guessed who that was, particularly after he offered an interest-free loan to Pierce to hire a PR firm to reclaim his and the *Hellbender's* tattered reputations. He even volunteered to dispose of the horrid images. Since no one wanted to touch them, he was applauded for his courage. Banker Bud had prevailed in every way and even managed to preserve a valuable piece of his collection.

About this time, Flotilla Hendricks's daughter Sabrina showed up on her mother's doorstep. It didn't take a mother to tell that Sabrina was with child and fairly advanced in the process.

"Where is he?" was Flotilla's first question.

"Who?"

"The guy that made this." Flotilla patted the protrusion.

"Not sure," Sabrina replied. "Could have been one of three or four or five, I guess."

"Silly child," was all Flotilla could muster behind tears and just ahead of the hearty hug she laid on her daughter. "Silly, silly child."

Didn't take long for all of Hardlyville to learn of Sabrina's condition. In the ultimate ego trip, Dill Thomas quickly and proudly claimed paternity, even offering child support to prove his point. Hardlyville laughed out loud. Flotilla was glad that her daughter had opted to come home for the birth and had neither taken drastic action nor given the baby away. After all, this would be Flotilla's first grandchild, and she was more excited than concerned about how, why, or who was to blame. Flotilla had given up on men long ago when hers had abandoned his young family, and she had done quite well without him or them.

Sabrina had fled Hardlyville the day after she graduated from high school, eager to have a real life. When real life became too hard, she fled again, this time to drugs and sex—seeking pleasure over purpose and finding neither. When she woke up pregnant, not knowing which of the three guys in two days or five guys in three might have fertilized her garden, her first thought was abortion. She wasn't ready to be a mom, to settle down, to face the real life she had left Hardlyville to find. She called her brother Chuck, who had fled for the same reasons two years earlier, to seek his advice. He had chosen a different path than Sabrina, gone to community college for an Associate's Degree, and was now in night school, seeking one in finance. He had a job waiting at a health care provider, where he was currently interning, when he graduated. Beyond an occasional beer, his life was sound and sober, and his girlfriend of two years seemed a logical choice to extend his with.

He worried about his sister, apparently for good reason now. He adored her. When asked, he immediately said, "Go home, have a baby, and get your shit together."

Sabrina wondered if Mom would take her back.

"Without question," he responded, knowing the courage and heart it took Flotilla to raise the two of them. He visited with his mother often, and she always closed with a prayer for Sabrina. He shared this with Sabrina and could hear her sob through her cell phone.

Sabrina didn't know if she could kick the drugs or indiscriminate urge to screw men. She did realize that her current state was empty and vacuous, and that giving it up couldn't be worse than continuing to wallow in it. She began the process of cleansing her body and mind and found new clarity in her thinking. She gave her two-week notice at the drugstore, her thirty-day notice at her cheap apartment, loaded her old Chevy with what few things she possessed, and chose Mom.

Flotilla hired Sabrina part-time at the little bakery and nourished her soul with love and affection. Most of Hardlyville seemed content with Sabrina's return and condition, though some whispered. Flotilla sent Sabrina to Doc Karst for a checkup, and he pronounced both baby and mom safe and sound. He would see them again in two months and then monthly thereafter. Sabrina settled back into the slow, natural, Ozarkian rhythms to anticipate the birth of her first born.

Banker Bud dropped dead of a heart attack. He had been fondling his customers' money and re-inventorying his photo collection after locking up one slow afternoon a couple of minutes before three. This was not his punctual norm, but Banker Bud was in a celebratory mood. He had closed the bank's monthly books that morning and showed a healthy profit, fueled primarily by unbudgeted transaction fees and unplanned for loan volume, all Big Pork sourced. He declared a dividend on the spot and would present it to his rubber stamp board tomorrow for approval. Another one of those "say yes or get less on your CD" decisions. As owner of all outstanding stock, dividend would go straight into his pocket and fund a new cycle of "run and gun" with his pig-raising buddy. Two junkets a year were within his grasp now and certainly well deserved.

His wife, Lois, called part-time lover Doc Karst when Banker Bud didn't show for dinner at the customary hour. Such a creature of habit did not vary from his norm. Doc suggested Lois bring a key to the bank to see if he was otherwise engaged. Lois confessed that Banker Bud had never offered her one, and she had never had the slightest interest in visiting him there. She much preferred Doc Karst's office examinations, she added with a sly giggle. Doc's mind moved to robbery, and he suggested they both ride out to Sheriff's house to seek his advice and assistance.

Sheriff Sephus Adonis was surprised to see the both of them together at suppertime, but he agreed Banker Bud's departure from routine was strange and perhaps suspicious. The three headed to the bank and, to no one's surprise, found it all locked up. It was always locked before and after hours, precisely to the minute. A light appeared to be on in the back, so after banging at every door for several minutes, Sheriff Sephus pulled out his revolver and broke the glass. *Funny*, he thought, as no alarm sounded, reasoning that Banker Bud must still be on the inside. Concerned now, he urged wife Lois and Doc Karst to stand back as he threw his considerable weight against the door, falling through to the ground as it gave. Rising slowing, he brushed dust and glass from his uniform, then headed back to the Office of the President.

He didn't have enough "shit, brothers" to describe what greeted him. Banker Bud lay flat on his back, with banded bundles of cash and old photos of nude ladies strewn all about him. He was clearly dead, which Doc readily confirmed. There were no signs of violence, but from the grimace on his puffy face, the passing must have been painful. It was then the sheriff saw one of the dreadful photos he had discovered in Pierce Arrow's bottom drawer. This one was particularly graphic and had brought nausea to Sheriff's belly.

"Bud was supposed to get rid of these," Sheriff Sephus muttered.

Then the air cleared, sordid mystery resolved. Apparently, they were part of his collection, just returned to the rightful owner. The son of a bitching banker was the insider on the Big Pork hit job on Pierce Arrow.

He continued to process, while Doc held Lois close, as she sniffled slightly and in a put-on sort of way. *No love lost here*, Sheriff deduced quickly, *and perhaps some gained*, he concluded. Doc was instructed to get Pierce Arrow on his cell phone, as well as Undertaker Bob, the mayor, and Postmaster PB. All had gathered within fifteen minutes.

A heart attack was diagnosed by Doc Karst.

"Dead, for sure," confirmed Undertaker Bob.

"No forwarding address for this one," was PB's weak attempt at humor.

"Win some, lose some," offered the mayor from behind his cheesy grin.

When Sheriff Sephus laid out his theory about the source of Pierce Arrow's child pornography, Pierce screamed in anger and frustration. Framed! Set up! Whacked! Kicked in the privates! He even called Banker Bud a bastard.

"Better keep him away from the mic at the bastard's funeral," whispered Sheriff to know one in particular.

"So who put him up to it?" wondered Sheriff. "We know Big Pork has a snout in this somewhere, but how did they get to Banker Bud. Bank examiners might find some interesting links, once they start digging."

He made a note to himself to secure the scene and call them first thing in the morning. He might even have to stand guard tonight with all this cash floating around.

Pierce Arrow's hands were shaking too much to photograph the lurid photographs, so Undertaker Bob assumed documentary duties. Pierce was already writing the *Hellbender's* next lead story in his mind, but would hold press until the bastard was covered with dirt. "Porngate" would be a new entry into the lexicon of Hardlyville history.

As Doc helped Sheriff move the stiff body to a conference table, his cell phone rang. When he couldn't get to it in time, it began ringing again, with a sense of urgency attached. He punched it up in time to hear Flotilla Hendricks screaming into the phone for Doc to come quick cause Sabrina and the baby were dying.

They all raced to Sheriff Sephus's patrol car and piled in on top of each other, leaving the stiff corpse, cash, and nude lady photos behind an unlocked door. Sheriff spun his tires and blew his siren in route to Flotilla's humble dwelling.

Even Dill Thomas could hear the commotion and came running down Main Street as fast as an eighty-plus-year-old man can fly. He turned the corner in front of the bank just in time to run smack into Dinky Douglas, sending them both sprawling. Dinky helped his elder up and saw the broken glass at the bank entry. He reasoned there had been a robbery and told Ol' Dill to stand guard while he went to find Sheriff Adonis. Dill's macho self got control of him and led him to open the door and charge in, assuring himself that he could handle whoever might be robbing the bank. He grabbed an umbrella from the front door stand and, now armed and ready, rushed the President's Office.

"Holy shit," he muttered, looking at the stacks of hundred dollar bills and nude ladies on the floor. "Holy shit."

He sat on his haunches, which is difficult for an eighty-plus-year-old man to do, and began running his fingers through the cash and over the naughty pictures. He had never seen such a treasure trove in his entire life—cash money and naked ladies. Maybe he had died and this was heaven, he concluded.

Just then Dinky came busting in, screaming what a fool Dill was. Sheriff was gone, and Dinky had told Dill to stand guard, not intervene. It was then that Dinky saw the stiff corpse on the conference table, rather than the mother lode on the floor, and screamed at Dill that he shouldn't have killed Banker Bud.

As a crowd gathered and the two old timers hurled accusations and insults at each other, one of Sheriff Sephus's occasionally appointed deputies pulled his gun and placed both under arrest for murder, grand theft, and hanging out with naked women. He read them their Miranda rights, with all as his witnesses, grabbed each by the back of his shirt, and trotted them off to jail, with Dill trying to turn his hearing aide up so he could find out what the hell was going on. He hadn't done anything wrong, unless running his hand over a hefty female backside in a photograph was against the law. Occasional Deputy warned the crowd that anyone who entered the bank while he was locking these old perverts up would face a similar fate.

Thus, a large group of Hardlyville's finest stood watch over a purported crime site of the most unusual and colorful nature. Someone would occasionally try and sneak a peek at the purported naked women that Occasional Deputy had mentioned and be pulled back into the crowd. One even claimed to have seen some really big titties but was shushed by the crowd for violating Occasional Deputy's admonition. Someone reported the claimant to Occasional Deputy when he returned, resulting in another arrest, this one for gawking, and incarceration followed. With Jimmy Jones already occupying the cell, the remaining detainees were thrown in together, with Jimmy begging to know what was going down.

Things were not going well at Flotilla's. Sabrina was laid on a bed, unconscious, with blood oozing from her nose. Doc said her pulse was weak and waning. He said he had read about something called an aneurism once, when blood bursts into the brain and drowns it, but he had never seen one before. He feared the worst for Sabrina. Flotilla asked about the baby. Doc said it was far enough along to take, but he would have to move quickly. What did Flotilla want him to do?

"Save the baby, and keep Sabrina alive," was her flat response.

Doc would have to do a C-section with whatever he had in his bag and hope for the best. They soaped up Sabrina's belly as he inserted a scalpel just above her panty line and opened her up. Her breath came in brief bursts before stopping.

"Sabrina's gone," Doc muttered and prayed to God he could save her baby.

Flotilla sobbed, and the rest gathered around her in an embrace. Doc reached in Sabrina's belly and pulled forth a tiny baby, coated in her blood, cleared its mouth and nose, and whacked it on the butt, bringing forth a gurgled but clear cry. The baby was still alive.

"Towel and hot water!" screamed Doc, who snipped the chord with kitchen scissors and wrapped the baby in a warm towel. He urged Flotilla to clean the baby in the bathtub, to get her mind off the now departed Sabrina, and he, Doc, would assure her daughter would receive proper and respectful attention. Sheriff helped Doc move his second corpse in twenty minutes to the kitchen table until Undertaker Bob could take over.

And yet another scream from the bathroom sent Sheriff running there.

"Is the baby okay?" received only a nodded yes. Then Sheriff got the picture.

"Shit, brothers. It's a boy, and he's black," Sheriff Sephus announced calmly.

Doc said, "He will need nourishment soon."

Sheriff looked at Pierce and asked if Lettie was still in her milk with the little yellow-eyed girl. Pierce nodded.

"Get her fast!" shouted Sheriff.

So with all the dead ends, there was one more new beginning in Hardlyville—a small, black baby boy. Hardlyville, in all of its long-storied history, and never had one of those before.

The entire village of Hardlyville showed up to lay young Sabrina to rest. They sheltered her stone under a large elm in a far corner of the cemetery, as requested by Flotilla. She wanted peace and quiet for her baby as she rocked Sabrina's own in her massive arms. Lettie wet-nursed on demand for as long as her milk came in and also became quite attached to the small, quiet, dark-skinned infant. It would be nice to have another for her Lucas and Vixen to grow up with.

Hardlyville residents were generally gentle with their comments about their newest resident, though several dropped the "N" word behind closed doors. Pastor Pat felt compelled to launch a special series of sermons on tolerance and the beauty of diversity. "Just Look at Nature" was a controversial message, but it paled in comparison to "Jesus, the Dark-Skinned Jew" on the following Sunday. Only Ms. Rosebeam bought into that one, observing that there were no white crackers or lazy hillbillies in early Middle Eastern lineages. Just Jews, Arabs, Greeks, and Romans, she proclaimed with impunity. No one disputed Ms. R's affirmation of Pastor Pat's theory, despite her obvious lack of historical grounding. Most simply shook their heads—didn't want to know, didn't care—so Pastor Pat quickly dropped his crusading ways and went back to more mundane forgiveness of sins. There was generally plenty of demand for his lead product.

Pierce Arrow even received a rare "Letter to the Editor" on the subject, handwritten in number two pencil.

Dear Editor,
Jesus wasn't no dark-skinned Jew.
He was poor hill folk, like me.
He just had a Holy Father, not a shit-bum like mine.

131

As for the black-skinned baby, he can stay, as far as I'm concerned.

Not his fault.

There was no signature attached.

It was the longstanding editorial policy of the *Hellbender* to not print anonymous submissions. But Pierce pondered over this one, trying to get to the bottom of it. Never could. Communication among his neighbors was sometimes a circuitous exercise. Something in the mash, he mused. In the end, he stuck to his policy guns and filed it away for the book he was writing.

State bank examiners descended on Bank of Hardlyville the morning after Banker Bud's demise. Sheriff Sephus returned from the tragic scene at Flotilla's house to personally stand guard overnight until they arrived. While they could not technically shut the bank down, something going back to FDR and his bank holidays, they opened several hours late to allow a big-city bank senior lending official time to drive in and assume interim CEO duties. In that there was only one other full-time employee, the Widow Greisidick—long-suffering teller/new accounts rep/senior administrative assistant/paramour to the deceased boss—and she had been placed on administrative leave as a suspect in whatever had gone down, business ground to a halt. The interim CEO filled the big chair, sipped coffee, and watched an army of examiners scurry around, seeking to balance the books.

Residents who needed cash were referred to the single cash machine outside the bank front door, and at times the line became quite long and unruly. Some didn't have a card nor had ever used the blasted machine, so they had to borrow short term from those who did, spawning a small cottage lending industry tied to handwritten IOUs. Charges of usury and fraud abounded. The state bank examiners said they didn't have time to regulate cowboy lenders and looked the other way.

All of Hardlyville was on edge. Beyond mourning poor Sabrina, there was a hint of scandal in the air.

In less than a week, examiners concluded that there was exactly fifty thousand dollars in cash missing from the bank. Other funds flowed back and forth in mysterious ways but balanced out to the penny. They also uncovered the extent of Banker Bud's Dominican Republic investment in Skunk Creek Ranch and the kickback loan fees that his best friend had laid on him for a below market borrowing rate. Foul play, indeed. They would follow up with his CEO friend once more details were confirmed.

Pierce Arrow got wind of these developments and began to piece together the conspiracy against both Hardlyville and himself personally, funded by Big Pork and executed by one of Hardlyville's selfless civic leaders. He would present a world class exposé, once the examiners gave him the green light. The whole sorry affair made Pierce sick to his stomach and inspired him to, at least in the back of his mind, start thinking about another run against Congressman Larrsnist. He had plenty of time to stew on it and focused his passion on investigative journalism, for the moment.

The bank examiners didn't know what to do with Banker Bud's world-class, antique pornography collection, and apart from slipping into the vault in ones or twos to ogle the evidence, steered clear. Ol' Dill Thomas only wanted to acquire the photo of the large derrièred lovely he had so gently fondled the night of Banker Bud's demise, so all looked the other way as he sought and absconded with it. What a marvelous piece of memorabilia from a night to remember. Ms. Rosebeam called him an old pervert to his face when she heard. He said he wanted to donate it to the Hardlyville Library when he passed on. She nearly passed out at that possibility, much to Ol' Dill's delight.

Sheriff Sephus Adonis whiffed enough criminal activity in the whole bloody mess to launch a formal investigation. He started with the missing cash. His gut told him that Banker Bud had absconded with it, but that was a literal dead end, so he turned his attention to the crowd that had gathered outside the bank that fateful night. Seemed that everyone he talked to was not present but knew someone who was. As he correlated lists of potential witnesses, based on at least three positive ID's from those who weren't there, he was able to narrow the list to about thirty attendees to interview. And while each denied having been in the crowd, all confirmed that no one had entered the bank in the absence of Occasional Deputy during his multiple jail runs that evening. Come to think of it, there was one exception. Ms. Rosebeam appeared on several lists as having entered to use the ladies' room.

Sheriff requested that Ms. Rosebeam appear at his office for a formal interview. She was grateful to oblige, but a little leery. She had heard tell of Sheriff's romantic bent and, while curious, was not buying. When she told Sheriff that she was not that kind of woman after opening pleasantries, he choked on his coffee and assured her that was not the point of his invitation. She still sat as far away from him as possible, glancing nervously on occasion at the shadow beneath his big belly, and blushing bright-pink beneath her caked makeup.

When Sheriff got to the point of the interview, namely had she, Ms. Rosebeam, entered the bank on the night in question, she became edgy.

"Yes," she responded, "but expressly to use the ladies room, and nothing else."

Sheriff asked if she had noticed anything unusual. She confirmed that while she made her way back to the ladies' room, which curiously Banker Bud had installed in his corner office next to the vault, she couldn't help but notice lots of money, piles of hundred dollar bills, strewn all about, amongst piles of wicked pictures of naked ladies. She was so taken aback that she immediately retreated to the front door, where she grabbed her purse and returned with it covering her face to protect her from the shame of it all. If she hadn't had to go so bad, she would have just left, but nature being nature, she had no choice.

To her horror, she soon discovered that there wasn't even toilet paper in the single stall, and she was forced to wipe with whatever she could find, which ended up being a stray hundred dollar bill just outside the door.

"Threw it back in the pile," she quickly added.

Sheriff Sephus asked if she had seen a body on the conference table. She hadn't, but even if so she would have had to go or piss her britches. Sheriff winced at that thought.

He wondered if she had touched any other evidence during her visit, and she responded with indignation that if he was referencing those awful photographs, she would have puked on them first. When asked if she was a suspect, and if so, of what, Sheriff Sephus waved her away and thanked her for her time. No way she could have done such a thing, he concluded.

The only other breaches of the suspected crime scene were by Dinky Doodle and Dill Thomas, and neither had seen the other do anything suspicious. Guess they could have conspired, but their combined intelligence quotient precluded that consideration.

So Sheriff Sephus Adonis was stumped. Someone had stolen fifty thousand dollars from the Bank of Hardlyville, and the principal suspects were a dead banker pervert, the village idiot, a senile self-proclaimed sex toy, and a matronly Latin teacher. No, neither Banker Bud nor Dinky nor Dill nor Ms. Rosebeam could have pulled off this heist in Sheriff's wildest imagination. "Shit, brothers" was about as close as he could get to the truth. So Sheriff Sephus did what he had always done best. He declared "case closed" and submitted his inconclusive report based on missing people, missing evidence, and missing minds. The bank examiners were none too pleased but lacked further jurisdiction, unless they wanted to call in the FBI and could imagine the rolled eyes and hearty laughter that would accompany that response. "Case closed" would stand.

Sheriff Sephus had realized one minor victory during this ordeal. Stoned Jimmy Jones had become a model prisoner after several straight talking sessions with the sheriff and two quick "roughing ups" with the nightstick. What had worked with Lucas had resonated with Jimmy all the way around, and Sheriff released him early on good behavior. Jimmy promised to walk tall in Cousin Lucas's empty shoes, and Sheriff's affection for Jimmy blossomed.

Jimmy was given another shot at his old gas station job, and he grabbed it with gusto. Same with Banker Bud's daughter, pretty little Sally Boswell. She re-embraced the boy, warts and all, and he grabbed her with gusto as well. After their first comingling in months, Jimmy noticed a difference. He observed that she seemed a bit "looser" than before and wondered aloud if she had paid a visit to Sheriff Sephus Adonis during his incarceration. She blushed colorfully.

"Just once?" Jimmy pursued. More blush, and even a small tear, confirmed her response.

"Well, you know that's going to have to change when you are my wife, don't you?" Jimmy casually observed.

This stopped Sally Boswell in her tracks. She asked if he was asking her to marry him, and Jimmy nodded yes. Her flood of tears said "yes," and they celebrated his proposal with an immediate remingling. She pledged her eternal loyalty to Jimmy, that she would never stray again, and thought she would likely grow tighter again over time. Jimmy acknowledged that he sure hoped so, but it wasn't a deal breaker. He even confessed to harboring no animosity toward the good sheriff, whom he now considered a mentor and a friend.

The final major change in Jimmy's immediate life was his decision to grow more dope and consume less. He broadened his planting palate, widened distribution channels, and was soon rolling in cash as Sheriff Sephus looked the other way. Good for Jimmy, and good for the local economy, he reasoned. Jimmy soon had enough financial resources to bankroll a wedding and honeymoon and sought formal approval from Sally's mom to sweep her daughter away to a small new house he planned to build in his big field. Mom's only proviso was that it be a double wedding, as she and Doc Karst were of a similar bent. Jimmy saw no problem with that and reasoned he would save some big money in the process, maybe even enough to fund another weed patch.

Jimmy the entrepreneur and Jimmy the family-guy-to-be was now finding inspiration from his beloved Cousin Lucas, beyond grief, escape, and self-pity. Jimmy still sensed Lucas around an occasional bend in Skunk Creek when he was fishing—looking on, maybe even breaking a grin. Jimmy Jones would make Cousin Lucas proud before it was all over.

A FRENCH CONNECTION

One winter's day, Pierce Arrow received a handwritten, out-of-the-blue note that would impact Hardlyville in ways Pierce never could have imagined. It was from his college roommate, Felix Feelgoode, now Dr. Feelgoode, Ph.D. They had been close in j-school, but Felix had always been "the one." Top of the class, cock of the walk, including Pierce's first wife, who never got over dashing Felix and ended up with him on a writing retreat—experimenting with erotic language and its aftermath—just two years beyond Pierce's marriage vows. Somehow Felix always managed to stay in sporadic contact over the years. For Pierce, there was always pain and personal hurt—jealous of the marriage wrecker but drawn to his magnetic field, nonetheless.

How Felix found Pierce in Hardlyville was bizarre. So was Felix. Pierce thought he had escaped his past, as well as Felix. Not.

Anyway, Felix wanted to come visit. His continuing education had earned him a Ph.D. in English and a starting position at Dartmouth University, which became a tenure tract and gained Felix the ultimate human protection next to a mother's womb, tenure, after a decade of service in cold Hanover, New Hampshire. He warmed many hearts and bodies along the way, including that of his department chair's wife, which led to embarrassing accusations and unfounded truths—and ironically to a promotion for Felix to chair of creative writing to shut him up about her brazen lust. Always the victim, Dr. Feelgoode earned and protected his academic credentials with passion and vigor. At least, that's what Felix told Pierce.

So Dr. Felix Feelgoode wanted to bring his current girlfriend, the French, third-tier actress Florence Hormel, to visit Hardlyville because she had never met a real hillbilly. Strange request, Pierce wondered, but read on.

Florence, Flo for short, was passing the winter in Hanover as a guest lecturer at the Hopkins Center for Performing Arts. Though she spoke no English, her weekly lectures were widely attended and wildly acclaimed, particularly among faculty circles, for their passion—and partial nudity, all in the interest of drama.

It had taken Flo a mere fifteen minutes to seduce Dr. Feelgoode. Soon thereafter, Flo transported her suitcases full of revealing clothing from the mundane dorm room to Felix's nineteenth-century farmhouse. While limited in opportunity to parade her ample wares around campus in the dead of a New England winter, she showered them proudly on Dr. Feelgoode and his increasingly well attended Sunday night faculty dinners. The administration heard rumors but were never included on the invitation list, so they chalked it up to just another exercise of the Liberal Arts.

Flo's curiosity about all things hillbilly surfaced as Dr. Feelgoode led his honors creative writing class through the dark Ozarkian novel *Winter's Bone* by Daniel Woodrell. Felix often shared his daily assignments with Flo to calm her after their madcap love-ins. He wondered how she could speak no English yet understand the language so well. With *Winter's Bone*, she claimed to have never heard such a story or of such gross characters. Felix assured her it was all true. All hillbillies were as described therein. Lazy. Coarse. Dirty. Illiterate. Primitive. Inbred. Diseased, particularly STDs. All told, an ancient, sorry, self-perpetuating, bottomless cult of savages, straight from the dankest slums of seventeenth century Ireland, fornicated to Scottish whores, and crossbred within on a whim. As a culture, they were clearly third world in standing, perhaps fourth, if there were such a thing. And he, Felix, actually knew one.

Flo swooned at this news and begged him to introduce her to it and its mangy colleagues. What a life experience it would be. Perhaps she could find a caricature to bring back to her Paris acting world that would resonate with critics and boost her beyond soft porn and horror into tier-two roles. Her career needed a boost, and besides, it had to be warmer in the Ozarks than in their godforsaken corner of the New Hampshire tundra, notwithstanding the dark novel's sinister title.

So Dr. Feelgoode reached out to his old friend, college roommate, and wife swapper, Pierce Arrow, executive editor of the *Hardlyville Daily Hellbender*. He wondered if he and his actress associate could visit during Dartmouth's spring break to introduce her to true Ozarkian culture—with an end game of sharing their traditions in Europe through theater and film. Plus, Felix had heard about the election scandal kiddie porn stuff on the national news and wondered if a little moral support might boost Pierce.

Pierce was baffled by it all. Moral was not a word Pierce associated with Felix. He hadn't heard from him in years, hadn't wanted to, hadn't forgiven him for snatching away his wife then dumping her for a college senior, and hadn't a clue what all this bullshit about Ozarkian culture and European interest therein was about. But what could a civilized classmate say? Come on down! Don't have a proper hotel in Hardlyville, he responded, but both could stay with Pierce if they would share a bed and bath in his guest room. Indoor crapper and warm water guaranteed.

"Sure," wrote back Felix a couple of weeks later. "How about we show up mid-March?" promising to be there unless he heard otherwise. "We'll fly in to wherever you recommend, rent a car, and drive directly to Hardlyville to meet you at the now-famous *Hellbender.*"

Pierce smiled to himself and saw a shot at humor in such a visit, amidst a subtle longing to get just a titch even for his lost wife. Felix always blamed the affair on her in subsequent conversations. Said she was ready for change, and if it hadn't been Felix, it would have been another. Nothing personal, Felix had said, and he hoped it hadn't damaged their longstanding friendship too much. Pierce always feigned disinterest and observed that with friends like that, who needed enemies?

Oh well, thought Pierce, *it will be interesting.* Felix was always worth the price of admission, and a French actress named Flo could only add color. Might even be worth a special edition of the *Hellbender.*

Lettie laughed out loud when he told her over supper one night. It was good to hear her laugh again, thought Pierce.

Spring sprung with warming sun and vibrant Ozarks colors. Sarvice, pear, redbud, and dogwood swarmed through greening woods and early morning fogged valleys. One late afternoon, as Pierce lounged around the *Hellbender,* contemplating his next move against Big Pork, he heard a horn blaring outside and opened the front door to a sight not beheld often in quaint Hardlyville. Behind the wheel of a bright-red Cadillac convertible, in the shadow of the sinking sun, was none other than Dr. Felix Feelgoode, sitting staccato on the honker, emulating the sound of pissed off mallard drake. He was fully clothed in robed regalia, including a puffy red academician hat, in an obvious attempt to impress those assembled.

However, he was wasting his time. To Felix's right was the finest set of female attributes, wrapped in gauzy silk, that Pierce had ever seen. There was nothing left to be imagined. Must be Flo, he adroitly concluded, before screaming at Felix to cut the racket.

A crowd quickly gathered, drawn by the commotion.

"Ils sont des vrais hillbillies?" Flo whispered to Felix, just loud enough for Pierce to hear.

"Yep," was his response, drawing an admiring sigh from his seat mate. This was clearly going to be fun for all involved.

Dylan Thomas was the first to come to his senses. He proudly walked to the passenger side of the red Caddy, buried his bifocal covered nose between Flo's bounty, sniffed loudly, then asked if they were real. Flo confirmed the obvious, pitying the old fool, and waving him away with a playful admonition in French to come back when he was old enough to handle with care.

Dinky Doodle quickly ripped off his shirt and jumped on the caddy's hood with a chest bump challenge.

"Mon Dieu," smiled Flo. Dill pulled Dinky from behind, complaining about him blocking the view, and once again the two crazed elder warriors were at each other's throats. Sheriff Sephus pulled them apart and patted each gently on the noggin with his night stick, nodding his approval to the lady he too would come to know as Flo.

"Yep," Felix whispered to Flo again, "these are real hillbillies."

Pierce invited both into the *Hellbender*, where he poured each a dollop of Ol' Dill's finest white lightning and raised a glass in welcome.

"Il fait trés chaud," observed Flo, slowly removing her gauze blouse. Between blushes, Pierce thought about offering to open a window in his upstairs office but decided against it when he observed Dinky Doodle perched atop a ladder, staring in with disbelief, and heard Ol' Dill Thomas clamoring for his turn from below.

Pierce and Felix quickly caught up with one another, and after a second dollop, Flo was pumped to meet some more real hillbillies. Pierce promised to take her on a walking tour of Main Street if she would put her blouse back on, and she quickly complied.

A veritable mob was waiting. Men, women, and children of all ages became her personal entourage as she passed the bank, the post office, the library, Doc Karst's office, and strolled all the way to Skunk Creek Bridge. She loved the look of the cool, clear water and asked Felix if she could hop in. With his nod, she was buck naked, in and out of the cold water, and back in his arms before the crowd could even gawk.

"Did you see that, Dill?" asked Dinky.

"She didn't have a hat, you blind SOB," responded Ol' Dill.

"I didn't say anything about a hat, you old deaf coot," growled Dinky.

"You're finally right about something, Dinky," Dill observed. "She does have really big toots. Even a fool can see that."

"Coot, coot, coot, not toots, and you are the fool!" shouted Dinky.

Felix asked Pierce if he would take them on a float trip, as in olden days. As he described a float trip to Flo, she broke into a huge smile and then began to reclothe.

"Voyage en bateau," she murmured in sensual tones that no floater had ever heard before. Pierce could only nod yes and confirm a float trip the next day, weather permitting.

Tour complete, Pierce whisked the happy couple back to their red Cadillac convertible to follow him home for supper. He also cautioned her admiring entourage to stay away or he would shower them with buckshot. Flo found this exciting and did promise in French that she would enjoy getting to know them better over the next week or so. And what a week it was.

Flo simply didn't like clothes and wore few, if any, around Pierce's house. She felt sorry for Pierce, not having a woman to keep him warm at night, and slipped into his bed to provide company and comfort immediately, until Pierce had to lie to her about his sexual preferences to keep her away. He didn't want Lettie to have the slightest suspicions about his intentions and slept in his snowsuit, rubber boots, and a ski mask after Flo's first foray.

Other's in the community were to be more hospitable to Flo's overtures, which they were delighted to acknowledge as her genuine efforts to repay her community hosts' many kindnesses.

The next day's float trip dawned to spring sun and warmth. It went forth without a hitch and without a stitch on beautiful Flo. Felix wore his academic regalia, including puffy hat, until Jimmy Jones tried to shoot it off his head with his new deer rifle, just grazing the top knot. Fiancée Sally was impressed, but Pierce Arrow wasn't and threatened him with a citizen's arrest unless he ceased immediately. Felix was shaken, but after a couple of cold beers, declared himself ready to float on.

Flo spent most of her time draped across the canoe gunnels mid-ship, soaking up sun on every navigable inch of her body. No tan lines there. Mayor had declared a Hardlyville Holiday in honor of the distinguished visitors, which allowed members of the community to paddle alongside or gawk from the treelined banks instead of being at work. The remainder gathered at the Skunk Creek Bridge take-out for photos and autographs. What a float trip it had been. Certainly, unlike any in Hardlyville's storied history.

While Felix took copious notes about hillbilly life to use in his next series of "Bone" lectures, Flo reached out to get to know the community. While she generally enjoyed sex, she more importantly viewed it as a tool in her goodwill ambassador's toolbox—a bridge to cultural exchange, a way to give back, a gift from France to the community, and a means to really understand a hillbilly. Once her generosity became evident, husbands were sent on out of town errands, and boyfriends were dispatched on college visitations, though none of the latter harbored the slightest intention of pursuing higher education. Some poor souls were temporarily tethered to front porches or locked in barns with the horses. Even with these distractions, Flo became well acquainted with the community at large.

Lettie and many of her friends found Flo likable. Several chose to keep her company and away from their men. Lettie appreciated Pierce's efforts at celibacy but told him she really didn't care if he partook of the unusual opportunity that presented herself. She was particularly amused with his snowsuit defense strategy.

The days flew by. Felix also tried his hand at cultural exchange but found few takers, beyond a couple of revenge encounters precipitated by Flo's affections. He was particularly attracted to Lettie, but she was not moved by his charms. She, in fact, carried her two youngest with her any time he was in range, which served as a useful deterrent and shield for her virtue.

Pastor Pat's fall from grace was swift and sure. Flo had paraded into his church in skintight shorts and a skimpy bikini top as he was practicing his Sunday message from the pulpit. She asked if she could listen so she could better understand what hillbillies do for religion. It was a missing piece of her market sample.

As Pastor Pat stammered through his dissertation on the Good Samaritan and how such noble and generous outreach to even hostile factions represented the best in spiritual purity, Flo was moved by his message and inched closer. It represented so well her philosophy of sharing and giving, and frankly, she was a bit surprised it was such an important foundation for hillbilly morality. She confirmed her admiration of this core value with Pastor Pat in French as she removed her spring wardrobe. And while he didn't speak a word of any foreign language, she soon translated in terms that were linguistically transformational.

Ol' Dill even got lucky and crowed like a banty rooster. Dinky tried but finally confessed to Dill that he just couldn't do it. Something about Flo bursting into laughter every time she said his name.

"That's what village idiots are for," Ol' Dill assured him.

And it didn't take long for the legend of Sheriff Sephus Adonis as the consummate Hardlyvillain lover to reach Flo's ears. Once veracity was established, Flo felt a need to delve deeper into this corner of hillbilly culture. Felix recorded it all in great detail to share with the faculty at future Sunday night dinners in Hanover.

As Felix and Flo prepared to depart back East, the community gathered again to offer a fond farewell. Felix sat gunning the Caddie's big engine, while Flo worked the crowd, kissing any lips extended, and accepting all parting gropes. She basked in the glow of Hardlyville's communal adoration and likely would have carried on for hours, if flight schedules had permitted. She sidled up to Pierce Arrow and planted a big one on his lips, squeezing Lettie's hand with hers all the while. Last, and definitely not least, Sheriff Sephus Adonis waited patiently. She kissed him with genuine affection and tears in her eyes.

"Adieu," she whispered and turned back to the car.

It was then she noticed Pastor Pat trying to blend into the crowd and leapt toward him, embracing him with legs wrapped around his midsection and a slight hump-da-hump. The good Pastor passed out and fell to the ground, while Flo cooed in his ear, something about what a benevolent Samaritan he was.

With that, Flo was finished with her entourage and returned to Felix's honking horn. A starlet's wave and a brief flashing of breasts put an exclamation point on a week in Hardlyville to remember.

"J'aime les hillbillies!" she screamed above the roar of the crowd.

Pierce Arrow had certainly never seen anything to rival it, and he mused how far the community had come from a She Devil forcing sex on Hardlyville's finest son to a sex kitten presenting herself with a passion and joie de vivre that restored hope and energy to a wounded community. A French connection, indeed, in the interest of global understanding and international relations. But Pierce also drew a deeper conclusion. The Hardlyville he had come to love and call home was underlaid with passion. Her citizens, in all of their irregularity and nonconformity, cared deeply about this place and each other.

Mademoiselle Florence Hormel had lit a spark that rekindled that passion and helped the village regain its swagger after a series of stunning setbacks. *Passion*, whatever that meant, was the one word that kept flooding his mind. He would need to think more on it.

"Au revoir et merci, sweet Flo," he whispered as she disappeared down the road.

PASSION

In the wake of Felix and Flo's departure, Pierce Arrow and Sheriff Sephus Adonis sat over coffee in the sheriff's conference room.

"Shit, brothers," was all Sheriff could say, over and over and over again. "What a lady," finally broke the sheriff's cadence.

Pierce pushed him as to what he meant and got the same response. Something had put Sheriff in repetitive mode. He could say nothing without repeating it at least once since Flo had marched gaily and proudly out of his office just minutes before their departure. Pierce never spoke to the sheriff about his personal doings but knew of his reputation. He had never seen the sheriff be anything but a gentleman to any lady in his presence and had certainly never seen him slip into a demonstrably amorous state. He had never seen him like this either.

"What is it, Sheriff?" Pierce queried again.

"She was just so passionate," Sheriff responded. "Passion," he repeated, "pure passion."

There was that word again.

"Passionate as in loving . . . or sharing . . . or living . . . or—?" Pierce prodded.

"No," Sheriff interrupted. "Flo Hormel was passionate as in giving. Giving of her all for the solitary purpose of pleasing, as if that were her foremost goal in life, giving pleasure—that nothing else much mattered."

"Strange," responded Pierce quietly. "Strange."

He had always admired passion, never been able to get his arms entirely around the concept, and had certainly not placed it the context of worldly pleasure.

Sheriff didn't want to pry but wondered if Pierce had sipped from Flo's cup of passion during her visit.

"No," Pierce confessed, "but not from lack of opportunity." Just other things on his mind, he guessed.

"Like little Miss Lettie," guessed Sheriff back to no response.

Pierce didn't even notice, as his mind was a bear-greased Möbius strip, with a vague notion of passion rushing by, around, and over, again and again and again. Now he was in repetitive mode, just like Sheriff Sephus and most others whom Flo had touched.

It was right then and there that Pierce became obsessed with defining and understanding passion, with a capital P. Florence Hormel had certainly set the village of Hardlyville on its collective ear with her passion, as Sheriff Sephus Adonis termed it. Pierce Arrow was determined to gain a deeper understanding of what had happened to and in Hardlyville the past week and what it might mean for the future—his and others.

He returned to the *Hellbender* where a huge crowd was waiting—well, maybe more enthusiastic than huge—to demand a special edition devoted to the visit of the divine Miss Hormel, including front page photos of her clad in her minimalist finest. Pierce dispersed the crowd with a promise of something soon and sat in his soft chair to contemplate passion.

When nothing happened after five minutes, he decided to consult Mr. Webster himself. What he found helped little. "Any emotion" was definition number one. That really narrowed things down. Got a little tighter in number two: "intense emotional excitement." Again, any emotion. Emotional emotion? There was even a Biblical reference. This was going nowhere.

Maybe it's the word, he reasoned. Try a different one. So out came the old, dog-eared *Thesaurus*. Replacement words seemed to focus on sex: "lust, craving, sexual excitement." Certainly, it was hard not to equate Flo with sex, but her passion seemed to slip those confines, at least according to Sheriff Sephus. He had spoken about "solitary focus" and "giving" in defining Flo's passion. Pierce had seen it, even if he hadn't experienced it. This drive, this focus, this commitment to an end or even another human, this inability to accept no. Pierce was knee-deep in it now. Perhaps he was even defining passion with his own obsessive insistence to try and define it.

What was Flo's passion, and why had it lifted Hardlyville above loss and mundane meanderings? Why was he so intrigued with it all?

It was almost as if a strange outburst, even infection, of passion had descended on his village at a time it was sorely in need of moving beyond fear and tragedy. A close-knit community suffers as one. A rising tide lifts all canoes. Florence Hormel had bridged the two platitudes.

Pierce had dinner with Lettie, helped her tuck in the kids, and walked home by way of Skunk Creek Shoal. He sat in the grass, the creek moonlit, and a large V in the rapids shining like a neon directional. He stared at the V, fixated on the fierce flow gaining momentum within its shrinking borders toward its focal point, then bursting through the narrow bounds to disperse again— kind of like an orgasm, he smiled. Hadn't had one of those in a long while, at least beyond dreams of Lettie. He slapped his hand mentally for even harboring such a heretical thought. She had all she needed to worry about without him reaching out to touch. He needed to help and support, not lust. *She is one fine woman, however,* he mused.

A car pulled through the field across the creek, and the headlights dimmed beneath happy laughter. He couldn't make out the celebrants but soon became aware of their sighs and grunts and pants and moans, then shared cries of pleasure. More like the *Thesaurus*, he noted. Was what he just witnessed passion? Pierce asked himself. What is the relationship of passion to pleasure, the difference between passion and lust? Obviously, neither participant was delving into their quick tryst with such intensity, smiled Pierce as they drove off to whatever home hearths awaited them.

If their shared pleasure was passion, it still fell well short of the magical momentum provided by Flo—unstoppable, irrepressible, confident, and at the same time curious, in an eternal sense.

Momentum . . . hmmm. Pierce had hated physics in college, but for some strange reason, a simple formula jumped brain front: mass x velocity = momentum.

Say what? Pierce asked himself.

What if Florence Hormel was *mass* and her passion *velocity*? At high torque, her momentum would spin off to any on her field of play and energize theirs exponentially. And everyone would feel good. He liked this theorem but needed to test-drive it.

Back to the neon Skunk Creek V. What if . . . what if the momentum of passion was equivalent to the compressed power of flowing water through a V in the creek? What if the flow of that intensely strengthening passion could burst forth just beyond the final point of constraint and disperse passion and energy to all within range?

Pierce stared fiercely at the flowing water tightening toward the point of the V and exploding in a moonlit spray and waves and ripples to blanket the immediate downstream environs. Is this what Flo had done to Hardlyville? Had she primed her flow with passion's momentum to touch all within her reach? Could the definition of passion be reduced to a simple algebraic formula? Flo's passion as *mass*, Flo's flow as *velocity*, Flo's impact as *momentum*—washing all in its glorious wake? fP x fF = fM?

Was there a case in support of this amended theorem? Pierce had certainly never seen Dylan Thomas move as fast in his ten years in Hardlyville. In fact, Ol' Dill's momentum had carried him to a dangerous collision with Ms. Rosebeam, as he had raced down Main Street screaming about how he had gotten him some of that sweet French stuff. The old dowager was unimpressed, and after pulling herself up, had beaten Ol' Dill around the head and shoulders with her large purse, drawing blood and blackening an eye. Ol' Dill smiled all the way to Doc Karst's office and back home, after a couple of stitches. He reasoned that, with all of this new momentum, he might make it to ninety. "Passion trumps age" would become his new mantra, and Ol' Dill was on call to prove it. All thanks to Mademoiselle Flo.

Pierce Arrow needed a drink after this brainwashing.

He would come back and ponder this another moonlit night. He would do so in the context of his passion for Lettie, which he simply could not deny anymore. For now, his adoring public was demanding a feature story on Florence Hormel, preferably a revealing exposé. Just how much skin could a Pulitzer guy show and not be defrocked? How little and not be run out of town? Ah, the perils of a small-town newsman. *National Enquirer* vs. *New York Times*.

Pierce himself had only two current passions—Miss Lettie and seeking justice for Big Pork. Once he understood more about passion, he would have to do something about both.

Pierce Arrow received a gushy, perfumed, ten-page thank you letter for Flo shortly after she returned to spring in New Hampshire. Predictably, it was in French, so Pierce ran it to the big-city newspaper for translation. He watched with humor as the translator, a stuffy young man with a snooty air about him, began to convert it into English on his laptop. He first blushed, then began to sweat profusely, and excused himself to the men's room several times thereafter.

In it she lamented not getting to know Pierce as well as some of his colleagues but had greatly appreciated his and the community's warm embrace. She was so proud of her immersion into all corners of hillbilly culture and relieved to learn that they were nowhere near as useless as the good Dr. Felix Feelgoode had made them out to be. She had found them to be warm and kind, gentle and well-meaning, and on average better endowed than their European counterparts. That most had descended from those very roots, their enhanced manhood must be attributed to the hearty lifestyle they had lived over the centuries—those marvelous float trips, the clear, homemade white lightning. Her new version of the stereotypical hillbilly was substantially more flattering than her original one. She would return to her native France with nothing but admiration and passion for "les hillbillies."

There's that word again, thought Pierce. Florence Hormel had generated enough *passion* to found a religion.

She and Felix had parted ways, though she would be eternally grateful to him for taking her to Hardlyville. She might even wish to return one day, if welcome. Pierce smiled broadly at that one.

The young translator was close to completion when he came up on a beautiful photograph of the author, sans clothes, and taped to the last page. He gulped and ran out of the room, pushing away Pierce's hundred dollar bill rendered for services. Below the photo, even Pierce could get the final words—"mon amour, gros bises," with *Florence* scribed in bold calligraphy.

What a letter, what a lady. Pierce would be careful not to excerpt too much in his feature article.

Pierce returned to the *Hellbender* and began to lay out the special issue. He found it hard to concentrate because of this new obsession with the word passion but plowed ahead nonetheless. That would be the theme of the feature article devoted to Flo and Felix's week of cultural exchange in Hardlyville. It would allow him to bridge culture and randy in a single provocative word, beyond the photos his readership was clamoring for.

PASSION would indeed be the screaming headline, with a lead photo of the two visitors in the red Caddy convertible. "What does passion mean to them?" would make a suitable subhead. He would focus on the joy and passion a young French lady could bestow on a community in need after a series of tragic and unexpected bylines—and the healing and inspiration she would leave behind. He might even conduct a few interviews but would have to be careful there. He would end with a poetic *quid pro quo*, namely the joy and passion a hillbilly nation could implant in one schooled in dark and foreboding preconceptions. She arrived seeking *Winter's Bone* and left singing "Yellow Submarine," in French, of course. Truth, passion, and the American way.

He would close with his favorite Floism—"hillbillies rock"—delivered with accent aigu, as befits her native tongue. He might even include a fuzzed out photo of her lying au natural, gunnel to gunnel, on the famous "voyage en bateau," as well as a closeup of her parting blown kisses, neck up. Dr. Felix Feelgoode would be a casual footnote. Not all would be happy with his treatment. Some would be offended, some would want more skin, and some would be relieved, but he would walk the thin line of journalistic propriety that Pulitzer professionalism would require.

He would also report the bizarre news that Ol' Dill's cat had gotten pregnant during the visit. This was newsworthy only in the sense that she was fifteen years old. As was his tendency, Ol' Dill immediately claimed paternity, then just as quickly retracted his claim. He was comfortable with his manhood now, courtesy of Mademoiselle Flo, and would no longer need to make absurd attributions to it. Doc Karst first claimed it impossible, then ended up delivering the kittens, most of whom survived. Pastor Pat stopped short of immaculate conception but was always open to divine intervention. Pierce Arrow simply chalked another one up to the passion that flowed through Hardlyville that unlikely week in her history.

Forgiveness
And Inspiration

One early afternoon as Lettie was putting the young ones down for an afternoon nap, a light tapping on the door got her attention.

"Just a moment," she whispered and slipped quietly out of their shared bedroom to the front door.

A short, shy young woman emerged from the shadows but said nothing. She stood quietly for a couple of minutes before asking Lettie if she could beg her forgiveness for an unpardonable sin. Lettie nodded and invited her in.

She began by saying she worked at Skunk Creek Ranch and was one of several members of a former religious group, who had stayed in the area after their congregation had disbanded. She carried the guilt of a great sin atop her shoulders and within her heart and was fearful of going to hell. This was hard for her to share, but she would do anything to get to heaven when her time came. And it was likely not far off, as cancer had attacked her body through her breast, and by the time she got to a doctor, it was too late. He guessed two to four months, if she was lucky.

She needed Lettie's forgiveness if she was to greet death with any hope at all. Lettie was generally the forgiving sort, and she had certainly gone down that road with Lucas after his occasional dalliances came to light. She had exacted a touch of revenge through Sheriff Sephus but had found forgiveness a brighter path than just getting even.

"Please continue," she had encouraged the young lady after rubbing her emaciated shoulders with caring concern.

She claimed to have been one of the last to see Lettie's husband, Lucas, alive. Furthermore, she had contributed to his demise by not standing up to a bully that had raped her. She described, in shallow tones, the events that led to Lucas's last stand.

She began with the day Lettie's husband, Lucas, and a big, burly fellow in a uniform came to Skunk Creek Ranch, where she was serving as a cleaning lady. The ranch manager showed them around the entire hog operation and said he would like to visit with the citizens of Hardlyville at some point, to allay any concerns they might have with a hog farm so close to their village and its pristine creek. The officer had confirmed that the invitation was an open one, but Lucas seemed very skeptical when he left. The manager had mentioned the religious order, of which she was a part, and the communal living quarters most shared not far from the ranch.

She had come to recognize that she and most of the member families were in some sort of a brainwashed or trance state or they would never have condoned the practices of the commune or the evil lady who served as their pastor. They were aware of the code of violence by which she ruled, but they were lured by the sex and gratification with which she funded their indebtedness to her. By the time the authorities descended and the commune was uprooted, including jail terms for most of the males, it was too late for them, and for poor Lucas.

"Ladies and children were spared as innocent bystanders, though we were all guilty of the worst sins by simply going along."

The pastor/high priestess disappeared and was never heard from again, though word filtered back to those who remained that she conceived a child through the seed of Lettie's husband. The child was left on his grave. Rumor claimed that the baby had yellow eyes, like the evil one did. Lettie shrugged slightly but smiled at the mention of the precious, yellow-eyed baby she embraced as her own now.

The lady claimed she had started to visit Lettie on several occasions but could not bear the shame of her complicity. The specter of death over one's shoulder trumps shame. She needed to tell Lettie of her husband's bravery in dying and apologize for not stopping it or not dying with him.

"The night before the raid, High Priestess had conducted an evil, high-voltage, group think-and-grope town hall meeting, promising to exact vengeance on the town of Hardlyville for the death of several of her henchmen, shot and killed, in fact, by your husband, Lucas. As I headed home, a cruel and vicious neighbor grabbed me, muffled my screams, and led me into the woods, where he forced himself on me. As I stumbled away to his threats of squealing on my infidelity, I stepped right on your husband, Lucas, who was partially dug in beneath a large rock. I screamed, then recognized him as one of the visitors to the ranch the previous day and identified him as such to my attacker. Your husband was a very handsome man and not easily forgotten, though I so wish I had said nothing. Perhaps the beast would have been easier on him. Not to be.

"He kicked your husband and his broken leg until he lost consciousness, dragged him through the woods to center stage, and reconvened the meeting, screaming at the top of his lungs that he had captured a rapist. He dragged me up front with him to confirm his accusations. He ripped the remainder of my bra, blaming the scratch he himself had inflicted on Lucas, who seemed to drift in and out of consciousness. He also displayed my privates, with his semen spread about, blaming Lucas as well. I confirmed both atrocious lies," she sobbed and tried to regain her composure.

Lettie urged her to continue with a gentle nod and tears dripping of her own.

"Lucas was then encaged on stage to await his judgment moment. I am so sorry," she wailed. "Your husband would be alive today if I hadn't stepped on him, hadn't ID him, or had told the truth at his mock inquisition. I was so scared. Scared of my rapist, scared of my husband, scared of the evil priestess, scared of my own community. Fright has given way to shame, and I beg your forgiveness."

Lettie assured her that she had it, without hesitation. She then asked the young lady if she could elaborate on one thing more. Her nod of approval cleared the way for Lettie to ask, one more time, about the final moments of Lucas's life, if she had been there. She had, she confirmed, and it had been one of the cruelest scenes she had ever seen played out.

"Your husband was essentially raped by this beastess, forced to copulate to stay alive. His staying power was beyond natural. His concentration on keeping her engaged and on fire like the animal she was defied definition. The crowd was berserk, which egged her on more, and he just did his job. Like an old plow horse, eyes clenched shut in pain and focus, teeth barred, silent in his strength, while she wailed like a banshee. This was not an act of sex but of courage. I saw what finally trapped him as the copters roared in. I was sitting in a seat of honor, front row, for my brave cowardice of the prior evening. She bit into his tongue, like it was a piece of sausage, elevating his agony again to the point of passing out. He was out cold when he unloaded in her, when she screeched her victory, and when she shot him—beyond pain and glory. Be proud of him," she begged, "he deserves your honor."

Both women were sobbing now, then hugging close for comfort.

"Thank you," was all Lettie could muster as they said good-bye. There was validation in hearing of Lucas's bravery from another source.

Lettie opened the door to the nursery and lifted both babies into her arms, Lucas's legacy intact. She held them close as they cooed slowly awake.

Lettie felt more love for Lucas Jones than ever before. And she was proud of him in the strangest way.

One morning Pierce opened the door to the *Hellbender* after a strong knock. Standing outside was a tall, slender, good-looking man who asked to visit. He was accompanied by an attractive women, introduced as his wife. He was considering relocating his business to Hardlyville. He introduced himself as Rifleman, which was also the name of his business. She was Steele.

His attention had been drawn to Hardlyville when reading of Pierce's crusade against Big Pork. He hated both, big and pork, and was touched by Pierce's passion. His business was such that he could locate it anywhere. He made custom persimmon rifle stocks by hand and really only needed raw material and hunters to survive. The Ozarks was flush with both, as well as, in this case, a serious porker problem.

Pierce extolled the virtues of Hardlyville, her citizenry, and the beautiful Skunk Creek, which ran alongside her. Rifleman acknowledged that, ironically, he didn't like to hunt, but he loved to fish. He had a passion for smallmouth. Pierce assured him he had come to the right place, and Pierce would do anything to make his move easy and productive. He even knew a young man who could introduce him to Skunk Creek brownies, as good a fisherman as Rifleman would ever meet.

Rifleman said he would like to start there. Could Pierce put him in touch with the young man as soon as possible so he and Steele might sample the creek? In thirty minutes, Jimmy was in front of the *Hellbender* with a john boat loaded in his truck, fishing gear for all stowed carefully in the truck bed, along with a beer cooler and sandwiches. Such was life in Hardlyville. Things moved quickly when priorities were clearly identified. Six hours and a couple of eighteen-inchers later, Rifleman knocked on Pierce's door, thanking him for the intro to Jimmy and Skunk Creek. He and Steele had talked it over and were prepared to move to Hardlyville from their current home in Eastern Tennessee.

He would require about two thousand square feet of space to house inventory, a production line, and living accommodations for him and Steele. Each of his stocks was hand carved to order, then sanded and polished to a dark sheen. He typically processed five to six orders at a time and earned enough to live comfortably. Pierce wondered if Banker Bud's old house might work. Lois had moved in with Doc Karst and Sally with Jimmy Jones, both prenuptial but blessed by Pastor Pat for purity of intent. A quick walk about the house confirmed acceptability, and Rifleman closed a handshake deal with Lois on the spot.

"Life in Hardlyville seems to work so easily," Rifleman muttered to Steele. They promised to return with belongings and cash within two weeks. Rifleman's final challenge to Pierce was to keep on Big Pork's sorry ass. Reinforcements were on the way.

Pierce was moved by Rifleman's admonition and rejuvenated to take up the battle again. He would publish back-to-back weekly exposés on hog farms, lagoons, and solid waste, and reboot the community's commitment to removing the upstream threat.

He would also announce his intention to challenge Larry Larrsnist in the next congressional election. He would recount, in great detail, the hit job on his campaign by Big Pork and the now deceased and discredited Banker Bud. He would seek national exposure for sharing the whole sordid affair, including the current incarceration of the former chairman of the State Oversight Board and the pending trial of Banker Bud's best friend and hog company CEO, both on charges of corruption. He would launch his campaign on the backs of these scoundrels and would run it on the same principles that brought him so close in the polls to Congressman Larrsnist last year, before the kiddie porn attack. He would rally his army to righteous action against fraud, corruption, and degradation of their backyard and precious creek. His heart beat fast, and his spirits soared.

And while he was at it, he would ask Lettie to marry him.

This sudden burst of passion had been lurking beneath Pierce's emotional surface so long that it took neither time nor formulation to take shape. His fixation on the word itself had lured him into study and away from action. Enough academic meandering. It was time to pursue his passions without fear or constraint. Passion is as passion does, or something like that from his *Forest Gump* memory bank, and he was inflamed to do it all now, right now. Whether it had been passionate Flo or resolute Rifleman who had triggered his final outburst, or simply a narrowing of focus, like the moonlit V in that Skunk Creek rapid of several nights past, Pierce was on point unlike any time since taking down the "Evil Coven." Beware world. Pierce Arrow was back. There were things he simply couldn't not do!

Pierce decided he would run his grand plan by Sheriff Sephus Adonis as soon as possible. He asked the sheriff to meet him after supper at the big rapid above Skunk Creek Bridge. Another bright moon greeted them as Pierce shared all his theories on passion within the metaphor of flowing water, including mass, velocity, momentum, and Flo.

Sheriff was confounded. Had Pierce Arrow lost his mind? What kind of gibberish was he talking? He had worried about Pierce since he refused to play with Flo and wondered if this was the breakdown that had resulted from his principled, if foolish, abstinence. Sex had always been Sheriff Sephus's answer to just about anything, and to go without would certainly have twisted his logic. He didn't understand a single thing Pierce had just shared with him. He did conclude that Pierce Arrow just needed good, old-fashioned sex before he blew his top. As hard as it would be, he would talk to Miss Lettie about it, as she seemed to be the only female Pierce would even lay eyes on.

It was then that Pierce began to lay his full agenda on Sheriff Sephus Adonis, seeking his counsel and advice. Sheriff breathed a heavy sigh of relief as Pierce started making sense again. He had flipped the "on" switch Sheriff had so come to admire and moved beyond esoteric flagellation to bold and beautiful. Sheriff said "absolutely yes" to taking on Big Pork again, to vanquishing that fraud Larry Larrsnist, and, with a wisp of envy, to wedding Lettie. He couldn't relate any of it in any way to the metaphor of the flowing water, as Pierce called it, but he had Pierce's back, whatever came of it. He didn't know who this Rifleman dude was either, but if he had sparked Pierce to get off his ass and follow his passion, he must be okay.

He asked Pierce what the hell he was talking about earlier, and Pierce simply smiled.

"The anatomy of passion," was all he said.

Pierce said he would start with Miss Lettie and asked Sheriff Sephus Adonis to be his best man. Sheriff smiled his confirmation.

Pierce stopped by Lettie's on the way back from Skunk Creek. The kids were in bed, and she was reading a cheesy romance novel to get her mind off the young housekeeper's visit and conversation. She seemed pleasantly surprised to see him.

This would be hard for Pierce, for as eloquent as he often was in full speaking mode on issues, personal articulation had always been very hard for him. It had taken him six months to propose to his first wife, nearly a quarter of the amount of time they were ultimately married. Every time he would start to ask, an embarrassing eye tick would present, and he would excuse himself for some reason or another until their next date. He had seen this happen to bad guys in movies and knew he wasn't one of them. Yet he couldn't move beyond it.

Wife one finally got it and started playing to it.

"Cat got your eye?" she would tease as his left eye squeezed open and shut like the flapping of a butterfly wing. "The eyes have it by a large margin over the nose," she would confirm, then laugh hysterically as Pierce fled in shame. She even threw in occasional Biblical references to removing the sty from his own eye before doing same with his neighbor, or something like that. And, of course, a blinking eye for a blinking eye, a friggin' tooth for a friggin' tooth, and on and on. He should have known their marriage was doomed to ridicule before he even got the question popped.

Lettie asked Pierce in and offered him a nightcap beer. He accepted and began to tell Lettie about all that was happening at the *Hellbender*. He sought her opinion on the "Passion of Flo" spread and the buffed up photos. She laughed and said it seemed to represent a less compromising position than a few of Hardlyville's finest had found themselves in. She repeated her admiration of Flo's lust for life and mankind. Pierce laughed at the latter. Flo's visit to Hardlyville was timely, constructive, and in a sense, healing, Lettie concluded. She still had trouble with the visual of nude Flo snuggled up next to Pierce in his snowsuit, ski mask, and boots, but Dr. Feelgoode had confirmed it. She admired Pierce's self-control, but questioned his rationale.

Pierce changed the conversation to his new crusade against Big Pork and plans to announce a second run against that pig Larrsnist, keyed to the corruption and graft that ended his first.

Lettie beamed at this one and spoke to Pierce of how proud she was of him. She offered to help in any way she could.

Well, he responded, there was a major role she could play, which was the purpose of his call this late evening.

"Lettie," he began.

"Pierce, what on earth is wrong with your eye?" she interrupted. "Are you flirting with me?" Lettie laughed. "Winking at me, perhaps?" she added. "Kind of cute," she smiled.

"Lettie," he gasped after chugging a good half of his nightcap beer, "Lettie, will you marry me?"

Lettie was laughing so hard at his flapping left eye it took a moment for her to grasp what he was asking. Once the question was out, his tick stopped, and she knew he was serious.

"I am so sorry," Pierce apologized, "but I get this embarrassing tick every time I ask a serious personal question, and Lettie, I'm dead serious with this one. I love you, and I want you to marry me as soon as possible."

Her smile was slight but genuine. She had half-grown kids, as well as two babies, and her life was totally invested in them. But she was flattered and touched beyond her ability to express. She would need to think long and hard about Pierce Arrow's proposal before she could respond.

"Could you give me forty-eight hours?" she asked.

"Only if you don't make me repeat the proposal," he laughed, fake blinking the offending left eye to her amusement.

"No," she confirmed, "once is enough," and thanked him with a very strong hug for a very little lady. "I'll get back soon with an answer," Lettie promised.

Pierce headed back toward the *Hellbender* to plan out his publishing schedule for the next several weeks. Sleep would not come easy that night. He felt a depth of love for Lettie he had never known before. He hoped she would say yes more than anything he had ever hoped for in his life.

The next day, the community lost another dear soul. Ms. Rosebeam died in an automobile accident when she lost control of her ancient Lincoln rounding a rain-slicked curve just outside town on the way to buy a new Latin textbook in the big city. She hadn't renewed her driver's license in years but drove around town nonetheless, occasionally sideswiping a mailbox or stray dog, but never inflicting personal injury, until now.

Sheriff Sephus knew she shouldn't be driving but generally looked the other way when he saw her creeping down the street to church or the Piggly Wiggly. He reasoned that at ten mph the worst damage she could do in that battle wagon of hers would be self-inflicted and repairable. Every time he tried to talk to her about hanging up the keys, she played the sex card and threatened to accuse the sheriff of harassment with intent to fornicate. Where she came up with this stuff was a source of amazement and laughter to all.

Between her and that sex-crazed Dill Thomas, every act, suggestion, or thought is reduced to sexual innuendo, thought Sheriff. *Probably ought to lock them both up in a single cell for a weekend and see what happens.*

Wouldn't be happening now. Her car was so old it didn't have seat belts, and she wasn't about to install them on her teaching salary. Her auto had flipped, and her head was crushed into the ceiling, assuring instantaneous death. All mourned her passing.

Pierce ran a single page tribute release before he began his blockbuster run of specials. He traced her roots back to Thomas Hardly and spoke of her passion for the community.

He interviewed several of her former students, who extolled her virtues a teacher, mentor, and mixer of magical toga party elixirs. All agreed that she was one of a kind. Even Ol' Dill expressed remorse at her passing and said he would miss her. Said she was the next to best lovin' he had in his eighty-plus years, the best being his most recent conquest, that hard to get vixen, Flo. With no one to dispute his "next to best" claim, it stood, particularly with his newly earned Flo sourced credibility.

Pierce saved the best for last. In going through her things, they found a handwritten note labeled:

LAST WILL AND TESTAMENT—ROSEBEAM

In a neatly handwritten note, Ms. Rosebeam left her home and everything contained therein or affixed thereto to the Hardlyville Library as a living Museum of Latin Culture and Studies. Funds endowing the museum and to acquire a unique collection of Latin classics would be found in a large purse beneath Ms. Rosebeam's bed. It was her final gift to her beloved community, which accepted it with deep gratitude.

Sheriff Sephus Adonis had been called in to take custody of the funds. As he emptied the contents of Ms. Rosebeam's bag on her bed, a large smile graced his face. He found five banded bundles of one hundred bills, which he quickly calculated to equal ten thousand each or fifty thousand in total. The old biddy herself had robbed the bank the night of Banker Bud's demise. He should have known when she complained about having to wipe with a loose hundred dollar bill.

"What a dumb shit I am," he laughed out loud without explanation.

All the hundreds were in bands of ten thousand dollars each. There were no single Franklins hanging around to wipe anyone's privates. She stole the fifty thousand dollar bequest for her beloved Latin legacy from that scumbag Banker Bud. Justice served. Case closed. Way to go, Ms. Rosebeam, he beamed to himself.

Lettie walked resolutely to the *Hellbender* as promised after her forth-eight hours of deep contemplation. She knew Pierce would be there working feverishly on his upcoming exposés. She knocked quietly before entering. Hearing nothing, she slowly pushed the door open and walked upstairs to Pierce's office. She found him sound asleep, head on his desk-bound forearm. She leaked a tear.

"He is so sweet," she mumbled.

Pierce heard and leapt to his feet. She walked slowly forward, and they embraced. Pierce started to kiss her for the first time ever, but she placed a forefinger on his lips.

"No, Pierce, I cannot marry you, now or ever. I love you too, Pierce," she continued, wincing at the downcast look that spread over his face. "I love you, Pierce. I admire you, Pierce. You set my heart to racing every time I see you, but I can't marry you. I'll sleep with you, have your babies, if you want, even go with you to Washington, DC, when you whip Larrsnist's sorry ass, if you'll let me bring the children. But I cannot marry you."

Pierce didn't know whether to do a jig of joy or simply cry, so he just sat down in his chair while Lettie continued.

Lettie shared with him the young housekeeper's visit and plea for forgiveness. She had recounted the story of Lucas's last hours, with a focus on her guilt and his bravery. Lettie finally understood why Lucas had to go down firing, how he was resolute in trying to survive to his last blast, which incidentally he never got to even enjoy because he passed out from the pain and never again awakened.

Lettie had confirmed her forgiveness to the visitor but stopped short of validating the news of an offspring from that frenetic coupling, the little girl with the bright-yellow eyes. She really didn't want that news circulating around the coven campfire, even if most of the bad guys were all locked up. That evil Devil Woman was still out there somewhere. Lettie loved the little girl with all her heart and sensed she would require more shielding and protection than her others.

"Anyway," Lettie continued, "I am bound to Lucas and his name forever. I will be Lettie Jones to my grave—in honor of my husband and in support of his children. They deserve that. He earned that."

With that, she arose, walked over to Pierce, and kissed him fiercely.

"I love you, Pierce Arrow, and will for the rest of my life. You are a special soul, and yes, you turn me on. I have not had a man since Lucas, and you will be my first and last."

They made fierce and passionate love on the floor of Pierce's office.

Next day Sheriff Sephus Adonis was at the *Hellbender* first thing to ask Pierce how it went with Lettie. Pierce's smile said it all.

"When is the big day?" Sheriff asked.

"It's not," Pierce responded.

"You're not getting married?" Sheriff asked in disbelief.

"No," smiled Pierce.

"Shit, brothers, why are you so friggin' happy?" Sheriff continued.

Pierce's smile said it all.

"You got lucky," Sheriff bellowed, "didn't you, sly dog. I knew that's all you needed to get normal again."

Pierce blushed but wouldn't acknowledge private matters to the sheriff.

"Do I have to subpoena you to get the truth?" Sheriff threatened.

"I'll lie under oath to protect the innocent," Pierce countered, "like any good journalist would."

Sheriff was perplexed but acceded to Pierce's wishes.

"Sit down," Pierce ordered Sheriff Sephus, "and I'll explain."

And he did, everything that is except the incredibly raw and pleasurable parts. That was and would be between him and Lettie only. Not even confessions of philandering out of wedlock to Pastor Pat. This would be their secret, even if poorly kept. Pierce had never known anything like it. Pierce was in love, in lust, and in cahoots with the love of his life. He finally understood passion and accepted his inability to define it beyond the word "Lettie." He had finally made it to the mountaintop, to the point of the V in the rapid, to the something he couldn't not do.

Sheriff kind of got it and hugged Pierce with his large arms and his old friend Lucas within his heart. He could barely suppress the fleeting question of whether Lettie was still bald or back to bear's back and smiled at the memories.

Pierce Arrow moved in with Lettie Jones the next day and put his house on the market. Tongues wagged and rumors flew, but in the end most saw it as just another offspring of Flo's short but passionate visit.

SECRETS

Sheriff Sephus Adonis returned to Ms. Rosebeam's home several days later with the part-time library director, a pretentious little missus, who mistakenly thought she was a big thing, per the sheriff's read. And Sheriff usually had a pretty good take on folks. He also felt that Bilious Bloom was an apt name. She wore tight little glasses on the tip of her nose, held in place by a wicked witch kind of wart, and even tighter little jeans everywhere she went. She seemed to fancy herself as a "player," though Sheriff had never actually met anyone who had asked her to play. She claimed to be college educated, though none were quite sure what that meant in her case. Nor did anyone care because the job was part-time and voluntary and could have been adequately filled by Dinky Doodle. Well, maybe that was a stretch. Suffice it to say that Miss Bilious seemed superficial, at best.

Sheriff was along because he had an eye out for more cash. He was seriously bemused at the old lady's brazen heist and subsequent purchase of a personal point of light in Hardlyville's historic gallery of stars. Who knows what else the old biddy might have pulled off? The library director was there to formally inventory Ms. Rosebeam's generous gift, beyond cash.

Bilious Bloom was kind of tittery over being alone with the sheriff but simply didn't know what to do about it. Should she play it cool and let the big boy come after her? Should she flirt, then skirt around the end game? Should she sneak up behind him and leap on his big back, begging for mercy?

Bilious Bloom just loved playing these mind games. After all, she was a virgin and had no interest in trading her remaining claim to fame for a well-worn commodity. She wouldn't mind a quick peek at the icon itself but had learned from years of experience that show and tell was child's play and rarely turned out well. She had always admired Ms. Rosebeam's obvious indifference toward the male species and set out to replicate it. "Sexy but staid" would be her mantra until the right one came along. If, indeed, he ever did. Just like Ms. Rosebeam.

They began to comb through her closet, a seriously dusty undertaking. Sheriff Sephus Adonis noticed an unevenness of floor covering in a far corner. He crawled beneath several of Ms. Rosebeam's dated gauzy gowns, promising not to look up her dress, in case the old biddy was still watching. He scraped away cheap plastic tile with his pocket knife to reveal a corner of a small trap door. Bilious Bloom looked on with a curious combination of admiration for his investigative eye and wonder as to how good he might really be.

The small floor door did not open easily and may not have seen light in decades. Sheriff finally broke the seal and popped it open. Bilious felt a sharp sigh escape her lips as she wondered if that was how a real popping might feel. Not with him at the helm, she guessed with a smile.

Enclosed therein were several stacks of handwritten letters, encased in fine dust. Sheriff needed help with this one and rang Pierce Arrow on his cell phone, asking him to join Sheriff

Sephus and Librarian Bilious in Ms. Rosebeam's closet as soon as possible. The strange request mused Pierce, but what's new in Hardlyville? He walked quickly to the Rosebeam house.

Sheriff Sephus greeted Pierce at the front door, Bilious at his side. Pierce felt a brief sense of relief they weren't waiting in the closet for him, buck naked and looking for another playmate. It was always hard to read Miss Bilious as wanton or winsome, and as for his friend the sheriff . . .

All nodded and followed Sheriff to Ms. Rosebeam's closet. Pierce was even more confused as Sheriff swept aside Ms. Rosebeam's gowns and pointed to the dark, dusty hole beneath. Sheriff felt that Pierce, as a genuine man of letters, was appropriately equipped to fairly and rationally deal with what lay within.

Pierce reached into the small vault and began to remove the contents, asking the librarian to record in detail. A first stack of letters wrapped in twine and still enclosed in envelopes were all addressed to Mrs. Hardlita Hardly Rosebeam, Ms. Rosebeam's mother. They carried a return address bearing the initials "O.R.," which Pierce took to be Octavia Rosebeam, grande dame of modern times herself. That address ended in NYC, NY. Postmarks dated the exchanges to begin in 1939. Wow, was all Pierce could think. Must be fifty of them, he estimated. The librarian recorded every word Pierce uttered. She was good at this, and it kept her mind off of having sex with Sheriff Sephus Adonis.

A second group of letters were encased in envelopes from an older era and bore only "PPH" in the top corner and "Octavia" in the middle. These were obviously hand delivered rather than posted. Pierce opened one to find an almost historical document, as opposed to a personal one, all from Grandma Petunia to her beloved granddaughter, Octavia.

"What a treasure trove of Hardlyville history," whispered Pierce as he estimated the stack to be one hundred notes deep.

The librarian wrote it all down, word for word for word.

A single rolled piece of paper lay beneath it all. As Pierce Arrow carefully unfurled a coarse, hand-drawn map, complete with north and south markings, the legend of Thomas Hardly's demise crept into the back of his mind.

Pierce, Sheriff, and Bilious were silent in the moment. Hardlyville's earliest recorded memories lay just before them. The magnitude of this discovery was not lost on any present.

Pierce asked Sheriff if he could remove the precious historical contents to the *Hellbender*, where Pierce promised to keep it all in a safe while he sorted through to provide context and relevance. Sheriff concurred, and the librarian wanted nothing to do with the whole dank, dusty mess, which, in fact, was her institutional possession. Sheriff loaded the contents into a cardboard box, while Pierce called for Lettie to meet him at the office as soon as she could get the babies over to Flotilla's day care.

Pierce was knee-deep in his tribute to Florence Hormel and his exposé of Big Pork, but this must take precedence. He and Lettie could poke through quickly to gain a rudimentary understanding of what Sheriff Sephus had just uncovered, then get back to share, as appropriate, with the community after the feature articles were run. Shouldn't take more than a couple of hours.

Lettie arrived about three in the afternoon of a beautiful early fall day. She and Pierce walked home together as the sun peeked above the horizon some sixteen hours later. And they hadn't spent the time messing around. The stories and secrets that unfolded in their hands were cosmic in the tiny Hardly-villian universe.

Lettie had begun with Ms. Rosebeam's letters to her mother from New York City in 1939. Pierce had just dived into Petunia Perfidy Hardly's handwritten notes to granddaughter Rosebeam when Lettie whispered to Pierce that he needed to join her pile.

As Lettie read the intensely personal chronology aloud, Pierce attempted to condense it into a narrative that took on a life of its own. It went something like this.

Hardlita and her husband, Herman Rosebeam, decided to send their precious daughter, Octavia, Ms. Rosebeam to all, to a private ladies school in New York City to study the classics. Herman was a wealthy man by Hardlyville standards, and Hardlita was astounded by her daughter's interest in and ability to self-educate herself in all things Latin. Octavia's goal in life, beyond making her parents proud, was to become a world-famous Latin scholar and teacher. She wanted a Ph.D. behind her name, to teach in America, and to live in Italy in her summer villa with whichever Italian lover suited her fancy at the moment. Where Octavia had gotten her passion for a dead language from an ancient empire, and attached romance to both, was beyond parental understanding. Herman cast a wary eye on fellow Ozarker Ms. Rose O'Neill, whose art, poetry, and love of most of mankind was scandalous to some but inspiring to others, including his daughter. Whatever. Passion is passion, and they sought to nurture hers.

Herman's spinster sister, Pornopoly, lived in New York City, where she made a living as an artist. When Herman's letter reached her, asking about post high school educational opportunities in the classics, Pornopoly's immediate response was to seek Octavia's admission to a finishing school for classical scholars just blocks from her row house. She also invited Octavia to live with her, a source of great comfort to both parents. New York City was as far from Hardlyville in every way as any place on earth, but family grounding trumped uncertainty and fear. Herman and Hardlita accepted with gratitude, and Ms. Rosebeam was soon on her way to New York City to pursue her dreams.

Lettie had stopped reading long enough to run home for a couple of slab bacon and tomato sandwiches for dinner and to tuck the babies in under the watch of her older ones. She asked Pierce not to proceed without her. There was too much here to gloss over, she felt.

Pierce complied and just sat for awhile, reflecting on the gumption and fortitude of all involved. This background sketch was discernible from Ms. Rosebeam's first letters to her mother, which also bubbled with gratitude for the opportunity and spoke to how comfortable she was with Aunt Pornopoly. She loved her aunt, she loved her studies, she loved New York, and . . . she loved a young Italian dancer named Sardo.

Ms. Rosebeam wrote that she hesitated to introduce Sardo so early in the equation but had also promised all honesty in her communications home. She was in love for the first time in her young life and wanted to share that with her parents.

"Sad that she didn't save their reply," noted Lettie.

"Maybe it wasn't pretty," smiled Pierce. Lettie nodded.

Ms. Rosebeam had met Sardo, who was ten years her senior, at a Latin-themed dance and was swept off her feet by his grace, his wit and charm, and his blatant lack of conversational English. They agreed on the spot to tutor and learn from each other and became inseparable, as confirmed in a playful P.S. to one of Octavia's beautiful letters. That learning led to fondling and comingling was soon apparent.

Included in a separate envelope was a different and bold writing stroke, penned in what Pierce recognized as Italian, which he had taken in j-school, oh, so long ago, at the urging of his first wife. She loved the spoken Italian word and had always responded to it favorably and intimately, at least until Dr. Feelgoode had one-upped poor Pierce on the creative writing retreat.

His grammar was long gone, but key words remained buried in the recesses of the romantic corner of his brain. Breasts, buttocks, and nipples were all part of the dialogue with wifey one and surfaced in the first two paragraphs of Sardo's letter to

Ms. R. more than once. Lettie blushed and smiled, maybe even a little turned on.

"Ol' Dill lied again," Pierce laughed out suddenly. No way he could have popped Ms. Rosebeam's original cork, as he had claimed several times since her demise. Octavia and her Italian stallion had cornered that IPO with joy and aplomb. Lettie blushed again and got more turned on.

"Later," she whispered to herself.

Happy letters, like happy feet in a clear creek bottom, continued for months.

Then, nothing—a void, a lapse without explanation, which must have left Hardlita and Herman gasping for answers. Several letters to Aunt Pornopoly also apparently went unanswered, as confirmed in a short, terse reply from her that ended the drought. Octavia had an accident that had devastated her and caused her Italian lover to leave, she reported. It had not been her fault, but she was paying a mighty price. She had dropped her classes and mopped about aimlessly for months, but now she was ready to share her tale of woe.

Over the next several weeks of letters, Octavia laid out the whole bloody mess to her obviously heartbroken parents. It was hard to read, and Lettie broke out in tears several times. Pierce winced and gained a new level of respect for the lady Ms. Rosebeam became.

Seems that Octavia had strayed into a dimly lit park late one night, walking home after a particularly glorious session of amore with Signore Sardo—full moon, lust and love sated, warm breeze rustling the leaves, alone with her passion and senses. She heard a rustling from behind as in a dream. The strong hands that wrapped around her neck awakened her to a real nightmare. Octavia was warned to be silent and comply if she wished to live. A knife at her neck replaced one hand and reinforced the point. The other pushed her to the ground, face down, lifted her gown, ripped aside her undergarments, and brutally assaulted her from behind.

Lettie sobbed out loud.

Octavia had stifled her screams of anguish, squeezing her eyes shut to keep out the pain and humiliation and the yellow that blinked beside her ear.

"Stop," said Pierce, asking Lettie to read that part from the letter again. Lettie repeated the part about the yellow blinking, then continued.

The yellow that blinked amidst growls and grunts bespoke evil. The hot breath on her neck had reeked of rot and death. And when it finished, it just did it again. And again. And again. She passed out more than once during the endless ordeal. And finally, when she awoke, it was gone. And the prior pleasant tingle of love between her legs was buried in waves of sordid mess. Octavia had been raped violently and repeatedly by the devil himself, she concluded, sobbing so deep that her hurt burst beyond the point of penetration.

Pierce Arrow and Lettie Jones could only stare at one another, mouths agape. Pierce could not wait to bring Sheriff Sephus Adonis into this bizarre cauldron of happenstance. Lettie gently picked up the next letter with trembling hands.

Octavia announced to her parents that this violation had impregnated her immediately, well beyond the certainty of protection her Italian lover always wore. The words on this page were smeared, teared by either victim or reader, Pierce surmised.

Ms. Rosebeam's Italian lover soon left her in disgust, blaming her for careless indiscretions and a professed fear of contracting deadly STDs. A devastated Ms. Rosebeam retreated to solitary confinement as she weighed her choices. She was not ready for a baby, she did not wish to raise the baby of a beast, and she actually had a sense of fear from what lurked in her belly. Violent kicks awakened her in the night. She belched sour fumes from time to time. Stomach gurgles sounded growly. She could neither sleep peacefully nor calm her anxiety.

With Aunt Pornopoly's assistance, Octavia found an anonymous adoptive family for the baby, conditioned only by the fact that she would never see the newborn. The moment the baby issued forth with a loud and somewhat guttural cry, he or she was whisked away to a waiting set of arms. Ms. Rosebeam had been brutally raped and had given the baby for adoption without the slightest knowledge of what she and her abuser had wrought. Another tear trickled down Lettie's cheek.

One last letter from New York City confirmed that she would be coming home after several weeks of recuperation with Aunt Pornopoly. No one would ever know, beyond immediate family. Her career as a Latin teacher would begin in Hardlyville, not Italy, and as her life as a hopeless romantic died. She would never entertain another man in her life, she claimed in her last letter. Another tear from Lettie. She never did. *Veni, vidi, vici.*

Pierce Arrow was fixated on her description of the rape. He asked Lettie to read that passage again. The blinking yellow light from behind . . . the growls and grunts . . . the insatiable appetite . . . *My God,* thought Pierce. He remembered Sheriff Sephus's account of his first meeting with the lady with the graying ponytail, how she had mentioned kinfolk or roots or something with a connection to that area of the Ozarks.

"It couldn't have been," muttered Pierce. "It couldn't be."

A genealogy of Lettie's precious, yellow-eyed baby, deeply grafted to Hardlyville's own root stock? The devil himself to Ms. Rosebeam to Demon Lady to Lucas Jones to now? Who could make that up? Fiction at its foulest. Lineage at its looniest. And a beautiful baby to boot. He let it all rest in his swirling subconscious as he and Lettie quietly strode home beneath the rising sun. They hadn't even made it to Petunia Perfidy's

179

historical notes. They were too tired to make love, but did so anyway, seeking to ground in something that made sense.

Next morning, Pierce Arrow went straight to Sheriff Sephus's office with the Rosebeam chronology. Yes, Sheriff confirmed, Demon Lady had said something in passing during their introductory chat about kinfolk. Could she have been talking about Octavia Rosebeam? they asked each other. How could she know? Could she have accessed birth records identifying her birth mother? Why would one so possessed even bother? The questions rolled on and without logical answers.

"This story has no end," moaned Sheriff Sephus Adonis, gory memories rushing back in his mind. It hurt in his heart as well. There was nowhere to go with any of it. Nor would anyone believe it. Simply one of those horrid and random dots on the spectrum of history. Hardlyville history, in this case.

AND MORE SECRETS

Pierce and Lettie were anxious to get back to the second set of letters. They appeared to chronicle the history of Hardlyville through the pen of Petunia Perfidy Hardly. Dropping everything, including the babies at Flotilla's day care, they resumed where they had left off just a few hours earlier. Sheriff Sephus joined them for this next chapter. Law enforcement and emergency management would just have to wait, as would tributes to French passion and attacks on Big Pork. This was stuff for the ages.

All the letters in this stack were in envelopes as well, but not addressed beyond name, nor posted. The first letter in the stack explained the purpose of it all.

It was a "Dear Octavia" letter, signed by Grandma Petunia. Between salutation and signature was expressed the hope that Octavia would know of her lineage and find grounding in it. Grandma Petunia had not, having been raised as a virtual orphan by an abusive step-father and cowed mother. Beyond that, she didn't exist, and it was only through the grace of her betrothal to one Thomas Hardly that she had been given a chance at life, difficult as it was—life with hope and adventure and even love, on occasion. No one had taught her to read or to write. She had earned that on her own. It would be different for her beloved granddaughter, Octavia. Grandma Petunia would do everything in her power to assure that. The letters that followed would place Octavia in place and time—and love—Grandma Petunia promised. And they proceeded to do just that.

As before, Lettie read and Pierce reduced to narrative. He was an editor, after all. One letter leaked into another.

Petunia's first recording of history began in Northwest Arkansas as she, the new and second wife of Thomas Hardly, prepared to leave their mountain farm and move north to be closer to flowing water. Thomas had lost his first wife to dysentery, trapped in a cycle of dehydration and vomit that was addressed too late. They had no children, and Thomas had felt a weight of loneliness beyond self-selected independence and freedom.

"Thomas found me," Petunia wrote, "in servitude to a business man in Little Rock. To say I was a kept woman was an overstatement, more willing dependent until I could fight my way out of the hole, which was the only inheritance left to me by the sorry couple who raised me. I cleaned house and did other domestic chores in exchange for room and board. I was shown respect, by both the businessman and his wife, that I had never known before in my short life. I expressed my gratitude by working hard and staying clear of trouble beyond their home. They treated me almost as family."

Thomas had come to Little Rock to seek property along the Arkansas/Missouri border—land along flowing, clear waters, land that could be farmed and perhaps, more importantly, developed into a sustainable community. Thomas had friends back in Western Tennessee who had relatives and acquaintances who shared a similar dream.

"He was referred to my businessman by the local banker," Petunia wrote.

"When he called first time, I was struck by his handsome features and the sadness in his eyes. He thanked me warmly when I served coffee and again when I placed fried chicken and gravy in front of him that evening as he returned for supper and negotiation of price for a large parcel the businessman had recently bought at auction that fit the description of Thomas's needs.

"They were still in discussions when I retired for the evening and was surprised to learn next morning from the misses that he had inquired about me and my background. I blushed noticeably when he returned for a second round of negotiation later in the day, which drew a warm smile from him. After their next day get-together, I inquired of the misses as to whether negotiations usually took so long, and she smiled gently, adding that generally if the topic of discussion expanded they dragged on. I soon learned that I was the topic of expansion she referenced.

"Mr. Hardly asked to meet with me privately the following day. My uncertainty mingled with a tingle of excitement as we entered the businessman's office, and he gently closed the door.

"He had a dream, he began, and then his words flowed like honey from a hive. He confessed to not knowing me but to finding me attractive and comfortable to be around. His dream was centered on a clear, cold Ozark stream and a small community of hardworking, kind, caring neighbors who sought independence and respect, shared when needed, and laughed often. Ozarks life would never be easy, but it could be rewarding and even inspiring, at times. Clean water would be the liquid gold that bound all together in that pursuit, and all else would take care of itself. His eyes blazed behind his softly spoken vision.

"He had just acquired from my businessman benefactor a home for his dream and a large, uninhabited acreage, bounded on its eastern flank by a beautiful creek called Skunk by locals. Never mind the name, he urged, as the businessman had assured that it could just as easily be called Crystal or Clear Creek, and he had come to trust my businessman.

"One of the foundations on which that trust had been built over the past two days, he confessed, was me. He shared with me the deep grief he carried from recently losing his first wife and the void he sought to fill. He saw in me kindness and industry, which his dream would require of all who sought to share it. He had asked the businessman about me, about my background, and sought his opinion of me as a person. My businessman didn't hesitate to share the roughness of my upbringing or the challenges I had faced in life. He said he did not want to lose me from his employment, but if Thomas's personal inquiries bespoke intentions, he could recommend me with the highest certainty and praise.

"Thomas Hardly carried on, as I could only listen in a haze. Thomas said he was neither wealthy nor over loving his first wife. He had to be honest about both. At the same time, he was attracted to me and needed a life partner if he was ever to feel full again. He apologized for being forward or rude, but time was short, and he would close on the property with most of his savings the following morning. He would return to his farm immediately to organize his possessions and arrange for its sale. He would proceed, thereafter, to claim the new property and invite friends and kinfolk from Western Tennessee, as well as others who expressed appropriate interest, to join him in building a community along the banks of Skunk Creek.

"He hesitated a full minute or more, taking several deep breaths before looking deeply into my eyes with his sad ones. A tear fell. He then asked if I would consider joining him in the pursuit of his dream. He wondered if I could make it my own, that we might share it for the rest of our days. He then asked me to marry him that very night and head out to follow his dream the next morning. He thought we could learn to love one another.

I sat in stunned silence, feeling the fool for not being able to utter a sound. I now had tears in my own eyes."

So did Lettie.

"No one, save those in my immediate circumstance, had ever accorded me a moment of respect. Never had anyone mentioned the word love to me. All was taken from me. Nothing given. And this man, this stranger, was talking about sharing. Sharing love. Sharing dreams. I asked if I might have the night to consider his gracious offer. He nodded, though with obvious disappointment. He promised to return first thing in the morning and said he hoped my answer would be yes. He opened the door and slipped through it.

"'Yes,' I whispered. 'Yes,' I said boldly and with certainty. 'Yes,' I said louder still as he returned to the room with the broadest and most joyous smile I had ever seen. I knew I loved the man then and there.

"He didn't pause or hesitate in grabbing me around the waist and lifting me strongly off the ground and into his arms. His first kiss was soft but hungry. It lit me in places inside that had never been touched, far deeper than those superficial locales so often violated. I had never felt such warmth, such passion, such raw joy.

"Applause wakened me to my senses. The Mr. and Mrs. were joining in the revelry of the moment. They even had their pastor waiting in the sitting room, *Bible* in hand. 'Let's do this before she changes her mind!' yelled Thomas in a burst of humor. My misses removed my apron and placed fresh cut flowers in my hair. My businessman gave me away under the arch between the dining room and the kitchen. Pastor asked, 'Do you?' 'I do,' I whispered into Thomas's waiting eyes. His telltale kiss left me quivering with anticipation.

"The misses shooed away the pastor and Mr. and led us quietly to my quarters. I submitted to a man voluntarily and willingly, not under force or threat, for the first time in my life. It was glorious, my dear granddaughter, Octavia," Petunia concluded in ending that particular letter. "I can only pray the same moment for you one day."

Lettie was bawling like a stuck calf now. Lucas and Sheriff were sniffling as well. All gathered to hug, literally smothering tiny Lettie between them.

"Help!" she gasped as they backed off, laughing.

"No wonder this Hardlyville place is so riddled with passion," noted Pierce. "It's genetic."

Sheriff Sephus was starving, and he offered to buy comfort food at Greasy Spoons. Pierce Arrow initially showed interest, but a wink from Lettie promised a nooner instead. She was feeling amorous after reading the emotional betrothing of Petunia to Thomas, and sex was better for her partner's health. They promised to reenter Hardlyville's past within the hour, though it took Peirce and Lettie more time to consummate than for Sheriff Sephus Adonis to obliterate a double order of fried catfish, fried potatoes, fried green beans, and Tiny's latest innovation, fried chocolate ice cream. Sheriff was anxious for Pierce Arrow to run for Congress again so he would have an excuse to diet again as campaign manager. At least he hoped Pierce would, for reasons far more profound than his bulging belly. All returned to task at hand with smiling faces.

Lettie opened another envelope as Petunia continued her euphoric journey to Skunk Creek. First stop was Thomas Hardly's mountaintop farm. Petunia knew immediately why Thomas needed to move on. The view from the log cabin back porch was breathtaking, but the sense of isolation and loneliness was oppressive. Thomas cried as they rode in on horses, apologizing again for hanging on to the happiness of his past. He said nothing about her, but Petunia could sense the bonds that still bound. She didn't mind. Thomas had been honest with Petunia about her. It was sad but not morose, as Thomas and Petunia both sought to start over. They slept together in a second bed, not the one he and she had shared. They made love more quietly than before, but the underlay of relit passion carried both. It was clearly time to move on, out of respect and hope.

"Thomas even left me alone with her memory one night as he sought help in selling the property from a banker in the nearest village," Petunia wrote. "He provided me with food, a roaring fire, and two loaded weapons before departing. I felt her presence, if only in my imagination, and sensed no malice, only faint envy. Who knows about that stuff? Not me. A cougar cry near dawn snapped me to attention and full arms. It was a lonely wailing, not a hunter's boast, and fit the moment well. I didn't like being apart from Thomas.

"On his return, we began to organize for moving. We would take only basics, camp in a large tent beside Skunk Creek, and lay out our new village and home. Thomas hoped to find help in the construction, but he had built his current home with little outside assistance so was prepared to proceed alone if necessary. I would assist as I could.

"A particularly poignant moment was when he burned his deceased wife's wardrobe. It was neither fancy nor extensive, but he handled each piece, large or small, personally before adding it to the flames. He cried, as did I.

"The remaining clean up was easier, and we even smiled and laughed on occasion. Thomas has a wicked sense of humor to go with his quiet ways, and I have become pleasantly accustomed to his sometime bizarre antics. I will never forget awakening from a deep sleep to the head of a black bear staring at me, barely six inches away. Thomas tried to growl but broke out laughing, sending me from a full throttle scream into convulsions of laughter.

"'Don't ever scare me like that again, Thomas Hardly,' I ordered when finally able to regain some semblance of sobriety. He noted, with a smile, that I had seemed to enjoy the moment. He then raised my gown to take advantage of my heightened sensitivities, again with a smile. When all was packed or disposed of, we loaded the flatbed wagon and hitched it to two mules. Thomas drove while I trailed with the two horses and single cow. A joyous parade came to mind as we headed toward our new home on Skunk Creek."

Pierce needed a pee break and a brief walk around, so Sheriff and Lettie sat a while. Out of the blue, Lettie asked Sheriff Sephus if he ever mentioned their single shared indiscretion to Lucas. Or to Pierce. It was the first time she had raised the topic with him since that afternoon coupling so long ago, while Lucas had slept just twenty paces away. Sheriff nodded yes, then no. Lettie smiled a thank you. She had guessed the former, which made her love Lucas even more. She was grateful for the latter, as she feared Pierce might think her a slut. She wasn't, she knew that, but she still wondered why she had done it with the man who had become a father and grandfather figure to her since.

"So much has changed since then," she marveled to Sheriff Sephus Adonis.

"Some for the good, some less," he nodded before noting that now, as in Petunia's time, good can come from bad, gain can rise from loss, and love can prevail over all, neither diminishing the past nor exaggerating the future. *Wow,* Sheriff Sephus thought to himself, *better share that one with Pastor Pat. Must be two or three sermons there.*

Pierce returned and asked why both were blushing. Sheriff shrugged, and Lettie shed a tear. Both were grateful for the here and now, and still sometimes anxious to return to the then. Lettie popped open another envelope, leaving Pierce wondering which of Sheriff's many dirty jokes he had missed.

Petunia Hardly described her first sighting of Skunk Creek as "cleansing."

"The crystal clear waters flowed deep and strong into a rock pocked shoal that channeled them into raw and frothy power at the point of confluence before dispersing into gentle ripples."

"My," said Pierce, "what a poetic description of Skunk Creek rapid just above Hardlyville Bridge." *Hasn't changed much over a hundred years*, he thought.

"Sounds just like Pierce's crazed ramblings the night he asked you to marry him, Lettie," laughed Sheriff.

"Just love," smiled Lettie, squeezing Pierce's hand tightly. "Just love."

Petunia's next several letters to granddaughter, Octavia described in detail the challenges of putting the dream to plan and then execution.

"Thomas walked off a village center with enough room to house a store or two, a bank, a post office, and several businesses," Petunia wrote. "We then selected a site for our house, which was to be of wood frame, not log. It would have two stories with our bedroom atop, facing beautiful Skunk Creek, with a small balcony to view it from. It would sit on a slight rise to afford a degree of flood protection and greet the rising sun each morning. We would start with four rooms on each floor to assure adequate room for a family.

"Yes, Octavia," Petunia continued, "I shortly discovered that I was with the child who became your mother, though I knew not at the time. Didn't take long, did it! We both hoped to have many children to raise in this beautiful place and space in time. Little did I know how forlorn that hope would become," Petunia concluded in that installment.

Pierce was confused by Petunia's time context. It was as if she wrote in both present, past, and future tenses. He concluded that her jumping in time likely reflected real time recollections, perhaps copied from a diary, as well as post traumatic reflections, filtered for her granddaughter's benefit. We'll see how it plays out, he mused, knowing that the end game for Thomas Hardly bore tragedy.

Petunia recounted the paths of those who trickled in to join them, how Thomas shared his dream with each, and invited them in only if he could sense their emotional and personal engagement. He would sell every parcel, no matter how large or small, at his cost plus 10%. "Fair is as fair does," he always said.

"One of the first to show up as Thomas was platting a new community was James Qingdao, a man of Oriental descent. He asked if he might acquire eighty acres of farmland on which to build and farm. He claimed to have helped lay the railroad west during the Great Expansion, after emigrating from China, poor and illiterate. He had saved and scraped enough to take a bride, Anny, and wanted to honor her wishes to be closer to her family in Kansas City, Missouri, yet far enough away to escape discrimination for his color. He asked if Thomas felt Orientals were inferior, and Thomas confessed to never even having thought about it. That was good enough for James Qingdao, who again offered to pay a fair price for eighty acres once the community was laid out. Thomas tried his cost plus 10% theory on James, who readily accepted. James would also assist Thomas in laying out a community plan, and they would cooperate to construct their respective dwellings. A deep relationship of trust was established with their first handshake.

"Thomas and James worked closely together over the next several months, organizing the unincorporated Village of Hardlyville, so named after community founder and your grandfather, Thomas Hardly. Thomas had objected at first, perceiving such self-indulgence as arrogant and without merit. He finally agreed, at James's and my insistence that he invest a personal name to provide roots and continuity and a sense of emotional ownership. I took great pride in both the name of my new home and my new life," concluded Petunia.

More settlers drifted in over the coming weeks, some fit to become neighbors, some not. Thomas was demanding in his requirements for Hardlyville citizenship and evenhanded in administering them. He would not sell land to those who did not meet his expectations.

His first large parcel sale was to his friends from Tennessee. They traveled together for safety and expediency, building several barges on which to float wagons, livestock, bodies, and belongings down the Tennessee River to the Ohio and then the Mississippi to a take-out point in Southeast Missouri. Their procession trekked west from there, fording several major streams to reach Hardlyville nearly eight weeks after departure. They numbered sixteen adults and twenty children, two fewer than they began with. One child had drowned after falling into the Mississippi. One husband left his wife and baby along the way, taking off with a woman of the night at a village rest site. All were tired and bedraggled upon arrival. They nearly tripled Hardlyville's population immediately.

Petunia added a P.S. to this particular note.

"You will note, dear granddaughter, that I have spoken of the close and mutually respectful relationship between your grandfather and one James Qingdao (pronounced Chengdow), a man of Oriental origin. They were often inseparable in their labors, despite their differences in color and background. At the same time, I have avoided much mention of James's wife, Anny Qingdao. The oversight is intentional, as she behaved in a manner unsuitable for any woman in her position, almost a guest in our home. I will share her indiscretions to explain the first major rift in Hardlyville history. It is something you should be aware of, Octavia, if you are to become the keeper of family and community logs into the future," Petunia said.

Pierce Arrow and Sheriff Sephus leaned forward expectantly as Lettie pulled out the next letter. It was written in a curious back-and-forth manner so as to put what next followed in a form of personal reflection by both Thomas and Petunia.

"Thomas had blubbered his way through a disjointed explanation," began Petunia. "He was clearly agitated and embarrassed."

"I was taking my evening bath, always upstream," he hesitantly explained, "just like I usually do. It was hot outside and refreshingly cool beneath the flowing water. I lingered longer than most times, almost slipping into a dreamlike state. As I swam to the base of the large sycamore to towel and dress, I noticed with a sense of panic that all was missing. It was then I heard a giggle downstream.

"What happened next was unfortunate," continued Thomas. "I must tell you everything that happened, no matter how embarrassing, if I am to be ever again trusted."

"I felt tears of fear welling in my eyes," Petunia wrote. "I had heard rumors and reports and would now learn the truth about how Anny Qingdao was caught in a compromising position with Thomas."

"I looked toward the noise," he continued, "and saw Anny Qingdao without a stitch of clothing on, arms thrust aside to reveal all. 'Cat got your clothes?' or something like that, she teased. I thrust my palms over both eyes to avoid the view, though enticing it was. I lost my balance and fell awkwardly, hitting my head on a rock. I remember nothing thereafter until waking up with my head cuddled against her bare chest, her lips on mine."

"Thomas was flushed and sweating at this point in his story," Petunia added.

"As I struggled to break from her, I glanced just beyond and observed my dear friend James Qingdao pointing the barrel of his rifle directly at my head. 'Don't, James, please, don't,' I begged. Anny Qingdao screamed that I had lured her into the water and disrobed her for sinister purposes, which I clearly had not. James studied the situation for a moment or two, our lives in the balance, before nodding to me and waving his wife Anny to the river bank. He threw the clothes he had stumbled on at her and ordered her to reclothe immediately and go home.

"James Qingdoa then proceeded to apologize to me on Anny's behalf, explaining that sometimes she has these urges that place her in difficult circumstances. He also apologized for drawing down on me. 'Sometimes it's Anny's fault, sometimes the guy's,' he calmly explained, adding that he had killed a couple of opportunists for taking advantage of her. Obviously not the case this time, as her clothes were carefully laid out behind a bush. The gash on my head also spoke to the fall I claimed. Again, he was sorry. 'I just love the girl, no matter what,' he smiled.

"Most of the neighbors were gathered as Anny reclad and James and I made peace. Said he felt that he and Anny better move on after this. He explained that once Anny got her mind on a man, she could be pretty devious in his pursuit. He asked if I would consider repurchasing his eighty acres at my cost, which would net me another bump in equity. I readily agreed to James's proposal, and he and Anny were gone within a week—to my great dismay, at least regarding James."

"All of this Thomas revealed to me in great detail and to my immense relief. The first reports of my Thomas frolicking with a buck-naked Anny Qingdao were overstated and now put in their proper place. I was not sad to see Anny take her amorous streak elsewhere but knew Thomas would miss his friend James. I would seek to fill a part of that void.

"Again, dear Octavia, the point in sharing this bizarre encounter is not to shock or embarrass you but to set the record straight. On occasion, I would hear Thomas's tragic death attributed to an irate husband—a rumor that was, is, and will forever be false. Thomas Hardly was true to me to his last breath, and me to him, forever. I can only wish a similar man for you," was how Petunia ended her extraordinarily long P.S.

"Guess that explains the rumors about infidelity and angry mates," observed Pierce. "No, it was not Anny Qingdao's husband, James, who brutally murdered Thomas Hardly. And, come to think of it, Hardlyville was more racially diverse at its founding than at any time in its history before the birth of Sabrina Hendricks's beautiful black baby, ultimately named Otis by Grandma Flotilla."

Petunia continued her letters to Octavia about the founding and early days of Hardlyville over a period of months. She wrote of Thomas's early efforts to build a business base in the town center, of his establishing a general store, despite a lack of retailing experience, and of the trips to larger cities to stock it. Livestock was brought in by settlers or acquired. Gardens sprouted at every homestead. The soil was thin and rocky but particularly hospitable to squash, beans, corn, tomatoes, and strawberries.

Thomas made a market for his neighbors' excess and often bartered milk, eggs, and produce in return for hard goods in surrounding towns. He built a sizable and diverse inventory of staples over time.

"I particularly enjoyed watching him pack eggs for market in the flatbed. A layer of straw, then eggs, then straw, and so on. It was a three day round trip, and he was able to gather enough product from neighbors to garner a good trade value. Water from Skunk Creek was potable and plentiful. Wild game and fresh fish abounded. The climate was gentle in the first year, with moderate rains and temperatures throughout.

"My first pregnancy proceeded without incident, and when a beautiful baby girl was born, the entire community celebrated Hardlyville's inaugural conception. I named her Hardlita, again in honor of the dreamer of the dream, a female iteration. Your mother was all I had ever dreamed of in a child, even in those rough years when dreams didn't come true. This one had. No later than my recovery from childbirth, Thomas and I set out to make a boy. Thomas Hardly Jr. would be his given name, and if it took a couple of more years and births to strike male, we would persevere. Our love ran as deep and strong as Skunk Creek, and even Thomas's first wife faded to respected memory from a source of grief.

"Thomas continued to play his practical jokes on me, keeping me in a constant state of anticipation and laughter. He once placed a small garden snake in our bed just before retiring for sleep. My shrill shrieks when it nestled in the space between our snuggling bodies ended all hope of frivolity that particular night and dissuaded Thomas from future reptilian adventures.

"Life was very good in Hardlyville, and apart from the Anny Qingdao adventure, neighbors modeled the vision that Thomas had sold them."

The pathos of Arcadian mythology went poof in Petunia's next several, and final, letters to Octavia.

"These are the most difficult words I have ever written," confessed Petunia. "I will spare you the worst descriptives," she promised Octavia, "but not the horror of it all."

The first of the last letters left no doubt as to where Petunia was headed. She spoke of their last happy day together in great detail, from the breakfast of fried eggs atop biscuits and gravy to sharing lunch at the general store to snuggling under the moon on a blanket next to Skunk Creek rapid before retiring to bed. She spoke of their love and happiness.

The next letter was a flashback to a strange visitor from a day or two past.

"He came to the house about suppertime, riding into town fast and hard, seeking Thomas Hardly. As was community custom, we invited the stranger to sit for supper, and he accepted. His name was Mr. Garth, and he came from points west. He had heard of Thomas and Hardlyville from Thomas's old friend James Qingdao, also a friend of his. James had told Garth he could trust Thomas above most men.

"Garth was an agent for the United States Government—a federal marshal, to be precise. He was on a mission for the secretary of the U. S. Treasury himself, one that demanded the utmost secrecy. With a nod from Thomas, I excused myself at that moment and retired to bed.

"I do not know what happened next, only that Thomas did not join me in bed that night and that he and Garth were huddled next morning over a small piece of parchment spread on the kitchen table, studying it intently. Thomas broke their silence by pointing assuredly in the direction of Skunk Creek and waving to the east beyond. Mr. Garth nodded, shook hands with Thomas, bowed slightly toward me, and left through the back door, which seemed awkward at the time. Thomas exited through the front door. I watched through the window as he led Garth's horse around to the back of the house. Garth accepted the reins and walked his horse quickly and quietly into the woods.

"Thomas motioned for me to join him outside, and we walked in the silent dawn along his beloved Skunk Creek. He pulled the parchment they had been studying together from inside his jacket, folded it into a small square, and handed it to me, demanding that I ask no questions. He asked me to hide it in a place no man would ever discover until Mr. Garth could return for it several days hence. He would be accompanied by U. S. soldiers at that time, and it would be safe to return this very important map to him upon arrival. Until then, our task at hand was to act normal in every manner and keep the parchment map to ourselves only. I quickly inserted the folded square in my undergarments, next to my heart. No man will ever go there except Thomas, I laughed. He chuckled back that he guessed that meant I was off limits to even him until Garth returned. I could only grin and dare him to try. He didn't, which should have underscored the significance of it all to me."

Pierce Arrow and Sheriff Sephus Adonis listened intently as Lettie continued to read aloud. Pierce even stopped reducing to narrative so that he might focus on Petunia's words more intently.

"Thomas walked to the store to open," Petunia continued. "I met him there with lunch and offered to cover the store while he returned home for an afternoon nap since he had not slept the night before. He kissed me deeply and walked tiredly toward the house. He turned and waved. It was the last time I would ever see his precious face.

"When he did not return in three hours, I asked our neighbor, who was shopping for a woolen shirt, to stop by and wake Thomas up as she passed by the house. I soon heard screams, and before I could digest their meaning, several village folks were rushing in that direction, toward our house. I closed up, locked the doors, and started there myself before my neighbor's husband walked toward me, ashen and somber. He warned me to stop and sit down on a nearby log, as villagers continued to rush by me.

"He was sad to deliver terrible news. The baby was safe, but Thomas was dead. He had been brutally murdered, perhaps even tortured to death, for no apparent reason. It would not be good for me to see him until they cleaned him up a bit.

"The scream that began in my heart arced all the way to Skunk Creek before leaving me empty and unconscious on the ground. At least, that's the way my neighbor's husband later described it. When I awoke, I begged to hold my Thomas, dead or alive, to feel his strong arms in mine and kiss his lips, cold or not."

Lettie could not continue. She sobbed and grabbed at Pierce to draw him close. Pierce took the letter from Lettie's trembling hands, pulled her near, and resumed.

"They would let me nowhere near my dead husband—or my house, for that matter. Several women took the baby and me to a cabin to provide comfort, while the men in the village split into three bands: one to deal with what was left of Thomas's body and clean the mess our house had become, one with arms drawn to scour the surrounding woods for killers or signs of them, and one to stand twenty-four hour guard around our citizens.

"The neighbor ladies finally gave up trying to reason with my fierce and violent objections to their restraint and tied me up, apologizing in tears for each knot. I remember little beyond wanting to die. Hardlita was too young to know what was going on but was in need of mother's milk, which I was unable to provide amidst my wails and gyrations. She too began to scream until I was finally calm enough to nurse. I remember steeling myself to the task, as she was all I had left.

"Some hours later, several men returned to say that Thomas's body had been sealed in a hastily constructed wooden casket and that enough order had been restored to the house for me and Hardlita to return home to share a moment with the deceased. I sat by the wooden box all night, squeezing it, pounding on it, kissing it until my lips bled, rubbing my tears into it. Several kind ladies sat with me to keep me from hurting myself. My dear Thomas was gone, dead and gone, and there was nothing left for me to live for—except precious Hardlita, the shared seed of Thomas and me, and some day to bear you, my Octavia.

"We put Thomas Hardly, founder of Hardlyville, savior and lover of me, and your grandfather in the ground the next morning. A part of me went with him, buried under dirt and rock forever. I have never known such grief and loss.

"Neighbors insisted on staying with the baby and me the next several nights. They confided that, beyond the shocking shell of a man the murderer or murderers had left, our house had been ransacked, turned upside down, as if seeking something.

I guessed it was the secret map that still lay next to my heart. I cursed it and clasped it close at the same time.

"Mr. Garth never returned to Hardlyville for his cursed map, which I enclose herein for you, dear Octavia. I know not what it means or stands for. Perhaps you will find out someday. No suspects, no clues, no motive ever surfaced related to the murder. I only know what I believe to be true, that the map I carried next to my heart cost me the love of my life and you your precious grandfather, Thomas Hardly. It can carry no commensurate value," Petunia concluded, "no matter where it leads.

"I'm out of words, dear one," Petunia began her last letter. "I had hoped to share many more, but my reason for writing is gone."

This would the shortest of her many letters to Ms. Rosebeam, Octavia Hardly Rosebeam, granddaughter of the noble dreamer and founder of Hardlyville, noted Pierce.

What a personal tragedy Petunia had to bear, and what a profound gift she left the community. Perhaps Ms. Rosebeam, in her personal sadness, had been unable to bring herself to share it. Maybe she had even forgotten about the secret stash. Whatever, Hardlyville owned it now, and the *Hellbender* would share it—beauty, love, vision, tragedy, and all. A community treasure would be unveiled once Big Pork was properly reviled, promised Pierce.

"What about the map?" remembered Sheriff Sephus.

Pierce reached to the bottom of the pile and pulled it out. It had been flat many years but still bore the fold lines from Petunia's story. Sheriff laid it out to face the northern directional letter. He shook his head. Then shook it again while nudging Pierce. They both recognized the rough sketch bounded on one side by a creek and on the other by rock outcroppings, connected by a branch. The "X" was in the vicinity of the coven's former lair, home base of the lady with the graying ponytail, place of Lucas

Jones's last breath, and sight of the seeding of Lettie's beautiful yellow-eyed baby.

"Sheriff Sephus Adonis is right," Pierce Arrow told Lettie. "This sordid tale has no beginning, no end, just links that connect and reconnect through time and place."

THE MYSTERIOUS MAP

Sheriff Sephus asked Cousin Jimmy Jones to join him and Pierce in his office the next morning. No, he was not in trouble again, Sheriff assured Jimmy. Jimmy was relieved in that he had tried really hard to stay on the sheriff's good side since hitching up with Sally.

Sheriff Sephus shared the map and its history with Jimmy and advised they would have to go back in one more time.

"Back in where?" Jimmy asked.

"The lair," Sheriff responded, "the nesting place of the evil coven."

Neither Pierce nor Sheriff had returned to the site since the fateful night of the raid. Too painful. Nor had they sniffed around Skunk Creek Ranch. Not welcome. Jimmy had never been and didn't much want to see the place where his best friend and icon, Cousin Lucas, had met his end. But each knew that while they didn't have a clue as to what they were seeking, or even if they would recognize it if they found it, they had to try. It was simply too important to the Hardlyville story.

Sheriff said they needed Jimmy in case the going got too rough. Sheriff Sephus was bigger than ever, and we're not talking about legend here, and Pierce Arrow was only young at heart these days. With all that rock to explore, both above and below ground, spry and nimble were valued allies.

The map didn't help much when it came to specifics. Whoever had drawn it either wanted it vague or didn't know much about map making. Skunk Creek was obvious, right down to the pools and rapids, as much as a small parchment would allow. Jimmy Jones could even pick out the general spot where Cousin Lucas had launched his brave attack on the float party assaulters. He shivered visibly at the recollection. It was one of his last memories of Lucas alive and was the stuff of heroes.

The map was less succinct on the other side of the page. It bore a multilayered attempt at a rock face with a small water flow leaking out beneath, tracking lightly to a merger downstream with a larger branch that flowed off the page, probably about where rotten-smelling Skunk Creek Ranch sat. Sheriff Sephus remembered following the stream with Lucas and Pierce toward the rock enclosed pavilion of the devil lady's showtime. They had conjectured it to be a spring issuing forth from somewhere beneath all the rock, though they never had time to source it. There had to be plenty of fresh water from somewhere in the rock fortress to support a crowd the size of her coven. The large "X" on the map was planted squarely on the roughly-drawn rock formation, with no hint at above or below. The contradiction between detail and blurred sections led Sheriff Sephus to lean toward an intentionally vague diagnosis, a clever charade of evasion that would make solutions difficult to obtain.

They questioned out loud what hidden secret could be so valuable as to cost Thomas Hardly his life. What could warrant the brutality of his dispensing? Petunia never provided graphic detail but implied evisceration and dismemberment, perhaps linked to torture. Someone or thing had wanted the map next to Petunia's breast in the worst way. Thank God they didn't know where it lay, or things could have gotten even uglier, observed Jimmy.

"So what were they looking for? Buried treasure?" offered Sheriff Sephus. Certainly, the involvement of a federal marshal as proxy for the secretary of treasury implied something of a monetary nature.

"But then again," countered Pierce, "this dude Garth never showed up again, according to Petunia. Maybe it was just a hoax to ensnare Thomas Hardly. To what end, by what means? Or maybe Garth did show up. What then?"

"Maybe it had something to do with the Civil War," offered Jimmy.

"What would you know about that?" teased Sheriff Sephus.

"Learned all about it in history class junior year," countered Jimmy.

"I repeat my question," Sheriff Sephus went on with a smile. "My recollection was that you were always stoned or diddling the banker's daughter, which didn't leave much time for history," snorted Sheriff Sephus.

"Hey, that's my wife you're talking about," sneered an offended Jimmy Jones, squaring into slugging position.

Pierce grabbed Jimmy with the admonition to settle down before he got back in trouble with the sheriff.

"Besides, I even passed," shouted Jimmy as Pierce led him out of the sheriff's office to cool down.

When Jimmy regained his composure and sheepishly wandered back in, Sheriff Sephus apologized for insulting his wife and his intelligence.

"Well, she weren't no virgin, and I made a D minus," confessed Jimmy, earning him a warm "shit, brothers" and a hardy pat on the back from the sheriff.

Pierce allowed that Jimmy might be on to something. Something stolen or abandoned in flight was a distinct possibility.

"Could have been coins or currency, or even gold or silver ingot. Either Yankee or Confederate, in this part of the land," added Sheriff.

"What if we find bones?" wondered Jimmy aloud. "Somebody or bodies kidnapped or murdered? What if there's a big mine or source of precious metal? Never heard of gold in these parts, but maybe silver."

The what-ifs rolled off their tongues until Pierce called for order. He would google all of these possibilities to see if anything popped out. In the meantime, they had all better prepare for a couple of days of camping out. They sure as hell didn't want to ask for beds at the pig farm, and the trip was too long to go back and forth. And they needed to get mentally and emotionally ready for a return to their nightmare. No one looked forward to that part.

Pierce Arrow found little substantive in his research. A few silver based rumors, both from the Civil War and early settlement days, surfaced. And the oft-repeated tale of hidden treasure from violent criminal Alf Bolin's time. But nothing credible. There were always plenty of bad guys and gunslingers flitting in and out of the Ozarks, from Jessie James to Bolin himself and beyond. Fact is, the area was pretty lawless in Thomas Hardly's day, with vigilantes and nightriders raising havoc as well. Thomas Hardly's vision of an idyllic enclave amidst the chaos of the times was naïve, at best.

Pierce shared his findings with the conclusion that they would just have to barge in and look everywhere for nothing in particular—all under the haze of frightful and poignant memories.

They would go in the front door this time, following the dirt track that led in from the pavement. Pierce wondered how many, if any, of the fanatics remained. The former ranch housekeeper, who had visited Lettie with her guilt-ridden confession several months back, would be one if, indeed, the cancer hadn't gotten her yet. Most of the men had been incarcerated for one reason or another. Probably just a few women and children, if anybody. He also guessed the reception would be chilly, at best, if someone recognized who they were. Very likely, given Sheriff Sephus's memorable profile.

What the hey, they don't own the place any more than we do, he thought. *But they could squeal to the ranch manager, who certainly could run us off, so Sheriff better take a search warrant. We could seek to camp on the premises, but who knows?* worried Pierce. He was dreading this trip.

The three loaded up the next morning with gear, food, and drink for a long drive back to hell. The last time Sheriff had been on this road, Lucas had been with him, paying a courtesy call on Skunk Creek Ranch. That had been ages and lives ago. They would leave the paved road earlier this time if, indeed, they could find the dirt track in. If not, Sheriff's truck could go cross-country.

The track was unmarked but obvious. Sheriff steered into it and slowed to a crawl. He followed it for several miles up and down before arriving at a large rock facing—almost a bluff, but not quite. The road ended there, and a narrow path led through a crevice in the rock. They locked the gear in the truck and set out on foot to breach the natural rock fortress. The path broke forth into a small clearing, the natural rock amphitheater where Sheriff had cradled Lucas's lifeless body next to his chest to the right. Sheriff Sephus Adonis sobbed silently. Left was where the crazed crowd had gathered.

The clearing opened beyond into various forms of shelter ruins—some log, some brick, some canvas, all primitive. The coven had indeed sacrificed earthly comforts for their leader's gospel of sex, violence, repentance, and otherworldly salvation. *What kind of strange, mesmerizing hold did she have on them?* pondered Pierce. There was not one soul in sight. They were all finally gone.

"We'll set camp here," Pierce announced.

An hour later, tents and food secure, they set out to search for water and an "X" in a rock stack. Water was easy. They could hear it gurgling somewhere close by. They stepped on stage and looked back and down to where her disciples had gathered each Saturday night. A sense of immense power embraced Jimmy from this vantage point. Pierce felt it too. Sheriff recalled the Demon Lady screeching and striding purposefully to the back of stage before disappearing forever. He led Pierce and Jimmy there, the sound of water growing.

What they found was beautiful, no, nothing short of spectacular. Vintage Ozarks. They pulled flashlights, descended into a cave opening, maybe six feet in diameter, and squat walked about thirty feet. This was not easy for Sheriff Sephus, who bemoaned his last two pieces of Tiny Taylor's cherry pie. The cave opened into a large room, maybe thirty feet tall, with a waterfall issuing forth from above into a beautiful pool below. Smaller cave entrances dotted the perimeter of the underground cathedral, as a pool overflowed into several of them. Pierce Arrow guessed the water flow to be constant and significant and to disperse into caves and caverns beneath the surface amphitheater. How this Swiss cheese of water and rock did not collapse upon itself spoke to ancient natural design or the Creator's hand, he mused to himself. Where all of this water sourced or where it went was the stuff of hydrologists and engineers. No question that some of it ended up in Skunk Creek, which owed a great debt of freshness and virgin purity to the cleansing karst filters.

"No sinister or provocative 'X' here," observed Sheriff Sephus. "Only glory."

Some of the water had to rise in the area for the former residents to access it, and Pierce guessed they would find a surface spring beyond the abandoned residential area. Sheriff presumed the same for some of the caves. It was now clear to him how the lady with the graying ponytail had simply exited stage rear and escaped the chaos that followed her dramatic encore. She obviously had known her way around this subterranean neighborhood, and it fit her clandestine comings and goings like a stone glove.

Jimmy crawled into one small, adjoining cave that seemed dry. He soon was backpedaling out as fast as he could backwards crawl, with a genuine look of fear exposing at his exit. He claimed to have seen tracks, big cat tracks, and fresh scat. He wanted to get the hell out of there.

Sheriff was hungry, and Jimmy was spooked, so all retreated back above ground to regroup and plan. They carried full canteens of spring Ozark water with them. It was almost sweet to the taste.

After supper, discussions turned to tackling the immense natural catacomb beneath them. Pierce cautioned against getting ahead of themselves. To assume that the "X" spot lay below ground may be overlooking obvious clues. First thing tomorrow they should undertake a thorough review of the upside, including detailed mapping of all crevices, indentions, and caves. To expedite the process, they would each take a segment. Jimmy would explore the rock face on both sides, Pierce would walk the entire amphitheater area to spare Sheriff Sephus the agony of his final memories there, and Sheriff would inventory the section where people had lived, the site of their camp.

All crawled into bedrolls early and slept fitfully. A cougar cry was clearly discernible about midnight, answered by another from some distance away. Jimmy's discovery in the cave was no fantasy.

They awoke at dawn, and after a light breakfast, too light according to Sheriff, they undertook respective searches with instructions to return by noon. Pierce cautioned each to note anything unusual, not sure what that might be, beyond instinct and gut feel.

By noon, no one had anything to report. Sheriff had finished in time to eat two lunches, raising questions about the thoroughness of his effort. Pierce found nothing out of the ordinary. The amphitheater had been scrubbed clean by investigative authorities immediately following the raid, and anything that passed as evidence had been processed and catalogued.

Jimmy claimed to have climbed over every inch of rock, finding no upside caves or openings, only the rock crevice that served as entrance to the compound. He did observe an unusual number of copperhead snakes lolling about, almost lethargic, and seemingly unconcerned with his presence.

"Almost like house pets," Jimmy laughed.

Pierce's memory bank rewound to the squirming bucket She Devil herself dipped a hand into the night he had watched her performance. The large copper-colored reptile she pulled out seemed almost mesmerized by her gaze. What could she possibly have to do with the domestication or muting of such dangerous and aggressive critters? No answers here. No "X" either.

"Must be multiple nests around," Jimmy concluded. "Best watch our step around the rocks."

Sheriff reported nothing but squalor and filth from his investigation. Fortunately, time had disposed of human waste, as he discovered no toilet facilities. Torn canvas, rotten clothing, a few discarded shoes, and rotting structures littered his field of inquiry. He did find the water source they had imagined yesterday. A piped spring flow had been roughly dammed to form a possible bathing area before leaking into a stream of water below. He couldn't imagine how cold those baths must have been.

"As for the emerging stream, nothing can stop water," Sheriff laughed. He guessed they probably gathered drinking water from the pipe before the water's degradation below. "These heathens lived as they might have a hundred years earlier."

It was time to go subterranean, Pierce announced after lunch. They would do this together, in the interest of safety and attention to detail. Sheriff's service revolver would be their peacemaker with any ornery critters they might encounter. Jimmy would lead explorations into the separate grottos. Pierce would attempt to map the substrata. This would take time, if they were thorough and attentive.

By the end of the day, Pierce had recorded seven separate exits from the grand cathedral room, including one directly behind the falls that particularly intrigued him. Several offshoots came to sudden ends, either from rock slides or solid walls. None showed any sign of disruption over the ages. Several went on for yards before narrowing to the point of prohibiting human access. Nothing there deserving of an "X." They saw no prominent veins of minerals, just sandstone, limestone, and occasional fields of chert. No signs of humans or additional critters either. They left the waterfall-veiled cavern for last. Tired and hungry after a long day of fruitless search, they agreed to wait for the next morning to explore it. It was their last remaining hope for something unusual or special.

They cooked on an open fire that night—venison steaks, steamed vegetables in foil, and even a paper cup or two of red wine. Sheriff complained that the meal was bland. Pierce countered with "healthy and nutritious." Sheriff grimaced over a lack of dessert or leftovers.

Talk turned to what they had discovered or the lack thereof.

"What if we find nothing tomorrow?" Sheriff said. "Would that mean that Thomas Hardly was killed for nothing?"

This was a conversation killer of the highest order. All drifted off to sleep, full but dispirited. Another big cat cry or two dotted their slumber.

Pierce Arrow led the way down the next morning. They would slip behind the large waterfall in search of "X." The opening was wide and deep, with several tentacles branching off. The first thing they noticed was that this particular sub cavern had been used.

A discarded and torn wolf skin spoke to the "by whom." This was where she had lived. This was where she cavorted with her subjects and who knew what else. There was a rotting mattress in a dark corner that still reeked of evil. There even appeared to be remains of fire, though none could figure how she vented it until Jimmy felt a cool rush of air from above the ashes.

"A natural chimney?" he wondered.

He lit a match and watched the smoke drift upward after it died. Animal bones littered the floor, probable leftovers from her nourishment. Large leg and rib pieces were probably deer. Some were small enough to represent squirrel or other rodents. They even found what appeared to be the skull of a pig. Blood money from the hog farm. Nut shells were also scattered around. She evidently existed on clean water, game, and whatever else she could scrounge from the adjoining woods. And took a cold shower whenever she wished.

Sheriff guessed that she had stayed a while after the raid. A major all-points bulletin had been issued by both state highway patrols, and she would have been a hard one to miss on the run. Strange that the authorities hadn't looked down here. Maybe they did and just missed the waterfall wing.

Pierce conjectured that she had birthed and nursed Lucas's baby here, which would have kept her around almost a year. That would certainly have fit the timing of her care package on his grave.

"The rotten bitch," growled Pierce.

He confessed to wanting to puke at the thought of Lettie's precious child nursing from the witch. Beats the alternative, was the only comforting thought. That she didn't murder the baby was a miracle in itself, given the unlikely and probably unexpected fact of her pregnancy. She apparently didn't kill anyone else either, at least based on Sheriff's recollection of no missing person reports. She was an animal of sorts, all agreed, though the concept of sex with a cougar seemed farfetched, even for her. More likely a legend she nurtured to enhance her aura of mystery and intrigue. Maybe even a fantasy of hers, Jimmy offered.

One thing for sure, she was long gone now. Far, far, away all hoped and prayed.

Jimmy started messing around in several of the tunnels adjoining the cave room. Two headed different directions and carried beyond earshot of Pierce and the sheriff. They became concerned when Jimmy didn't return from one after fifteen minutes. Pierce tried to follow but achy knees and a stiff back stopped him in the narrowing passage before he could get far. Sheriff couldn't even make it through the opening. Their yells went unanswered.

One could imagine their surprise when Jimmy suddenly appeared in front of the waterfall behind which they waited. Actually, surprise was an understatement. He had followed the one small tunnel to daylight, probably half a mile away. He surfaced next to Skunk Creek Ranch and had to crawl part of the way back to avoid detection. He guessed that the facing tunnel also served as an exit. He ducked in and disappeared, returning through the waterfall a short time later. Even quicker to daylight this time. He confirmed a dry walk out from the low rock face into the thick woods.

All marveled at the witch's ingenuity, beyond her evil ways. Sheriff guessed she just strode offstage after shooting Lucas, ducked around the waterfall, and exited through the tunnel that dumped her into the thick woods the night of the raid. Probably hung out there until the coast cleared and troopers moved out before she returned home. Oh, he wished he could have gotten his hands on her that evening. Probably would have killed her on the spot, he guessed.

"If I didn't know better," shared Pierce, "like the fact that Octavia Rosebeam was likely Demon Lady's mother, I would wonder whether the "X" might relate to her. Such timelessness would place her squarely in the supernatural and beyond simply evil, though the latter was, or is, certainly bad enough."

A murdering lady of the night might have earned a federal marshal's attention back then and warranted a raid. But the Rosebeam Chronicles were too compelling to ignore. That Octavia Rosebeam bore the She Devil with the bizarre genetic fingerprint from the seed of an evil rapist was nearly irrefutable. Thankfully, Lettie's baby evolved as a kinder, gentler iteration, owing no doubt to the dilutive effect of cumulative kind and gentle strains, owing to Octavia and Lucas.

Pierce was out of ideas. They had combed above and below in search of anything that might warrant a brutal murder almost a century and a half past. They had hoped for booty or bodies or both to bring closure to the tragic and seemingly senseless death of Thomas Hardly. Instead, they had found only signs of a current day real killer, whose own rampages had produced other senseless deaths. No tie to bind beyond senseless.

Pierce Arrow handed the useless map to Cousin Jimmy, not even sure of its historical significance anymore. He was sorely disappointed. Jimmy tucked it gently into his shirt pocket, still not sure there wasn't more to it all. He would have to stew on that a little later.

Pierce led Sheriff Sephus and Cousin Jimmy up top to break camp and go home. He hoped never to return to this place of tragic loss and faded memories, despite its great beauty. The Ozarks are like this in so many ways, Pierce mused. Majestic landscapes rich with flowing clean water and kind people—and evildoers and tragedy. Life was never easy here, but its natives persisted, leaning on humor and each other to survive. He could use some of both right now.

Sheriff Sephus Adonis mounted the stage one last time. He slowly walked to where Lucas had laid, clumsily fell to his knees, sat in a prayerful pose for a few moments, then kissed the very spot where Lucas died, a wrenching and tearful tribute to a man he had come to love. He rose with help from Pierce and Jimmy, hugged them both, and asked once more why he hadn't ordered the troopers to charge just five minutes earlier. The question would forever dog and haunt his life whenever he allowed it breathing room. He had no answer, nor ever would.

Instead of heading left to Hardlyville, Sheriff Sephus turned right on the highway and right again on Skunk Creek Ranch Road, newly paved and widened to accept large trucks. He stopped at the last crest before the descent to the ranch, stepped out with his binoculars, and trained them on the ranch house. No young beauties sunbathing topless on the lake dock this day, like with he and Lucas. Just the smell of hog waste and the snorting of pigs. And the ranch manager staring back at him through binoculars as well.

"Just want them to know we're watching," announced Sheriff Sephus as he fell back into the driver's seat. "They had better not fuck up," Sheriff warned no one in particular.

Despite the sheriff's passion for the act, it was the first time Pierce had ever heard him use the word.

The drive home was low and slow. Jimmy tried to banter with Sheriff on occasion, but Sheriff Sephus wasn't biting. Pierce Arrow was mulling over in his mind how to handle the story of Hardlyville's founding that had no proper ending. He wasn't sure what to do with Octavia Hardly Rosebeam's tragic tale either. He would sit on both until his Flo and Big Pork projects were complete. He would then lean heavily on Lettie for advice and counsel, sensitive to the needs of long deceased principals as well as the historical grounding of the community.

Sally was waiting for Jimmy with a newlywed "come and get me" look. Jimmy quickly thanked his seniors for including him in the search party, then went and got her. Sheriff and Pierce were both grateful that Jimmy Jones had turned the proverbial corner, despite living on the edge of the law. He was a good kid, and Sally was helping him grow up.

Sheriff Sephus dropped Pierce Arrow off at his front door with a pat on his back and a muted thank you. Pierce hugged Lettie. He advised her that she would never believe the outcome of their investigation. Thomas Hardly died for nothing. No map. No treasure. No nothing.

Lettie listened to Pierce's frustration, then showered it with kisses. He could be so damn intense when it came to closing loops or righting wrongs. Loose ends did not settle well with Pierce Arrow. She needed to help him push this one aside for a while and did so with fervor and passion. Pierce responded with more of the same.

As they lay in the shadows of shared pleasure and the children's afternoon nap, Lettie looked at Pierce's craggy profile while he drifted into a nap. She had never known a man so passionate or so giving. Then again, she hadn't known many men. She had been loyal to Lucas, despite his occasional failure to return the favor—excepting, of course, Sheriff Sephus Adonis. And Pierce Arrow made three, the only lovers in her life. And Sheriff really didn't rate a spot on her scorecard. One and done for the sake of curiosity, not lust or passion, didn't count in her loyalty point calculation. She still didn't understand the why of that one, but doubted she would burn in hell for it. Comparing Pierce and Lucas was a loser's game as well. She loved them both: the memory of childhood sweetheart Lucas Jones and the present of Pierce Arrow.

She thought of Lucas less often these days. The deep love she had felt for him had merged into the horizon, ever present but distant. Some memories still made her laugh. Lucas was an ornery cuss, a practical joker, a physical kind of guy. His kisses were hard and aggressive. He wasn't sweet and cuddly, more of a "slam bam, thank you, ma'am" lover, with a staying power that could make you quiver. Her Lucas could go for hours if she was up to it, as often she was. She smiled at the memory of one marathon session when Lucas had too much beer and had to pee at least every fifteen minutes, pleasuring her before each interlude, traipsing off to the john for his relief, and returning armed and dangerous from every visit.

We must have carried on half the night that way, she smiled to herself.

Pierce was different. He was a thoughtful and patient lover, always looking out for her interest beyond his. No one she had ever been with treated her with such reverence, almost worshipful at times.

And here she was playing her self-proclaimed loser's game of comparative lovers. She laughed out loud at her voyeuristic meanderings, waking Pierce from his cat nap. He asked her what was so funny. She half-truthed him.

"You," she smiled, inquiring with a mischievous smirk if he was still mourning Hardlyville history or up for another round.

Later that evening, Pierce safely and happily tucked into bed with all the rest in her house, Lettie sat down with her laptop and began to google.

She started with Federal Marshal Garth. No response. She dug a little deeper into the time frame in question. Still nothing. Didn't mean much, but she had found other federal marshals listed by name. Maybe he wasn't one.

James Qingdao was next on her list and scored a hit. He was pretty much as represented in Petunia Hardly's history—an unusual Oriental man with a wife named Anny and a lot of home

215

towns. A vagabond of sorts, owing to his wife's preoccupation with the opposite sex, she guessed.

Then she tried Anny by herself. She was stunned to find more about her than the other two. Anny had been indicted on charges of being an accomplice to murder on at least three occasions. Early feminists had taken on her cause as a persecuted damsel in distress, which had gained her a degree of notoriety and ultimately a dismissal of charges in each case.

The facts varied, but the nature of the murders was similar. Seems Anny grazed while James toiled, the latter accepting her infidelity as the price of poker, so to speak. No mention of him shooting any of her lovers, as reported by Petunia, only of her employing current patrons to take out those few who spurned her overtures. Anny Qingdao must have been an intensely narcissistic and insecure woman, reasoned Lettie. To turn down her advances was to personally insult her beauty and allure, almost akin to attacking a perverted sense of integrity. Questioning integrity got one killed in some circles back then. Fold in a current lover named Garth and one who turned Anny down named Thomas and a circle is complete. If Garth posed as a federal marshal and conned Thomas into complacency, it would have been simple to slip back in and take his life. Perhaps the brutality of the act was done to disguise the simplicity of it. Lettie was proud of her detective work and relatively sure of the validity of her conclusions. That said, it was a sad and sordid act and fate.

Pierce would be pleased to know, upon waking, that Thomas Hardly was likely killed for his virtue and loyalty to Petunia. His ending was tragic but noble, not wasted. If only Petunia had known.

Pierce was grateful to Lettie for bringing a positive spin to a dastardly deed, probably the worst in Hardlyville history next to poor Lucas's murder. He then asked about the map. Lettie had nothing to add to his state of confusion.

Right And Wrong

Rifleman and Steele returned on schedule with a small trailer that served to move all of their earthly goods, including production line and packaging materials for Rifleman. Little did they know what awaited them.

Sheriff Sephus had rotated occasional deputies for several days up the main road into town to assure they didn't arrive by surprise. In that no one could remember the last time, or even if ever, a real, live, legal manufacturing business had relocated to Hardlyville, civic leaders were out in full finery to greet them. Hardlyville didn't have much of a Chamber of Commerce in that Banker Bud had been de facto chamber chair, but Mayor would seek to fill the void. With all the powers vested in him, Mayor declared it Rifleman Day, to include a police escort and a celebratory parade, featuring the Hardlyville High School Marching Band and the Hardlyville Nursing Home Spoon Quartet.

The four spots in the latter were hotly contested positions, and some enterprising denizens who didn't even reside in the home would sneak in for a night or two so as to be eligible to try out. Ol' Dill got away with this tactic until he was caught bringing special mash product into pre-performance practice. Lively rehearsals

217

gave way to spoon fights and R&B renditions of standard spoon songs, which left quartet director Edward R. Ding apoplectic. Ol' Dill was subsequently banned from all Spoon activities. The Spoon Quartet played at major civic gatherings from the Bulrush Festival to Nativity Night and were considered by most to be a unique and invaluable community treasure.

A podium had been erected at the western city limits sign. This one registered Hardlyville's population at 301, and was much preferred over the east entrance's 253 census count. No city official had ever been able to reconcile the difference, and Mayor refused to spend money to conduct a recount because no one really cared. Postmaster Bond (PB) and Undertaker Bob would join Mayor on stage and dutifully applaud his short, platitudinal speech. All three were eager to impress Rifleman because they were hopeful he might join the civic leadership team as a representative of business to replace Banker Bud. If Rifleman was interested in being a civic leader and knew how to play seven card, roll your own, high low poker, he would fit right in. And no more head covering paper bags with eye and nose slits to distract from a love of the game.

Sheriff Sephus met Rifleman at the city limits and asked him to sit tight until the mayor arrived, as he had prepared a formal speech of welcome. Rifleman said he didn't want no speech, but Sheriff threatened to arrest him on charges of trespassing if he refused His Honor's formal welcome. Both laughed at that one, and Steele urged Rifleman to just sit tight.

Mayor ran to the podium, million dollar smile frozen in place, and began with "It's a beautiful day in the Ozarks" followed by "A straight rifle and a hard man are good to find." He finished with "You can bend Steele but not break her." He was proud of the personalized nature of his remarks and was applauded wildly by the podium party. Rifleman and Steele could only look at each other in disbelief. Sheriff leaned in to assure them Mayor was well-intentioned and wanted only to be liked.

"Cut him some slack for his inane comments, and he will do anything for you."

The civic leader delegation came forward with their invitation to Rifleman to become a civic leader if he knew seven card, roll your own, high low poker. Said he didn't, but Steele was damn good at it and would be happy to serve. This set civic leadership scrambling. The thought of a woman in their august group and weekend game had never crossed anyone's mind, and theirs ground to collective gridlock.

Sheriff Sephus Adonis, sensing a civic crisis, quickly accepted Rifleman's kind offer of Steele's services, and before civic leaders could blink, their vacancy was filled. Undertaker Bob, always the grease on the wheels, was first to congratulate Steele on her non-election to office and to invite her to join in this Friday night's game, as well as to come and go through the weekend as her schedule allowed. She expressed delight and offered that she might do more going than coming this weekend, due to setting up the new house and shop, but looked forward to taking their money. Civic leadership froze again, and even Mayor's smile crinkled.

"Just horsing around," she smiled even broader than Mayor.

Pierce Arrow, who was providing press coverage, laughed out loud. The wheels of government may well never spin in old ways again, he mused, and that couldn't help but be for the better. *Might make a good lead story once we get beyond the Big Pork exposés,* he mused.

One final formality remained, and Flotilla Hendricks and Dylan Thomas stood at the ready. They presented their new neighbors with the traditional pawpaw cake and mason jar of Ol' Dill's finest mash, with Pastor Pat's prayed admonition that they consume both simultaneously and not sequentially.

That done, Sheriff Sephus Adonis cranked up his siren, spun his flashing lights, and provided a memorable police escort to their new home.

Rifleman and Steele went to work immediately, transforming a discredited banker's stuffy residence into a production line with all the comforts of home. Rifleman noted someone driving back and forth in front the first couple of days and finally waived down Jimmy Jones in his truck. Rifleman recognized Jimmy and asked him to take him fishing again. Jimmy would be delighted to do so the coming weekend and also wondered if Rifleman needed any help around the shop. Couldn't pay much at first, Rifleman warned, but added that if Jimmy was as good with wood stocks as he was with smallmouth bass, he knew he could use him. Jimmy gave his notice at the gas station the next day and was soon learning a real trade, one that was even legal.

Pierce ran his Flo "Passion" Special to great acclaim. Only one dissatisfied customer, Ol' Dill Thomas, complained publicly. He had insisted that Pierce Arrow interview him about the full range of his exploits with Miss Flo, and Pierce had refused. Pierce did not consider him a credible source, and Ol' Dill was gravely offended. He said he would tell his story himself, but after the first three guffaws to three separate iterations decided to just sit back and savor the memory of a moment that might never come again.

Pierce and Lettie were in heaven together. At least that's what Pastor Pat claimed. He even forgave them of their sins of cohabitation and adultery, though none in town felt they needed his blessing. He longed to formally marry them but couldn't get them to budge on that one. He lived on memories of Flo and anticipation of the coming Bulrush Festival. Perhaps Lettie and Pierce will contribute a baby Moses one day, he smiled.

Pierce attacked Big Pork with both barrels in the coming weeks. He researched hog Concentrated Animal Feeding Operations and industrial pig farms in great detail, even driving up to Iowa for several personal calls on unsuspecting farmers. What he found only elevated his levels of concern. His new and expanded vocabulary reeked of nursery barns, grown-out barns, free-range pig farming with mud wallowing pits and rooting gardens, field application runoff, sewage lagoon overflows and collapses, phosphorus and nitrogen rich hog waste, ammonia, methane, and hydrogen sulfide emissions, and hog carcass disposal.

And his most favored/least favorite descriptive: intensive piggeries. It sounded almost sweet, like a nursery rhyme. This little piggery went to market . . .

Pierce Arrow had nothing against farmers. Most he knew were honest and hardworking, like most Hardlyvillains. He really had nothing against pigs or big pig farms. He, in fact, loved to eat pork. Chops, ribs, bacon, tenders, and cutlets fried in bacon grease were all specialties of Lettie's kitchen and comprised at least four of his seven suppers every week.

What chapped Pierce to the core—beyond the deceit of a greedy banker, a crooked pork producer, and his slimy lobbyists—was location, location, location. There is no way in hell an intensive piggery should ever see the light of day in the watershed of a beautiful and nearly pristine Ozark stream.

What worked in Iowa sure as hog shit wouldn't work in the limestone karst strata of the Ozark Mountains. Iowa is no Ozark when it comes to what lies beneath the ground to absorb and filter what sits or flows atop it on the way to the groundwater supply. Pierce was no expert, but he knew enough to know that something nasty was going on—and that something bad would come of it.

And if he heard or read one more time about baseless fears of "what-if" scenarios, he might just drop his drawers and defecate on the source material personally. This threat made Lettie giggle, but the rest of his expanding narrative didn't.

There was no way there should be a ten thousand pig operation in the Skunk Creek watershed. There was no way four million annual gallons of manure and wastewater could go anywhere but downstream eventually. There was no way Skunk Creek would not be permanently harmed and degraded by the selfish acts of a few whose return on investment lay upstream and east. No "what-ifs" here. This was no family farm with a pig sty.

To accept that barns, sewage lagoons, and manured fields were the last line of defense to an environmental disaster for a community's prize natural resource was lunacy. It was a matter of wrong and right, and it was dead wrong.

Lettie began to assist at the *Hellbender*. It kept them close together, and she added an element of organizational structure and efficiency that Pierce had always lacked. Who would understand the need for efficiency and structure better than a mother of four children, including two babies? Thank God Flotilla Hendricks had opened a day care to supplement her bakery income. She needed to keep that beautiful, black baby boy of dear Sabrina's in good health and well fed. And Lettie needed her. She loved having Lettie's babies involved in her program and sensed a natural affinity among future playmates. Pierce was a writer not a businessman, and he was now freed to do what he did best.

He ended up doing four consecutive "reveal alls" instead of two, including the details of his kiddie porn trashing by Big Pork and partner Banker Bud in the previous congressional election. National media picked up his features, and he was soon on the Pulitzer list again. Lettie also had an innate feel for marketing and made certain each story or revelation birthed another and fueled momentum within Pierce's passion.

The buzz began without instigation from Pierce. Not *if* he was going to run again but *when would he announce* so his army could reboot. These were the "grassroots" Pierce so admired as an antidote to corruption. They were primed and ready.

Piece Arrow scheduled a press conference barely a year ahead of the next election. It was covered by most regional media outlets, and Hardlyville was swamped with cars and bodies. He presided from the front porch of the *Hellbender*, using a lavaliere microphone because of the crowd size and owing that he was more comfortable wandering among that crowd than speaking to it. He butterfly-wing-eye winked rapidly and intentionally at Lettie to calm her nerves.

He began by thanking all of those present for attending. He noted that what he was about to announce was probably not a major surprise. He then asked Lettie to join him as he returned to a small podium. All waited in rapt attention.

"My friend Lettie and I are happy to announce," he pulled the front of her simple smock up to just below her bra line to reveal a baby bump, "the due date for our first child together."

The crowd went berserk, and ultimately even national media scrambled to pick up a quick take of Lettie's tiny but clearly popping midsection. This was hardly national news, but it would surely sell.

Ol' Dill asked Dinky why Lettie was baring her breasts to the TV cameras.

"It's her belly," Dinky corrected, noting that the old fool needed to put his glasses on as well as turn up his hearing aid.

"She's showing her ass next?" he whooped in disbelief, pushing through the crowd for a better view.

"Not her ass," screamed Dinky, "your glasses, retard."

"They're both showing their asses?" he puzzled. "Who in the world would want to see Arrow's backside?" he wondered aloud.

"How can you possibly be so slow?" Dinky screamed, wagging his finger at Ol' Dill.

"He's bringing back Flo to run his campaign?" Ol' Dill cackled. "Brilliant!"

Dinky had all he could take and tackled Ol' Dill from behind, dragging him to the back of the crowd where Sheriff Sephus Adonis awaited them.

"What are you idiots doing now?" Sheriff demanded.

"Just trying to keep Ol' Dill from embarrassing hisself in front of all these strangers," proudly confirmed Dinky.

"Better arrest them for indecent exposure," Ol' Dill bellowed. "At least him. Hers was pretty decent, come to think of it."

Sheriff delivered a couple of gentle nightstick knocks, out of range of the TV cameras, and sent the boys on home with a threat of another night in the clinker if they didn't obey.

"Oh, and by the way," Pierce Arrow added to the crowd, "Miss Lettie and I plan on serving as your next elected representatives to Congress come a year from November."

Another wild outburst.

"How can that be?" one reporter asked over the din. "You can't both be elected," he followed.

"We sleep together, and since I will represent my constituents from home, as I promised last run, we will proudly serve together," yelled Pierce, thrusting Lettie's clasped hand to the heavens.

Another roar from the crowd. Rifleman started firing rounds into the sky while Steele handed out Rifleman business cards right and left. She was not about to let this marketing moment slip by. Mayor Cheshire Cat grinned from ear to ear until a dead crow fell on one of his brightly-shined shoes, evidently a victim of Rifleman's barrage. He quietly kicked it into the crowd before picking up the smile where he left off. God forbid he offend anyone.

The most unorthodox campaign for office in the entire U. S. of A. was underway.

The Garden

Jimmy Jones had stuck the old map from the failed expedition in his bedside table drawer, crammed with condoms and fishing lures in need of repair. He and Sally were contemplating doing away with the former in favor of parenthood. Jimmy felt they could afford a couple of kids with local weed prices at an all-time high, as his cash coffers were overflowing. Damn, he wished they had more than a failed bank in town so he could quit having to bury it all in his subterranean strong box. Besides, he was tired of making babies without the babies, dirty deed or not. As for the damaged fishing lures, they assured that the old map was in good company.

Jimmy pulled out the map to look at it from time to time, still baffled as to its linkage and relevance. He had studied it from every angle, noting that one arm of the "X" seemed to point at what would appear to be due east.

Jimmy recollected in a hazy dream one night that while he had been scrambling around atop the rock face that sheltered the natural amphitheater, dodging large, lethargic copperheads here and there, an isolated stone extension had caught his eye. He had forgotten about it because at the point of discovery he had stepped on one of the slithering bastards, drawing a strike to his leather boot. He had kicked the serpent off the bluff in anger and moved on, forgetting about the unusual rock formation.

In his dream, Jimmy revisited the stone, which carried a long crack through which the sun would surely shine at some time or season to rocks below. He further observed that the rock crack presented a vertical and horizontal span, a truly unusual piece of heavenly handiwork. He awoke with a start.

His first conscious thought was "what if?" What if a sunbeam cascading through an abnormal rock opening could take its form and plant it at some spot below as an "X" surrounded by shadow? What if that "X" could be the one on the old map? What if there was something beneath that "X" of great value?

Jimmy needed a joint to ponder this to its logical conclusion. It was only six in the morning, and he had long ago given up daytime toking in the interest of full employment and wedded bliss, but . . . Besides, he didn't report to Rifleman's production line until nine, so a couple of strong cups of coffee would dull the buzz to a manageable level. Mix in a little mouthwash, and no one would ever know. Beautiful Sally lay in deep sleep beside him. So he grabbed his papers, rolled one full of his finest stuff, and moved outside to sit in the porch swing and light up.

Jimmy inhaled deeply and accelerated his nascent theory to the next level.

He wondered if, indeed, the sun could strike the rock-borne "X" to a solid ground target, how he could guess when that might occur, and what he might find beneath. Buried treasure? Buried bodies? An underground alien installation? A whole tribe of naked, yellow-eyed demon ladies with gray ponytails and tattoos on their butt cheeks? His imagination knew no bounds.

As to how to estimate when the magical mark might appear, Jimmy hadn't a clue. He even wondered if his dream was timed to coincide with a cycle of light. Ironically, today was the shortest day of the year, he remembered. Only one way to find out.

He dialed up Rifleman and said he needed a day off. Smallmouth might be on top water at this temperature, and he would let Rifleman know if they were. This was a language Rifleman could understand, and he wished Jimmy good luck.

Jimmy then tapped Sally lightly on her bare shoulder and told her they were going on a picnic. She nodded a confused affirmation and pulled him close for a kiss. Not just yet, he smiled and headed to the kitchen. An hour later, Jimmy's truck was loaded with the faithful, old army surplus blanket, cold beer, venison sandwiches, and the Bobbers as he left Hardlyville behind in the rearview mirror. He also left the condoms behind.

They headed east toward the former digs of the evil coven and the sad site of Cousin Lucas's last breath. Jimmy shared none of this with Sally, who was quietly celebrating this eruption of spontaneous romance. They shared an early-morning beer and joint and were transported back in space and time to a simpler life when only love and lust mattered.

They arrived at their destination midmorning, lay aside picnic makings, and climbed atop the guardian rock fortress. Sally was a little confused by Jimmy's callous disregard of a couple of lounging copperhead snakes, unusual to encounter this time of year, and followed closely behind, Bobbers warily bringing up the rear. She was really in a loving kind of mood and feeling a little hungry as well.

The first day of winter showed bright and felt unseasonably warm atop the rock. Jimmy checked his watch, eleven forty-five, and decided to stall until noon, a nice round number. He explained to Sally that this was where he, Pierce Arrow, and her good friend Sheriff Sephus had come with the map. Sally blushed before asking why this place, with all of those painful memories, qualified as a prime picnic location. Jimmy assured her the natural beauty above and below ground would win her over, but that just now he needed to test out a theory. He pointed to the stone with the large horizontal and perpendicular cracks.

Jimmy glanced at the sun and cringed at the cloud cover that was racing its way in the wind.

"Just five more minutes," he breathed to himself, then two, then one.

Suddenly, there it was, the sun perfectly aligned behind the cracks at high noon. Jimmy gazed down the shaft of light to a neon gold "X" striking a shadowed rock corner maybe twenty feet below. He marked it in his mind and hurried Sally and Bobbers down to ground zero, which had already lost its luster. Jimmy poked and probed desperately among the rocks.

"This has to be it!" he screamed, causing Sally to jump and Bobbers to pee.

And then it was. A mid-size boulder was a prime candidate as Jimmy tugged at its edges, moving it ever so slightly. Sally pitched in, and soon it tumbled aside, revealing only a deep hole with no visible bottom. Jimmy raced back to his truck, grabbing a long rope and two flashlights, asking Sally to stand guard. Over what, she was unclear.

Jimmy tied the rope to a nearby tree and asked Sally to shine one flashlight beam down the shaft while he grabbed the other. He then descended slowly along the rope. She heard a splash as he hit bottom and then a "Holy Shit" that carried a sense of awe with it as his own flashlight lit the subterranean scene.

He assured Sally she wouldn't believe what he was looking at, adding that he feared he had died and entered heaven. Now Sally was really spooked and ordered him to get his ass back up to her immediately so she could be sure he was still alive. The jerking rope confirmed he was on the way. He crawled out of the shaft with a dazed look of wonder and glory. His words tumbled out in bursts and vivid descriptives, sending Sally to wondering if he had been toking down there.

He closed by proudly announcing that he had found the perfect spot for their picnic. Sally wanted nothing to do with climbing down a rope into a big dark hole, but she was hungry and accepted his invitation. Jimmy grabbed the trusty blanket, sandwiches, and a couple of Bud Lights, and carried them below. He then returned for Sally, descending with her in his arms, her lighting the way.

She gasped when they bottomed out, feet in a frigid, clear stream issuing from a bubbling, rock-sourced spring, fuzzy natural light seeping in from some fissure above or around, and a subtle hint of subterranean warmth. She then screamed when her light revealed two ugly brown-and-green creatures in the stream slipping over her bare feet to thread between small boulders for cover.

"Hellbenders," Jimmy whispered with reverence, "real hellbenders. And look at those albino crawdads," he murmured, explaining their blindness and vulnerability to even the slightest of unnatural intrusions.

Jimmy told Sally that they had stumbled into a true Ozarkian Garden of Eden, where even the most vulnerable of God's creatures could survive mankind and his excesses.

Jimmy then noticed that the stream flow seemed the opposite of other subterranean springs he had observed on his previous visit. Almost like the water was running upstream. This amazed and confused him. Maybe a deep and different sourcing?

Jimmy's face would have been radiant if Sally could have seen it in full light. He led her to a smooth mud bank, spread the old blanket, kissed her fully and deeply, and for the first time in their many renditions and iterations of doing the dirty deed, Jimmy went unprotected. In the Garden of Eden. In the shadow of last seen alive Cousin Lucas.

As they lay, regaining their breath after their trip to the mountaintop, they gazed in wonder around them, eyes adjusting to the gentle light. No need for artificial illumination in this paradise. Jimmy confirmed that he had not worn a condom. Sally nodded her approval. She wanted to know what they might name it, if indeed they had struck pay dirt in this unusual place and time. Adam or Eve? No, countered Jimmy. He favored Lucas or Lucessa. Sally nodded yes again.

They spent the remainder of the day poking and prowling around their newly discovered subterranean wonderland. Jimmy wondered aloud when the last human might have intruded on the sacred spot. Maybe not since Thomas Hardly or whomever shared the map with him. Otherwise, how could it have survived in such pristine condition? He found other unusual creatures swimming or crawling around, some he had never seen, which was saying something given his time since birth hanging out in creeks and streams. He chose not to explore much with a flashlight for fear of disturbing, even slightly, the fragile balance of life within.

Jimmy had only seen one hellbender through all the years, one Cousin Lucas had stumbled on trying to retrieve a lure from among some boulders on upper Skunk Creek. Lucas had grabbed the slimy creature, and both had looked in wonder at its beady eyes and mottled skin, perfection in ugliness and camouflage. Lucas had gently placed the salamander only a mother could love, as he called it, back in its hideaway after a moment or two, rubbing the goo off his hands with a kind of reverence.

Jimmy had seen at least four of the critters today, but he had hesitated to pick one up. They were too comfortable and unsuspecting in their safe haven. Jimmy tried to pinpoint the source of the soft, natural light that seeped in around the corners of the rocks but couldn't get there. Same for the sense of warmth. It was as if the dim glimmer was cleansed of all harshness and tenderly radiated along its journey from the sun to there. Jimmy halfway wondered whether it lingered through the night but was too weirded out by that thought to pursue it further. He and Sally wore not a stitch of clothing during the entire term of their trespass and lost total track of earthly time to wonder and bliss.

Jimmy couldn't wait to share the news with Pierce Arrow. Pierce wouldn't believe what the "X" telegraphed and how Jimmy had found it. Nor would he be able to grasp the natural beauty that lay beneath the stage of tragic memory until he saw and felt it.

They finally reclothed and, with some regret, exited paradise lost. Sally thought she remembered a book of that name, maybe from Ms. Rosebeam's studies, but Jimmy didn't think it sounded very Latin-like. He also reminded Sally that they both received a D minus from the beloved village matron, so it was not likely that much had seeped in.

Jimmy climbed the rope once, carrying every human thing back where it belonged. He then returned for Sally to ferry her back to reality. He pulled up the rope, untied it, and rolled the disguising boulder back in place. He pushed and shoved to seal it tight and swept their footsteps away with a branch.

This secret playground would remain theirs until Pierce Arrow determined otherwise.

Jimmy had another of those strange feelings that Cousin Lucas was watching him as they headed back to the car at dusk. He hoped he was right.

Jimmy and Sally went straight to Pierce and Lettie, who had just gotten the babies to bed and were sharing a glass of Ol' Dill's finest on their porch, contemplating campaign strategies. Pierce couldn't remember if Jimmy and Sally were legal but poured them a snort anyway. Pierce had never seen Jimmy so animated in his young life.

They sat mesmerized by Jimmy's account of discovering a true Ozarkian Garden of Eden buried deep beneath the coven of evil's old stomping grounds. A place where "X" truly marked the spot if you dug deep enough, where strange creatures crawled, and water ran the wrong way.

"The cold, crystal stream even had hellbenders!" crowed Jimmy, noting that Pierce had named his paper after a critter he had never seen.

Jimmy shared his sense that Lucas had a hand in the discovery, from dream to reality, and that if Sally ended up pregnant from the day, the offspring would bear his name. This was a little too much information, all agreed, with Sally kicking at Jimmy's shins, so Jimmy went back to sharing the natural wonder of it all.

Pierce Arrow sat quietly for the most part, attentive but reflective. It was true, he mused, he thought he was naming the *Daily Hellbender* after a mythical creature that only existed in theory in Skunk Creek and its surrounds. This was potentially a game-changing discovery, particularly in the context of a huge hog CAFO located less than a mile away. His mind whirred, and his campaign for congress gained additional focus.

Jimmy carried on for an hour with a vivid and detailed description, even earning a second tumbler of Ol' Dill's finest, Sally nodding all along the way. Jimmy asked Pierce what to do next. Pierce said he needed to think about it, but he was already headed to conclusions.

Then Jimmy added that he had found this, flipping a coin to Pierce. It looked like a silver dollar but not really, he observed, especially the sexy lady with the big bosom on the front. He said he found it in the beautiful stream.

Pierce stared with disbelief at the coin bearing the date 1803 and, as Jimmy had observed, featuring an alluring lady in profile, bountiful breasts draped just above decency, cleavage on prominent display beneath an attractive face and hair flowing back, all centered just under the word LIBERTY.

Oh my, thought Pierce as he flipped the coin to the backside, not sure what to expect. THE UNITED STATES OF AMERICA bordered a somewhat scrawny looking bird that appeared to be a cross between an eagle and a wild turkey, reminding Pierce of the fierce debate between Founding Fathers over the national bird. Benjamin Franklin had lost that one, Pierce recalled.

This additional contribution from the garden changed Pierce's calculations of where to go next. An 1803 silver dollar in a pristine stream, surrounded by nature's most fragile creatures in a dimly and naturally lit grotto buried deep within the karst alleyways of mother earth. *Wow*, he thought, *who could have dreamed this one up? And how many more coins are down there?* he wondered, passing the coin to Lettie.

Pierce thanked the kids for coming to him first and begged them to tell no one of their discoveries. Both agreed and headed home in exhausted ecstasy.

Pierce and Lettie stayed up all night discussing the "what next."

The immediate question was how to fold a threatened subterranean paradise set just beneath a stinking giant piggery into language that would alarm as well as resonate with voters. The discovery of hellbenders therein provided a natural link to a crusading voice of the same lineage. Would announcing their presence seal their doom? Pierce didn't know.

And then there was the single silver dollar of times long past. Taken in the context of Petunia Hardly's tale of the map and her loss and Lettie's research into Anny Qingdao and her lover Garth's intentions, there had to be more of them. Somewhere.

Lettie amended her theory on Thomas Hardly's murder, closing loops faster than Pierce could write it all down.

What if Garth was a total impostor of a federal marshal, as originally deduced? What if he had stolen or acquired a map that promised an invaluable cache of old silver dollars hidden deep in the remote Ozarks?

What if Anny Qingdao had nothing to do with Garth's visit to Thomas Hardly beyond, perhaps, helping him through husband James's name-drop to gain credibility with Thomas? Didn't much matter if they were lovers or not under this scenario.

What if Garth sought out local native Thomas, posing as a federal marshal, to gain his help in deciphering a map of a strange corner of the world? What if Thomas promised to lead him there when Garth returned with his troop of soldiers? What if Thomas refused to do so when Garth returned, instead, with a couple of thugs to steal the loot rather than redeem it for the U. S. Treasury? What if they brutally murdered Thomas for his recalcitrance, first torturing him to gain directions and access to the map, then tearing apart his house in their search before running off to hide? What if the map lying next to Petunia's breast had contained all the answers to the questions that were never subsequently raised?

Pierce concluded that Lettie's "what-ifs" created a tragic and credible story line, and that there lay both great natural and potential monetary wealth in the heart of the garden.

Pierce felt a sudden surge of sadness and fear. He deeply regretted the cruel and unnecessary death of village founder Thomas Hardly and the subsequent pain carried by Petunia and his heirs. He feared what might happen to the Ozark's own Garden of Eden if either its pristine condition or possible financial windfall reached the public domain. As much as disclosure of the former would be a natural and powerful extension of his campaign, adding reality and urgency to his efforts to shut down the Skunk Creek Ranch CAFO as soon as possible, it could do more harm than good. If Pierce leaked even a peek, everyone from well-meaning scientists and environmental advocates to coin collectors and common thieves would descend on paradise, and, indeed, it would be lost, in the true Miltonian sense.

No, Pierce would need to think beyond his immediate and personal needs and buy time for a far greater good. If Pierce could not win on the merits of his arguments, he should lose. As for the possible fortune buried within the garden, mankind had done without it long enough to prove it inconsequential in the grand scheme of things. Let it all rest easy for now, especially the precious hellbenders of Skunk Creek watershed.

Lettie agreed with his conclusions and admired Pierce for his integrity and foresight. They would have to convince Jimmy and Sally to take the highroad of confidentiality and nonintervention and to essentially forget their amazing discovery. Pierce felt he could make a case that would appeal to their roots and best instincts and to what would be in the interest their children and grandchildren to come. They seemed to understand that perspective as well as any young folks he knew. Well, except for their occasional forays into too much weed. He would sure as hell try. This was a clear cost-benefit calculation that didn't balance.

Jimmy and Sally agreed with Pierce and Lettie's analysis to not share the secret further, but they balked at a promise never to return to the garden.

"When you've sipped the magic, you are addicted for life," was Jimmy's conclusion, and besides, he owed it to Lucas to not only preserve and protect but to stay in touch.

He and Sally would revisit every now and again when romance needed a nudge, life more inspiration, or Jimmy needed a pat on the shoulder from his all-time best friend. A baptism in the precious waters seemed only natural and an appropriate gesture of great gratitude, if and when one was needed. They would take every precaution to avoid detection and not smudge a drop of slime on the back of a hellbender.

"Funny thing," Pierce shared with Lettie later, "they didn't even mention the silver dollar."

He guessed that confirmed the true nature of their attachment to the garden, a noble and pure attraction, beyond dollars, in this instance.

So the Garden of Eden of the Ozarks would remain the beautiful little secret of those four who understood its timeless significance. This garden didn't need a big "X" on its back, map or not.

MESSAGING

Pierce Arrow was not a deeply religious kind of guy, at least in the organized sense. But when he had heard "O Holy Night" blaring from the jukebox over breakfast at Tiny Taylor's Greasy Spoons this Christmas Eve morning, he had burst into tears. Lettie had looked at him with concern and confusion. Had the fried squirrel been too hot? Had Lucas Jr. dropped a big one that she couldn't smell yet? Had she forgotten to kiss him good morning, as she had every day of their life together as a couple?

No, Pierce shared, after regaining his composure, the music had carried him back to a time and place in his youth where Father had sung the song in church, and Mother had placed a warm arm around his shoulders. He had known love and grounding that too soon slipped away with her sudden death from an aneurism and Dad's descent into grief-fueled alcoholism. The memory of that moment of joy and comfort had flooded his senses.

He went on that he had not known a moment like it since, until he had admitted his passion for Lettie and she had reciprocated with her own. And as he sat there today in tiny Hardlyville, a world away from that former place and time, surrounded by a new generation of love and grounding, he felt a circle close and embrace him and those he clung to. Now Lettie let her own flood flow.

Sheriff Sephus saw this all play out and rushed over to see what was wrong. Even his eyes teared up when he saw Pierce grab Lettie's small hands, then release her to encircle Lucas Jr. and Vixen in their high chairs, smiles radiant and tear-splashed cheeks beaming. He didn't know what message they were sharing, only that he had no business intruding on their special moment. Pierce muttered that all was well, all was love and gratitude, and that they even loved Sheriff Sephus Adonis himself.

Sheriff Sephus returned to his counter seat with a smile trickling out of the corner of his mouth alongside a drop of Tiny's biscuit gravy.

Later that morning, Lettie asked Pierce to go with her to Pastor Pat's Christmas Eve service. Pierce had never been because of his fear of crowds and religious doctrine. Lettie always attended with Lucas because generally one or the other was praying for forgiveness for some thing or another. It seemed only natural that their first Christmas together move beyond their separate pasts and celebrate their new beginning together. Pierce reluctantly agreed if she promised not to make him sing.

Pastor Pat gathered his flock for the community's traditional Christmas Eve service. Next to the Bulrush Festival, this was the highlight of Pastor Pat's year. He did not rank the birth of the Christ Child as lesser in significance than that of Moses. He just felt the latter was underserved by humanity, and with his keen sense of equanimity, he enjoyed highlighting another special Biblical story.

No, the Christmas Eve celebration was the pinnacle in terms of sheer joy. Whether a few of his parishioners believed or not was hardly the point. Most loved a happy tale and reason to gather for festivity. Life in the village was hardly ever easy, and Christmas Eve offered respite from daily toil. Everyone in good health and a reasonable state of sobriety gathered to fill Skunk Creek Church of Christ to the brim and beyond.

Pastor Pat had honed his message tightly to the existing circumstance that night. Life is clearly a battle between good and evil, he began, noting that Hardlyville had seen more than its normal share of the latter this time around. Village losses had been substantial, from Lucas to Sabrina to Octavia Rosebeam to others. He failed to mention Banker Bud by name, but he counted the presence of pigs just upstream as an evil tied directly to him. The Demon Lady also went unacknowledged. Most knew of her story, though it had never been openly discussed. For the public record, Lucas's death and that of the young lady floater had been attributed to her male followers, but her shadow clung to the village like a wet piece of tarpaper.

And yes, there had been sin, he lamented. Some of it circumstantial and more enjoyable and excusable than others, hinting at a certain visitor from France, but all forgivable from the Christ Child's perspective. And Pastor Pat was just getting warmed up.

Jimmy Jones sat with Sally all aglow, lit up with love and the sweet scent from his visit to a genuine Garden of Eden earlier in the week. Jimmy could concentrate on little else beyond these reasons to be thankful. At least until he heard a familiar rant rising from the pulpit.

Pastor Pat had worked himself into his annual frenzy over the "wages of sin." Jimmy Jones had never understood this one. Something about getting paid to do wrong, paid to make mistakes, or even do the dirty deed where or when you weren't supposed to didn't resonate with the entrepreneur buried deep inside. *What is the message here?* Jimmy wondered. Wages were wages in his world, and he sure as hell wouldn't pay anyone to sin. Sally sensed his agitation and grabbed his hand to place it on her belly, where she was convinced a new life of its own was beginning to stir. She hoped so. This was a message Jimmy could understand and relate to.

Ol' Dill began to snore. Tiny Taylor reached over his shoulder from the pew directly behind and gently pinched his ear, causing him to snort and jump. Several giggles could be heard beneath the pastor's soaring rhetoric. Maybe there was something going on between the old coot and the little lady, Sheriff wondered.

Flotilla Hendricks always dressed up for Christmas Eve services. Tonight she wore her first and only wedding dress. She had let it out in recognition of her middle-aged spread and had managed to cram every inch of her body into it. She glowed with the promise of a newlywed, grandbaby Otis snuggled against her breast in deep sleep.

Doc Karst puzzled over her choice of wardrobe. There was surely a message there. Her marriage had been a short-lived disaster, with son Chuck and daughter Sabrina as the only dividends. Surely she wasn't commemorating her betrothal. Her recent and sudden loss of daughter Sabrina, after reconnecting with her after several years of exile, had spiraled Flotilla into depression, which Doc had medicated. At least until Flotilla's affection for baby Otis had finally kicked in as she saw hints of her daughter's early childhood in his smiling, dark face nearly every day. Maybe that's it, Doc concluded. Perhaps Flotilla is reassuring us all of her own rebirth as a blessed mother on this eve of celebrating the same. Doc grabbed new wife Lois's hand with gratitude for Banker Bud's demise, then reframed the thought in more civil terms.

Librarian Bilious Bloom listened to the good pastor intently, seeking direction in her own life. She was lonely and yet inspired by her dearly departed mentor, Octavia Rosebeam, whose gift to the community had given her, Bilious, new focus as well. Ms.

Rosebeam had clearly messaged the community that its roots and history were its lifeblood, and Ms. Bloom was intent in jamming that message down every living Hardlyvillain's throat every waking moment of every day.

Pierce Arrow sat quietly, trying to decipher what Pastor Pat was attempting to say. If it was a message from God, it was surely transposed by this earthly emissary. Maybe he is dyslexic, Pierce wondered to himself. The reporter in him then asked, *Who? God? Pastor Pat?* Or Pierce himself? This was not an internal interrogation he would share with anyone, even Lettie.

And so it went. Pastor Pat babbling on in a stream of consciousness kind of way, leaving a sea of confusion but sense of hope in his wake.

It seemed that all of Hardlyville hugged this Christmas Eve, as they had most past. And apart from an occasional lustful thought or too much of Ol' Dill's finest, no one sinned, paid or not. Tiny Taylor even closed Greasy Spoons after breakfast to eliminate yet one other temptation.

This Christmas Eve in Hardlyville, believers and non, and those caught betwixt, celebrated their brotherhood and sisterhood, their resilience, their courage, their interconnection, and their links to those gone, as well as they that gathered. Such public acknowledgement of God, religion, love, and their placement on a historical continuum had served them well since the founding days and would be sorely needed going forward.

Where else could one hear "O Holy Night" on a jukebox? Pierce Arrow mused to himself. Little Lettie Jones sat snuggled in next to him in a single metal chair in the narthex, surrounded by pistols and shotguns parked in their cubbies for safekeeping. Another "where else" formed on Pierce's lips.

"Only in Hardlyville," he whispered in Lettie's ear, answering the questions she hadn't heard.

She muttered for him to stop flirting with her in public, let alone church, and to wait until they got home if he wanted a more receptive audience. Her message was clear and left Pierce Arrow with a Christmas Eve smile on his face.

This Christmas Eve in Hardlyville was one of hope.

O Holy Night, indeed.

JUSTICE SERVED

She strode boldly into Sheriff Sephus Adonis's office and asked if she could visit with him in private. She introduced herself as the owner of Skunk Valley Show Horse Farm. She was dressed in only the finest and looked hot in its highest iteration.

"You the wife of that guy who sits in jail on charges of corruption and got caught boinking his aides in the big raid?" Sheriff asked.

"Yes, but that's not today's point. He is a shit and is where he belongs."

"He hurt Skunk Creek and Hardlyville, you know?" Sheriff asked. "The bastard sold us out."

"Yes," she responded, "but that's not why I'm here today, Sheriff Sephus Adonis. I could never make amends for that and have only goodwill in my heart for your citizens and their beautiful creek. I have even fenced my show horse pasture on lower Skunk to keep the herd out of the creek.

"Let me get to the point. I'm a show horse lady, through and through, but I have heard from several of my local friends that you have a tender side, a deft touch, a gentle way, and a stallion of note that you share with them on occasion."

"That so?" Sheriff responded quizzically.

"That's so, Sheriff, and if you are willing, I am ready for a test drive."

Sheriff placed the sheriff "out" sign in its slot outside the office and opened the conference room door.

"Ladies first," he nodded as she began to dismantle her expensive wardrobe and fold it neatly on the conference table.

As she freed ample breasts from La Perla's hold, she asked Sheriff where the Adonis came from.

"God of love," he smiled. "Formally changed my name after high school when it became clear that such was my lot in life."

She nodded, completed her disrobe, and reached for the wheel with a sigh of admiration.

"Over easy or sunny-side up?" smiled Sheriff Sephus Adonis.

Summer turned to fall and Hardlyville resumed a sense of normalcy—but for the ten thousand pigs perched east and upstream.

SHE

She sat on her haunches, gnawing from the leg bone of a deer she had roasted on a fire just outside a small cave that she called home for now.

It had taken her several weeks to travel by foot, mostly under cover of darkness, to this remote parcel of land in Eastern Tennessee that she had mentioned to her last tribe of disciples before their disbursement and disbanding by the fat sheriff and his army of allies. She neither knew of nor missed a single one left behind.

Beyond harvesting game, she had not killed on her sojourn—with two exceptions. One she had picked up in a seedy bar to pleasure her for several days and nights before tiring of his idiocy. She had dismembered and disemboweled his hearty carcass before throwing it into a remote farm pond. The second had offered her a ride as she walked a back road one rainy evening and angered her with his prying questions about the color of her eyes. She had slit his throat to shut him up, lit up his car, and pushed it, burning, into a deep ravine. Beyond that, the trip had been mundane.

She was happy to be here and now. Her existence seemed timeless and solitary, except when she was moved to organize in the interest of sex and evil. Perhaps out of habit. Perhaps out of boredom. She simply knew how to draw riffraff together, unite them under a subservient banner of fealty to holy icons, and fill them full of her hatred and lust. Most were willing vessels and became loyal subjects.

Her last coven had stayed with her through several decades and maybe two moves, she couldn't remember exactly. They had followed her without question or doubt, killed and raped at her command, and subconsciously elevated her to status of icon itself. She had called this one the Sacred Mother, though in past iterations her titles had been gender non-specific. They had humored her with their wanton and salacious devotion to a single-minded pursuit of sex with and beyond her. It had been fun while it had lasted.

Not so much fun had been the delivery of a baby. This had never happened to her through the generations. The man Lucas had looked good and felt good to her, as had ending his silly life. But a baby? She had no idea how that had come to pass, only an internal assurance of never again. Maybe it was his fault, not hers.

She felt it stirring several months after their remarkable encounter as she waited for the tempest to die down before attempting to move on. She gave some thought to terminating the fetus early on, but a cloying desire to raise, train, and empower one of her own and in her own image prevailed. She delivered a yellow-eyed little girl effortlessly and nursed it for several months before determining that motherhood was not for her and depositing it on the grave that was all that remained of him. She would return one day or year or decade to reclaim her spawn and mold it in her own image. She would also exact revenge on the pitiful little town that had dared to challenge her.

Her thought processes were garbled beyond that. She had no sense of origin or destination, only of hatred and pleasure. She knew not who, what, how, or why she was. Her memory stretched for miles, but without recollection. Survival was her instinct and lowly humans her pawns in that struggle.

She sat naked as she played man games over in her mind. She looked at the deerskin bag in the corner of the cave and resolved to reclothe in something to draw a mate for the next day or two. It was time, and she was ready. He would pleasure her, then she would decide whether to kill again or let him go. It seemed too early to start building another following, though there were advantages to variety and subservience. She would wait a while, for now.

—THE END—

BUT WAIT! THERE'S MORE ...

Don't miss books Two and Three in the Ozarkian Trilogy!

Available in print and ebooks.

SWINE BRANCH

~ BOOK II IN THE OZARKIAN FOLK TALES TRILOGY ~

Who knows what lurks in the deep, dark corners of the Ozarks?

The residents of Hardlyville! And what do a local environmental disaster of unprecedented proportions, a series of ghastly murders, corrupt state politics, a bedouin shivaree, crooked investment bankers, and Noodler's Anonymous have in common? Skunk Creek!

For Sheriff Sephus Adonis, congressman Pierce Arrow, and his true love Lettie Jones, justice is no longer an intellectual concept, it's a matter of life and death. From Hardlyville city hall to Washington, DC's halls of government, to the international stage, resilient Hardlyvillains wage a fierce battle to protect their precious waters and way of life. Hilarity abounds in their madcap and unorthodox rush to remain alive—and relevant.

Swine Branch is rowdy, irreverent, insightful, and grounded in Ozarks waters and history. It confronts and entertains amidst some of the most vexing questions of our times. A worthy follow-up to *Skunk Creek*.

GET YOURS NOW AT
WWW.PEN-L.COM/SWINEBRANCH.HTML

DONNY BROOK

~ BOOK III IN THE OZARKIAN FOLK TALES TRILOGY ~

Who knows what lurks in the deep, dark corners of the Ozarks?

The colorful characters of tiny Hardlyville are thrown into a panic when brutal murders, environmental disasters, corruption, and threats to their beloved and pristine Skunk Creek arise and up-end their bucolic lives. Larger-than-life Sheriff Sephus Adonis, devoted newspaper editor Pierce Arrow, libidinous librarian Billious Bloom, and Hardlyville's most influential citizens are forced to contend with a community divided by greed and self-interest to solve the riddle of a mother's love vs. inherent evil.

Will the Hardlyvillains stop the murders and save their indispensable water?

ABOUT THE AUTHOR

 TODD PARNELL began writing non-fiction during his years as a banker and educator, including published books *The Buffalo, Ben, and Me*, *Mom at War*, and *Postcards from Branson*. He is an award-winning author inducted into the Missouri Writers Hall of Fame in 2012. He tried his hand at fiction upon retiring as president of Drury University and hasn't stopped writing since, completing the Ozarkian Folk Tales Trilogy, published by Pen-L Publishing, and is hard at work on a second trilogy, Children of the Creek.

In his own words, "I've had great fun writing about the Ozarks and tackling important contemporary issues in that rich and captivating context!"

Parnell is a civic leader, environmental advocate, co-founder of the Upper White River Basin Foundation, and retired CEO of THE BANK in Springfield. He recently completed his term as Chairman of the Missouri Clean Water Commission. He holds Masters degrees in Business from Dartmouth University and History from Missouri State University, and is a graduate of Drury University.

Born in Branson, Missouri, Todd is a sixth-generation Ozarker. He resides with Betty, his wife of forty years, in Springfield and is blessed with four children and five grandchildren, so far.

CONNECT WITH TODD AT:
www.ToddParnell.com
Facebook: Todd.Parnell.7

Dear Readers,
    If you enjoyed this
book enough to review
it for Goodreads, B&N,
or Amazon.com, I'd
appreciate it!
        Thanks, Todd

Find more great reads at
Pen-L.com